A Daring Pursuit of the Dream

A young Saint Lucian-Cuban flees Cuba to pursue the American Dream—and her dream.

BOOK ONE

Monica Victor

Copyright © 2021 Monica Victor

All rights reserved.

No part of this publication may be reproduced, distributed or transmitted in any form or by any means, including photocopying, recording or other electronic or mechanical methods, without the prior written permission of the publisher, except in the case of brief quotations, reviews and other noncommercial uses permitted by copyright law.

Dedication

For my sister Leona Oscar, whom we call France, who dared to pursue the American Dream, paving the way for my mom. And for my mom, Sigrid Victor, our beloved Nennen, who in turn, led the way for me.

For my sister in heaven Delisha, known as Nazy, whose life was cut short by Lupus on March 2nd, 2015, two weeks shy of her 31st birthday. The sound of her voice saying Gloria and laughing at her antics echoes in my mind's eye as I write, a mix of emotions covers me. Wish you were here to read the finished product, Naz.

And for every immigrant who survived or sadly lost their lives in pursuit of the American Dream.

Acknowledgments

It is said that nothing worth having comes easy. And what a whirlwind getting here has been, which most certainly was not a solo endeavor. It would be remiss of me to not mention those who played a part in helping me achieve this feat.

God for the grace, favor, wisdom, grit, and creative mind to pursue this writing thing.

Wenda Jn.Baptiste, who when I was babysitting and desperately yearned to be in school introduced me to Stratford Career Institute, a vocational correspondence school. And Mildred Rainey, a creative writing instructor at Stratford whose feedback on one of my creative writing pieces 17 years ago read, "Monica this is a very moving story, nicely designed and developed. You still have a bit too much plot for a short story—this could easily be turned into a novel…" leading me here. Look, Mildred, a short story to novel.

Michael Koretzky and his students Hope Dean and Kristen Grau from my alma mater, Florida Atlantic University (FAU), who endured one of my early drafts providing feedback, forcing me to improve. Go Owls!

Meghan Alard for edits, feedback, and suggestions on everything from grammar to layout, opening my eyes to developmental and plot holes that I had overlooked.

Treanna Lawrence, for enduring one of my earlier drafts also opening my eyes to blind spots.

My cover illustrator, my beautiful niece Nyeisha Oscar who delivered just what I ordered. Gina Morelli, for the feedback, design element best practices, and tips.

My Sister Germaine, who on top of listening to Gloria's every endeavor day in and day out, fed me on the days that I was cooped up writing; and my beloved niece Makaela, the girlie, who served and entertained me, forcing me to take much-needed breaks.

Victor Solas, a coworker who once told me my book sounds like a movie, promising to purchase the first signed copy but whose life was sadly cut short by COVID-19 before publication. Thank you for motivating me to hurry and get this thing out. Thank you for motivating me even in death and helping me realize truly that time and tide wait for no man.

My friends, my dear friends, and all who were probably tired of hearing, "Oh My God, the same thing happened to Gloria," completely disregarding Gloria as a fictional character (facepalm). Thank you for bearing with me, for allowing me to insert Gloria's story into our everyday conversations as if she were a real person.

And to my other friends who constantly asked, "When is the book coming out, when is the book coming out, when is the book coming out?" or "I can't wait," forcing me to get over my Imposter Syndrome and just release the baby into the world.

To all of you and countless others, I say, THANK YOU for motivating me, thank you for taking an interest in my work. My cup overfloweth, my heart is glad knowing that I have an army of supportive folks in my corner, cheering me on.

My gratitude to you—each one of you—is eternal, immense, and immeasurable.

Salut!

"Nothing happens unless first a dream."

— Carl Sandburg

Chapter 1

DECEMBER 13TH, 1993

A knock on my bedroom door forced me to divert my attention towards it. "Happy birthday, mi hija!" Mom and dad emerged with the candlelit cupcake they had just splurged on at the pastry shop down the street—Patsy's Pastry and Cake Delights—the best here in Cuba.

"And happy freedom day, too!" my parents added with a nervous giggle, handing me an adult diaper. Another teardrop escaped my eyes dotting my pajamas.

"You know, these tears won't last forever, Gloria Grace," my dad encouraged. "Leaving us is the price and sacrifice for freedom and fulfilling your purpose in life. God has blessed you with an extraordinary gift. You can't bury it under a bushel, my child. You have to go out there and use it, bless others with it.

"There's no room for growth here. You've seen it, you've lived it. Dreams are crushed and suppressed under this regime. You are incredibly talented, Glo; staying here won't allow you to blossom to your fullest potential.

"Go out there and be the best you that you can be. It's what life is about, eh—taking risks and chances, making sacrifices, helping others, showing compassion, love, and empathy, fulfilling dreams, and prospering. You have too much talent and potential to waste it away here. Your mom and I can't let that happen," my dad said, drawing me closer and hugging me tightly.

As a little girl, I often performed for my parents in the cozy living room of our two-bedroom house. The expression on their faces during my antics and their reaction following every performance and character change reverberates still in my mind's eye. The resounding cheers and applause following my numerous bows echo still.

They always marveled at how animated, artistic, and expressive I was. Asked what I wanted to be when I grow up, I'd confidently say—an actress! But Cuba was not accommodating of my dream.

In my gut, I knew dad was right. I had a fire inside me, a burning desire to act, dance, sing, dramatize, and be on television. I had experienced the oppression and the stunting of dreams he lamented.

In Cuba, freedom of speech and expression were non-existent and neither were freedom of politics and freedom of religion. I witnessed those who dared speak against the regime silenced and those who dared to express themselves get arrested and thrown in jail for a day or two—one of my biggest fears and that of my parents, too. What there was, though, was access to free healthcare and education, a policy that earned me two degrees – one in Linguistics and another in Performing Arts.

Still in his arms, dad reassured me, "It'll be fine, Glo. You will be fine. We will be OK. Your destiny is beyond the shores of Cuba."

"I guess," I sighed, slowly freeing myself from dad's tight embrace. "I hope the world is ready for me, padre," I chuckled looking up at him and mom. Using the back of my hands, I wiped away the tears in my eyes and took several deep breaths in an attempt to pull myself together. On the brink of tears, too choked up to speak, my mom GloryAnna embraced me – and then the floodgates opened; she too began to cry.

Deciding to escape was risky. The stories of people losing their lives on the treacherous journey from dehydration and hunger, exhaustion and drowning because of sketchy rafts were ever-present in my mind. My parents knew it was a gamble and they too had run through the gamut of emotions. The day had come – they hoped for the best and hoped that someday their only child would gain real freedom, rise to stardom and perhaps make a way for them.

In a matter of hours, I would be embarking on the risky 90-mile journey in pursuit of the American Dream. I prayed I lived to tell it. I'm not quite ready considering I'll be leaving my family behind, but my parents say go—go spread your wings they say. I could've gone back to my birthplace Saint Lucia, but they agreed that neither Saint Lucia nor Cuba would be accommodating of my acting dreams.

When my parents left Saint Lucia and decided to settle in communist Cuba, I was still in diapers, could barely walk and talk, I was one. Now, seventeen years later, December 13th, 1993, I'm making a big move again. Only this time I'm an adult in a diaper, traveling solo, illegally by sea, and will have a recollection of it all— if I survive it that is. Described as the greatest country on earth, a bastion of hope, where dreams come true, where freedom reigns and Lady Liberty resides—I'm going to America!

My parents had paid Juan, a local fisherman, U.S. $2,500—their entire life savings—to take me to Key West, the southernmost city in Florida. Two thousand for him and $500 for his friend in the U.S. to help me with the immigration process and provide shelter until I get on my feet. Juan is more expensive than the other smugglers but he's got the best track record for getting Cubans to Key West safely and successfully. Still, inside me emotional turmoil builds. I'm scared of traversing the Florida Straits on a canoe. I feel guilty about taking all my parents' money. I feel guilty leaving them behind.

But they insist, "Do not worry, mi hija, freedom and opportunity await on the other side of the ocean. You go on, become the movie star that you were born to be. We love you so much and want the very best for you, Glo. Go, fulfill your dream. It can't happen here in Cuba."

Remembering the sobering words from my father, a voltage of electricity coursed through my soul, a pang of guilt jabbed through my heart, a knot at the pit of my stomach threatened to paralyze me. Fighting hard to climb out of the stupor and to control my emotions, I shudder. Then, the tears trapped in the lacrimal lake of my eyes escaped splattering onto the page of my blue diary.

Out of my trance, I glanced outside my window in time to see an assemblage in progress there.

A bird flew from the mango tree that stood erect at the back of the house and landed near my windowpane. Another, another, and then several others. Soon my window was littered with the grey and white colored feathered creatures—twenty pigeons at least.

I was surprised to see so many of them at once. They used to be plentiful once-upon-a-time but for some reason, the population is dwindling. My mind instantly flashed to the legend that birds flocking to or flying into your house is a bad omen—a bearer of bad news, bad luck and foretells the death of a loved one or resident of the household.

Boodoom, boodoom, boodoom. The rhythm of my heart changed. Like a drum, it beat as beads of sweat broke through my forehead.

A few feet away madre and padre are cooking up a storm. I do not want to alarm them so I'll keep my worries and bout of superstition to myself. The aroma emanating from the kitchen permeated throughout the house. As if in direct response, my stomach grumbled and growled reminding me that it's time to break my fast. But I wasn't ready yet. I had a diary entry to complete.

At the time, we received rations from the government. All families did after the revolution. Each month, mom and dad and I made our way down to El Paso's Market to collect our reduced-priced groceries—rice, beans, sugar, fish, coffee. We didn't get milk though. Only families with children under seven and pregnant women qualified for milk. So, to supplement dad worked the land around the house he inherited from his deceased parents, mis abuelos.

At the embankment of our house was a garden. A produce garden, a nursery, and a miniature animal farm co-existed there. Dad planted crops—fruits and vegetables and ground provisions. Yellow yam and white yam had their spots there. And so did the sugarcane, cassava, sweet potatoes, lettuce, tomatoes, avocados, a couple of banana and plantain trees, celery, peppers, green onions, mangoes and guavas, oranges and tangerines, and limes. Under the house was a coop; a mini chicken coop of about eight fowls—five hens and three roosters cohabited there. That was Dad's livelihood.

Dad worked the land all week and sold his produce on the black market to neighbors, passersby and whoever else had money and was willing to take a risk. At the time, Cuba was a monopoly on food distribution, and selling produce to the neighbors and the locals was illegal. Dad knew that. He knew the consequences of being caught all too well for it was this very practice that left his parents imprisoned at the height of the revolution and subsequently murdered inside there. Dad was 25-years-old at the time and their only child. The trauma and the grief that ensued following the loss of his parents were too heavy to bear. To cope and counter the feelings of aloneness, dad pursued monastic life. A man unafraid to show emotions, he still cries for them to this day. Dad promises to tell me details someday, but when he's ready, he says. I'm unsure of when that day will come.

And mom—once a teacher in her native Saint Lucia—had traded students and blackboards for cutting boards and a family. Now a housewife, mom took care of me, dad, and the house and planted flowers in the yard.

Fresh out of universidad, with a bachelor's degree in theater and a master's in linguistics, I offered free theater and English classes to the youth in my community. In addition to performing in plays at the Globe Theater in Havana, teaching theater afforded me the opportunity to express myself, to feel the excitement and adrenaline rush of performing, an opportunity to nourish my dream. Mimicking my antics, my students often joked how over-animated I was. I can't even refute their claim. It was the only time I felt alive.

It was a Monday afternoon. I had my birthday meal, my favorite—a fusion of Saint Lucian and Cuban cuisine—pumpkin soup, moros y cristianos y pollo (black beans and white rice and chicken), green fig salad, macaroni pie, lime squash laced with banana essence to 'wash dong de food,' arroz con leche (rice pudding) and pasteles de guayaba (guava pastries) for dessert. It was my last meal with my parents before embarking on my journey. But as much as I'd have loved to feast, overindulging was out of the question. Staving off the need to go number two on the water had to take precedence.

At around 3 o'clock—as ready as I could ever be and with my diaper on—I headed to the beach to catch my chartered canoe. As my stomach churned, I stepped back one last time to take a good look at my parents—the sadness on their faces visible, the pain reflected in their eyes palpable.

"Oh madre y padre!" I inched closer and hugged them both. "I love you so much and will miss you more than words can say. You are my everything. I wish we all could go. But you say I have to go without you, go ahead, go fulfill my acting dreams. I'm conflicted about leaving you behind but I will. My desire in life is to fulfill my dreams, to make life better for us, and to make you proud. And I will. See you when I send for you—soon. Adios, madre y padre. Te amo mucho."

My parents' eyes welled up again. Much tighter than we ever had before, we hugged one last time. The bus bound for the beach came to a screeching halt, forcing us to break up the embrace. My parents looked on as I boarded the bus. Making my way to one of the few available seats near the window, I turned back to wave goodbye one last time but by then they had enveloped each other and didn't see me. As the bus drove through the streets, I tried to register the route and sites in my mind's eye. For there were no assurances I'd ever see Cuba again.

Within a few minutes, I was at the beach.

Oh, such a glorious day it is outside, I marveled, making my way to the huge rock at the shoreline. It was a stark contrast from the emotional turmoil going on inside me. *If only my heart could illuminate like the sun and sing melodically like these chirping birds right now. If only my heart and my head could somehow synchronize. I'd feel OK.*

In a struggle to find congruence, my head kept saying go and my heart said otherwise.

Within two to three hours, the noise from sea bathers and fishermen pulling in their canoe was subsiding; darkness was falling. The crickets emerged from their sleep, and the sound of the waves thrashing against the rocks seemed to have grown in intensity, fueling my dark thoughts, prompting a pep talk.

"Positive thoughts, Gloria, positive, positive," I kept reminding myself. Determined to make a name for myself, I fought hard to not allow fear to cripple me. I had a dream to fulfill.

Around 6:21 p.m. or so, a black painted canoe pulled up onto the sunset beach. A tall, dark, and skinny guy probably around 34 or 35-years-old donned in a black sweatsuit emerged near the rock where I was sitting.

"You must be Gloria, Gloria Estevez," he said, lowering his counterfeit aviator sunglasses, revealing his light brown eyes and the vertical scar that sat right below his right eye. "¿Qué bolero?" ("What's up?")

"And you must be Juan, Juan Gonzalez," I replied, extending my hand to him for a handshake.

"Ready? Let's row!" Juan's cheerful disposition, wide smile, and energy temporarily eased my anxiety a bit. "Oh, one more thing," Juan leaned closer to me, lowering his voice. "At some point, before we get to you-know-where, remind me to give you Sandy's contact info."

"Who?" I whispered back.

"Sandy. She's the woman who uh, the one who uh. She's my contact who will help you get settled over there."

"Oh, OK." The word contact and thinking about the whole operation erased the little bit of ease I had just experienced upon meeting Juan. Fear rising in me, Zig Ziglar's FEAR acronyms, 'Forget Everything And Run or Face Everything And Rise,' reverberated in my head. I chose the latter.

"¿Lista?" ("Ready?") Juan asked.

"Vamonos." ("Let's go."), I whispered. Holding on to the two sandwiches mom and dad had prepared for Juan and me, two gallons of water, a rosary, fanny pack, my blue diary wrapped tightly in plastic, prayers on my lips, hope and faith in my heart, I followed Juan to the canoe.

"Some set up you got there, uh, Juan. What's all that on the sides?"

"These? These are styrofoam bars, my version of outriggers. They help the canoe float better and prevent it from tipping over."

"Oh! When my parents said I'd be going via canoe I imagined a wooden vessel much like the one our neighbor hides underneath their house—flat bottom, shallow with paddles. I also imagined I'd have to help you row, and how it would take us forever to get there because, acere (dude), I barely ate."

"Why didn't you eat? It's a long journey," Juan looked at me puzzled.

"Because um, you know. I don't want to soil my diaper," I sheepishly divulged, looking down at my feet.

"Ah!" Juan threw his head back and laughed. "Well, anyway, this canoe has a shallow-v bottom, deep inside, and see how flared the sides are? With the flared sides it's less likely to take on water."

"This is pretty cool, Juan."

"Yeah. The one your neighbor has is probably for shallow water fishing and leisure excursions. But this one is customized for deeper waters. The v-shaped bottom helps to cut the water. That way the boat can sit deeper in the ocean for more stability when the big waves come."

"Oh, nice!"

"And uh since I use it for the long journey, I invested in an engine so it could go faster. Shh...don't tell Fidel though," Juan whispered. "It's illegal to own such things as motors. Anyway, so no worries Gloria, you won't have to row," Juan smiled.

"Guau! Eso es impresionante!" ("Wow! That's impressive!") I smiled feeling somewhat relieved.

"But you do have to help me do one thing though."

"What's that, uh?" I asked, curious.

"Launch it into the water," Juan said.

"I can do that. How fast does it go?"

"5-6 miles per hour."

"Key West is 90 miles away, so 90 divided by 5. So it should take us uh what, 18 hours?"

"Oh! That was quick Gloria." Juan looked at me shocked. "About that but most often more like 24 hours depending on the weather conditions."

"Hey Juan, I didn't go to Fidel's free schooling for nothing, you know."

Juan and I made eye contact then snickered a little.

"So, you're an engineer?" I asked him.

"Well..." Juan let out a long drawn-out sigh. "Not exactly, but uh, I got into some trouble so uh, anyway." A look of uneasiness reflecting in his eyes, Juan deflected. "Yeah, my biggest fear on these trips isn't about safety, but being caught on the water by Cuban authorities or the U.S. Coast Guard. But like I told tu madre I've always been lucky around this time of year. Hope we're lucky this time. Anyway, ready?" Juan asked, rubbing his hands to get rid of the sand on them.

"Sure," I replied timidly.

"Vamonos!" ("Let's go!") Juan exclaimed.

My eyes opened wide in response. "Wish I were as excited and at ease as you are, Captain Juan, but OK," I muttered through my teeth as I prepared to push the canoe into the water.

Is he really not terrified? Hm... I think he's putting up a brave front to ease my anxiety because there's no way, no way one can be so unafraid or calm or whatever it is, embarking on this dangerous journey. I mean...

"Ah! But first." Juan let go of the canoe, slapped his forehead then reached for both of my hands, interrupting my thoughts.

Bowing his head and closing his eyes, "Guide and protect Gloria and me, oh Lord, as we embark on this dreaded voyage to America.

The smuggler prays! My eyes popped, my jaw dropped. Flabbergasted, I couldn't help lifting my head to stare at Juan.

"Keep us safe, dear God, and carry Gloria and me on the palm of your hands, not only on this trip, Lord, but throughout life's journey. Bless and protect our families and loved ones we left behind. This we humbly ask in your precious and Holy name. We both say Amen!"

"A-A-Amen!" I stammered.

Surprised and impressed at the same time, I readied myself to launch the canoe into the water towards the Florida Straits. After working up a sweat, success. Before hopping in himself, Juan picked me up, all of my 125 pounds, and gently placed me inside the canoe. And we're off. I looked up to see Juan looking in all directions, making sure the coast was truly clear. It was.

Chapter 2

"The journey is essential to the dream."
— Francis of Assisi

A few miles in and after Juan had established that he was in "safe" waters, he repeatedly asked how I was doing and whether I was comfortable. We had cleared the 12 miles from shore owned by Cuba and patrolled by officers, so getting caught by them was no longer a concern. The U.S. Coast Guard still was though.

This smuggler is really like no other, an unconventional one—he prays, does not overload his canoe, he seems caring, and appears to be genuinely nice. Who is this guy?

"You're so uh, so uh, you're so nice, Juan."

"She says I'm nice," Juan responded, throwing his head back, erupting in laughter.

"What? You're not?" I asked, drawing my brows close.

"Wait till you get on my wrong side, mami."

Huh! I thought, perking up.

Placing his glasses over his head, Juan turned around to look at me. "See this scar?" he asked, pointing to the one below his right eye. "Well, I wasn't born with it and I didn't get it from good behavior, either."

"Oh!" I jolted. Juan's admission and devilish grin are scary. But that didn't stop me from asking how he got it.

"Don't really want to talk about it," he responded. "Don't want to scare you."

Eyes opened wide, clasping my imaginary pearls, I perked up. "Somehow I uh, I, I don't believe you're like the other smugglers, though."

"What makes you say that? What do you mean?" Juan asked.

"Well, for starters, smugglers are, you know, typically thought of as bad guys. Criminals who are hungry for money, criminals with little regard for human life. But here you are praying, making the trip with one person at a time, not overloading your canoe and very, uh, dare I say, caring and sweet?"

"Um." Juan laughed, clearing his throat. "One, if I overload my canoe, I'm putting my life in danger also. Two, people are seeking a better life, have families to feed, dreams to fulfill. How can they fulfill those duties and dreams if they don't make it to America, hm? See what I mean? You folks are humans, not goods or drugs or merchandise. And I myself, I don't want to die. I don't want to die li-ke my da-d did," Juan choked up a little. "I have a family to feed."

"So sorry about your dad, Juan. How, how did he die?"

Juan told me when he was 17, his dad Mateo left him, his mom, and his little brother to cross the straits in search of a better life in America for himself and them. The plan was that his dad would cross first, get settled, then make a way for them. Mateo had tried to go to America the legal way but was denied a visa, denied refugee admission, and he never won the diversity lottery or the Special

Cuban Migration Program (SCMP). So as a last resort, Mateo decided to take a chance and cross the unforgiving ocean, like many before him.

The smuggler his dad contacted owned a rickety makeshift vessel that he often overloaded and would carry anything or anyone who had the money. Juan said his dad had paid U.S. $500, he and at least 11 other refugees—men, women, children, pregnant women and their unborn children, crowded the raft bound for America. About halfway there, 50 miles in, they ran into trouble. It is unclear exactly how it happened, Juan said, but they believe a massive wave must have rushed in, picked up the raft, tipped it over and that was it. Under the crack in his voice, he said, "It could've been a shark attack, too. No one knows for sure what happened. No one survived, not my dad, not the kids, not the smuggler."

Then silence. Deafening silence. Taking deep breaths, lots of deep breaths, determined to tell his dad's story, Juan persisted. "Some bodies were recovered. My dad wasn't among them. He never made it to America and he never made it back home."

Imagining the emotional toll it must've taken on him and his family, my heart broke into several pieces for Juan.

"Rescuers searched for days but to no avail," he said. "They came up empty."

I hope my parents never have to experience this grief, Lord. Spare us, Oh God, please, please, please...

As Juan recounted his story and with my mortality flashing before my eyes, I couldn't help think of the parents I left behind.

Everything inside me was now churning, forming a mishmash of emotions. I wanted to know Juan's story and why he was the way he was, but the details were beyond anything I had imagined. With goosebumps covering my body, chills running down my spine, and consternation growing inside me, I was not sure knowing the details while embarking on a similar journey myself was a good idea but

I'd asked. I wanted to know and I couldn't un-hear the details of his story.

In my quest for consolation, I compared and contrasted the similarities and differences between the two trips. Juan's snazzy canoe was no rickety raft, I was his sole passenger and he invoked the name of the Lord, so perhaps we were safe, I told myself.

"Must've been hard on your family, Juan, and your mom, my goodness," I asked, swallowing past the lump in my throat.

"My mom was struggling with everything," he said. "Losing my dad, immense grief, trying to raise my brother and me who started lashing out, following the wrong crowd, and dropping out of school, adding to her stress. It was a lot. Growing up I got into trouble a lot. I ended up getting arrested and spending some time in jail for, um, for, um, anyway..."

Oh! He just stopped short of revealing what he was in for. Did he? Did he...

"I saw a lot in there—fights, rape, bullying, you name it," Juan continued.

He told me that while in jail he had a chance to reflect on his life. How sorry he was for the way he has treated his mom. And how he always felt his dad was looking down on him disappointed.

"The last thing I ever wanted to do was disappoint my dad," he said, running his hand through his hair. "But it was my way of coping, you know?" he added, then paused. "I was angry. Angry at the world, angry at God for taking him when all he was trying to do was get a better life for himself and his family."

Juan recounted that one night he got ganged up on and beat up so badly in jail that he decided this wasn't the life he wanted to lead, making a concerted effort to turn his life around.

"I tried to stay out of trouble as much as I could but sometimes trouble would just find me. My cellmate was an older gentleman, an engineer, and a teacher who was jailed for his political views. He was always studying and I was always asking him tons of questions.

"The day he was released, it felt like I was losing my dad, a father figure, and mentor all over again. He had books, lots of books on engineering and English literature that he'd sometimes let me borrow. He told me to study. Don't let my life waste away in jail. Going to jail shouldn't be the end of my life. He said I had a good head on my shoulders. I had a knack for design and that my curiosity and thirst for learning would get me far. He truly saw the best in me and gave me a boost in confidence to continue school in jail. I will never forget him and will be forever grateful to him for giving me my life back."

"Aw, Juan!"

"Upon his release, he left me a couple of books to study. My favorite was one about rafting by Thor, Thor, um, Thor something. Can't remember the last name now. Thor… Anyway, that's how I learned to build things. A few years after that I got released with my bachillerato certificate in hand. But, finding a job with a record was difficult, as you can imagine. It was then I said if no one is willing to hire me, I have to hire myself."

Juan told me one day while swimming at the beach with his buddies, he hit a goldmine – a sunken canoe.

"Mi camaradas and I pulled it ashore and we paid a guy with a truck a few pesos to transport it home for me. Finding materials to repair it was difficult, I couldn't just go to the hardware store to buy materials because one, they were not readily available and two, having building materials could raise suspicion of you trying to escape and you know what could happen. So, on many occasions, I would go down to the beach to collect styrofoam washed up from the cruise ships, and whatever else I could find, to rebuild and repair it.

"I worked on it little by little for years until it was ready for the water. So I used it for fishing and to supply a guy who had a little restaurant with fish on the black market, of course."

"Wait! Is this the canoe, Juan?"

"Yep. A few years later I met the love of my life, we got married and had twin boys."

"Aw! How precious, Juan."

"They are my life. Anyway, so one day while pulling into the bay after a disappointing fishing trip, the catch for the day was no more than a couple of flying fish and sardines. A gentleman approached me and complimented me on the boat, the design, and everything. He seemed to know a thing or two about boats. He asked if I could take him to Key West for U.S. $5,000."

"What!"

"That's what I said, trying to process the amount. Stepping back to look at him, I asked 'Did you say U.S. $5,000?' I wanted to make sure I had heard right. 'Yep, cash' he confirmed. 'That's a lot of money,' I said scratching my head.

"I was no stranger to the sea, and deep water fishing was my life. At the time I was living in a shack in a Shantytown, struggling, struggling to feed my wife and kids, and very disappointed by the catch of the day. Without giving it much thought, 'When?' I asked him stroking the two strands of hair on my chin at the time. Then something clicked in my head. 'Are you working undercover for Fidel?' I asked him, stepping back to make eye contact once again. 'Oh. No, no,' he replied, placing one hand on his chest and pointing the other towards me.

So I asked him, 'Are you carrying drugs or…' 'Nothing like that,' he assured me. 'I just want to move there to start over, you know?' I believed him. I agreed and we shook hands on it. But I had never been more nervous in my entire life.

"The guy said he could swim so I could drop him off a few miles offshore and he'd swim the rest of the way. Sounded good to me. I went home and told my wife. She was upset that I had agreed to this deal before discussing it with her first. She was also petrified, for it was that very route that my dad had perished on. She had a point, well two. I understood her concerns but couldn't let fear keep me from making a better way for us. I didn't have much time and I didn't want to lose the deal.

"Five thousand U.S. dollars is a lot of money, Juan!" I said.

"Oh yes, a sum that could get us better housing, and perhaps move out of that part of town and closer to Havana.

"The following day I met the guy. He paid me, I gave the money to my wife and off we went. He told me about his life. Like my dad, he had tried everything to go to America the legal route but was met with tough luck. He had just gotten out of a 15-year marriage, had an older son, and was running a cigar business that he would pass on to his only son. 'He said he just wanted to leave Cuba and the shame and embarrassment of being cheated on behind. He took the chance and it worked. He got a chance to start a new life in America and I was able to move my family out of a very poverty-stricken area of Cuba and into a better neighborhood."

"Wow! A win-win, huh Juan?"

"Oh yes indeed! That's what started this whole operation. It's a risk, no doubt, but everything in life is. Every trip after that became easier. I realized that there was a need, people wanted to get to America safely and alive. I mean it's one thing to escape, but what good is it if you don't make it out alive, huh? I don't want people to suffer the same fate as Dad, so here I am providing a service – an illegal service some might argue but a service nonetheless."

"I know what you mean, Juan." The thought of being intercepted on the water weighed heavily on my mind just as much as drowning and being attacked by the unforgiving jaws of sharks. It is impossible to make the crossing without feeling terrified of the whole operation. I wondered if Juan felt the same. I had to ask him. "Do you fear getting caught?"

"Of course. If it ever happens, I will just say that I'm out here fishing and hadn't realized that I had traveled so far, something like that, some mierda, some bullshit that will hopefully work." He grinned, "I mean I've done nine successful trips so hopefully, it remains that way. So aye, if we get caught, just follow my lead and say we're out fishing."

"OK, Juan," I responded, looking at him sideways. "And now you're telling me?" I asked with an eye roll. "Anyway, how come you never stayed?"

"Where? America?"

"Yes and then send for your family."

"I love Cuba. I mean I have two jobs if you count this one," he snickered. "Free healthcare, free education. Growing up without a dad was not easy and I have vowed to be with my kids always. I decided I'd never leave them."

"You're a real family man, Juan."

"You know, there's this guy who told me he left, got settled in Miami but decided to come back. He said he was working paycheck-to-paycheck, all his money went towards bills, bills, and more bills. His family was doing OK over here, they had a business he'd someday own so he came back and has never regretted it.

"I kind of understood where he was coming from. I mean, I work hard. I'm employed, and sort of have two jobs, you know? They're both risky jobs, but I can feed my family and I'm offering a service to people. The sense of accomplishment and adrenaline rush I feel after each successful trip, Gloria, is indescribable. Helping people truly makes me happy."

"Aw, Juan. I notice you move alone, no partners, no comrades."

"The more people you involve in your operations the greater your chances of getting caught or being ratted out, you know? I've been doing this for close to ten years and have never gotten into trouble. I refuse to transport arms, drugs, or anything like that. Keep it clean and simple, you know."

"See, I knew you were an unconventional smuggler, Juan. You're a good guy."

"Ah if you say so, Gloria." Juan turned around flashing a warm smile.

"Do you see yourself doing this forever?"

"I said after 10 trips I would stop, so who knows, you might be my final trip."

"Aw, aren't I lucky?"

"I've had my good luck moving my family out of extreme poverty and all that so now it's time to stick to fishing and be home with them."

Juan's story was scary and heartwarming at the same time, forcing me to get into my head.

"You got quiet, Gloria. I'm talking you to death, aren't I? Oh, 'death.' I probably shouldn't use that word. I'm probably boring the hell out of you. 'Hell,' can I say hell? I probably shouldn't say that either."

"Funny, Juan." He was right though. The thought of death lurked on my mind throughout the journey. But, I whispered to God every so often pleading for guidance, protection, and a successful trip. My faith had me believe that it would be so. For the Father in heaven says, 'Ask and you shall receive.'

By now the sun had set and traded places with the moon. Overhead it shone beautifully surrounded by a vast galaxy. The stars sparkled like diamonds refined for resale and the light green airglow in between made for a perfect city in the sky. Beneath us the sea was calm and the canoe floated masterfully on the blue waters below. For a moment the pits of my stomach quieted and I could hardly feel my heart beating.

"It's ok. You can take a nap, Gloria," Juan said.

"Nap?" I questioned Juan's absurd suggestion even though my eyelids had become too heavy to keep my eyes open. "No way I can close my eyes. I want to keep you company. We can keep talking."

Juan and I spoke about God and family and life and everything under the moon. Tired and spooked by Juan's story about his dad, I fought hard to stay awake. I had left home at 3 p.m., waited for Juan for three and a half hours, and we had traveled eight hours. It was a long day but the sailing was smooth. In the midst of the calm, I remembered Juan had told me that his name means 'God's gracious gift.' And I told him how Gloria means 'a manifestation of God's presence.'

Trusting we were in good hands, in the hands of a higher power, I surrendered to sleep. According to Juan, I dozed off several times, the longest-lasting almost a full sleep cycle. I'm almost certain his estimation was a gross exaggeration.

Fifteen hours, approximately 75 miles into the trip and it was smooth sailing until it wasn't. Out of nowhere, a strong gust of wind rushed in, startling me and forcing me to open my eyes, causing my heart to thump in my chest, throat, and ears. As Juan struggled to maintain directional control, a 5-foot wave gushed in, picked up the canoe, and spun it at 180 degrees.

Coldwater covered me from head to toe. I screamed. Before the end of the scream, another wave came in, filling my mouth with salty water, causing me to choke and sputter. I blinked through the saltwater dripping down my face from my drenched hair and madras headwrap, but my saltwater-burned eyes stung mercilessly as I strained to open them.

Now facing the opposite direction, the canoe rocked from left to right, back and forth, bouncing Juan and me around like soccer balls. Eventually, Juan surrendered, allowing the storm to run its course.

"Hold on, Gloria. Lay flat and whatever happens, do not let go of the canoe," Juan instructed, his voice laced with panic.

A sinking feeling of fright swept over me. I endeavored to follow Juan's directions but the violent motion forced me to release my grasp. The wind was hitting us head-on, blasting the canoe, forcing Juan out at the helm, and falling on top of me.

"Ow!" I screamed as Juan's weight forced my head to the bottom of the canoe.

"Sorry, Gloria. This wind is a Mother…!" Juan cussed as he struggled to sit up.

Above us, a dark mantle of clouds floated. The prospect of what was about to happen, a recipe for disaster. Before long, the sky lit up with lightning and then a BOOM followed by clack, clack, clack... a thunderous roar infiltrated our eardrums.

"No bueno, no bueno, no bueno...!" Juan yelled frantically as sheets of rain pelted down, directly upon us.

Through the chaos, I remembered it was the Spirit of God who closed the lion's mouth for Daniel when he was thrown into their den. It was He who parted the Red Sea for Moses so he could lead the Israelites to victory. And it was this same God who parted the waters of the Jordan River for Joshua so the Israelites could cross over into the land of promise.

If He could do it for them, He sure can do it for me. I broke into fervent prayer to calm myself.

Soon, the force of the wind weakened and Juan attempted one more time to turn the canoe around. A few minutes later, but after what seemed like an eternity, the rain cleared up, the sea calmed, the wind quieted, the canoe stabilized, and Juan and I were finally able to breathe again.

"Oh My God, Juan! That was terrifying! Is it always like this?"

"Not always but this one was, whew," Juan opened his eyes wide and exhaled. Releasing the air from his puffed cheeks, he shook his head adding, "By far the roughest I've ever encountered." He sighed and shuddered.

"WOW! Must have been Fidel himself!"

With a creased forehead and raised eyebrow, Juan glanced back to look at me.

"Water, Gloria?"

"Huh?"

"Do you have water to drink? I'm so pissed. I forgot my water, food, and rum on the hire that dropped me off at the beach."

"Rum?"

"A lil' something to drizzle my throat, you know?" Juan laughed.

"Here's the water. I have no rum, though, sorry. But my parents made sandwiches for us."

"They must love you so much, Gloria," Juan reassured me. "Not just any parent would do this for their kid, you know?"

"Do what, sandwiches?"

"Nah use their entire life savings to make their child's dream come true."

"I kn-ow." My voice cracked a little. "Here. Drink. I'll get the sandwiches."

"Gracias, Gloria Grace."

"OH NO!" my jaw dropped. The cheese sandwich disintegrated as I held it up to show Juan. The look of disappointment reflected in his eyes broke my heart. He was hungry. I was too.

"Give it to me!" Juan pointedly extended his hand.

"No! It's disgusting!" I protested.

"Give it to me!" he demanded, again. His stern voice startled me, so I handed him the waterlogged sandwiches. Jamming his hand into the bag, Juan fetched the cheese out and handed me a piece.

"Here."

"No thank you, Juan. That's gross."

"Sure?"

"Couldn't be more sure."

"More for me then," he rejoiced.

Just then my stomach growled, reminding me that I needed to eat. I swallowed the saliva in my mouth and agreed to have some saltwater cheese. Astonished, Juan quickly turned back to look at me. With his jaw still agape, he handed me a piece.

"What's that on your face, Juan?" I burst out laughing.

"What?" he asked.

"Are you devouring the soggy and gross saltwater bread?"

"Un-un." Juan shook his head, struggling to keep a straight face.

"So, uh, what's that all over your face?"

Smirking, he rolled his eyes and turned back around, "Well, at least I don't have to drink water. Look at it this way—it's like taking a bite of bread and then a drink of water with the bread still in your mouth. Same thing."

"Awa, Juan, so not the same thing." I laughed.

"Only difference is it's salty water, well, just like salty food—woo! That was gross!" Juan smacked his lips and shuddered. "What's 'awa'?"

"It means 'no way.' My mom, who is Saint Lucian, says it a lot."

"Oh, you guys speak another language, Gloria?" Juan asked.

"Patois. French creole. How about you, Juan?"

"Spanish and English."

"Yeah, your English is pretty good, Juan."

"I learned in school and jail."

"That cheese just made me hungrier, Juan."

I drank some water, hoping it would keep me until I made it ashore. Poor Juan would have to wait until he got back to Cuba to eat and drink. Knowing that, I sipped it sparingly so he'd get the leftover for the voyage back.

"How many more miles to go, Juan?"

"About 15."

"Whoa, 15!" I exclaimed. The excitement and anxiety were a balancing act. We had now traveled about 75 miles of the 90-mile voyage. It was smooth sailing again but Juan and I were never completely at ease. The atmosphere was changing. The wind was chillier, the clouds overcast, dark, and gloomy. And the U.S. Coast Guard was ever-present on our minds.

"Think we'll be lucky today, Captain?" I couldn't help but search for consolation.

"Hope so, but keep praying," Juan responded with a snicker. "If we get intercepted on the water, we both will be at Fidel's mercy."

In the distance, masses of land and outlines of buildings were now faintly visible. Key West was grey and gloomy and cold, a stark contrast from the bright, sunny and warm weather we had left behind in Cuba. It was freezing.

Although Juan had made several successful trips, he grew increasingly nervous as we approached Key West.

"You know, you never get used to this part, Gloria. Butterflies flutter in my stomach every time." Juan's admission terrified me.

Sitting at the edge of my seat my head bobbed from left to right, back and forth searching for signs of anything. Then after a couple more miles, the announcement came, "Looks like we made it! We made it Gloria!" Rejoicing, Juan turned around and high-fived me.

"Woohoo! How long did it take? How long did it take?"

"Um." Juan reached for his pocket clock. "Twenty-two hours. Not bad."

"Not bad at all considering the bad weather we encountered."

"Yeah, that slowed us down quite a bit. But we're here. Hop off, hop off."

"Huh!" My eyes popped. "Here? Nah it's too deep, too deep, Juan!"

"You can swim, right?" Juan asked, glancing back at me with a puzzled frown.

"Nope!"

"What? Your parents told me you swim like a fish!"

"Me? Un-un," I said, shaking my head violently. "I only eat fish and don't even like it."

"Oh, mi Dios! Oh my God! You think it's funny?"

"Can't swim to save my life," I admitted pulling my lips back in a grimace.

"¡Que cojones!" ("What the fuck!") Juan threw his hands up in aggravation. Rage rising in him.

"They fuckin' lied to me?" Considering that one of the main requirements of his trip is that escapees can swim, Juan became irate, falling into a swear-induced frenzy. Juan grew angrier, and understandably so. The joy he had just experienced was now marred by deception. The more agitated Juan got, the faster my heart raced.

Oh, God! Juan's heart is going to stop.

"I'm sor-ry, Juan," I apologized for the lie—everything. Juan shook his head. "OK, Gloria," Juan glanced at me and in a calmer tone said, "a few feet more and you have to hop off."

With my heart racing, chest tightening, and breath shortening, I reluctantly agreed.

Guess I'm gon' learn to swim today. But I'm not coming this far to die by drowning, I reckoned internally.

"Here!" he said, expecting me to jump out as agreed.

"What?" I asked, pretending to not know what he meant.

"Gloria!" Juan huffed. He kept going. "Here. Think you can swim from here?"

"A little closer, a lil' closer, Juan. That looks deep."

"Gloria! You can! Girl, I swear if I get in trouble I will wipe you guys out!"

"You guys?" I blinked rapidly.

"You and your entire family. Hop the fuck off now!" Juan snapped, his eyes growing cold.

"Juan!" I screamed.

"Gloria, listen to me," Juan said, lowering his voice and glasses simultaneously, looking directly into my eyes. "My life and yours are at stake here. You have to hop off. If we get caught we'll be thrown in jail or even..."

"But, Juan! Sharks!" I protested.

"Gloria, hop the fuck off!"

"JUAN!"

"Oh my God! Gloria, I'm more scared of the shark back in Cuba and the U.S. Coast Guard! Off now. Now! Now! Now!" Juan yelled, repeatedly jerking his index finger pointing downwards.

"Ok Juan, keep going. Let me put my rosary around my neck, make sure my diary is still secured tightly in the plastic so I can put it in my sweatshirt, and make sure my fanny pack is securely fastened around my waist."

"Oh my God!" Juan screamed, raising both hands and placing them behind his head in frustration. The wrong side Juan had spoken of when I met him was beginning to rear its head. "Gloria, the closer I get to shore, the more likely I am to get spotted. Do you not understand that? I have to head back to my family!"

"Juan, I'm scared. Still too deep. I can't swim."

"Well, you'll learn today. Hop the fuck off now or…"

"Or what, Juan?"

Whoosh! And splash!

Juan picked me up and threw me overboard. "Sink or swim! And you better swim!" he admonished.

Gulp, gulp, gulp. I swallowed a half-gallon of seawater and another and another. Now it feels like the whole sea is inside me. I struggle to keep my head above water. I have to make it ashore. To my surprise, I was able to barely touch the ocean floor on my tippy toes. I glanced back to look at Juan.

"¡Chao pescado!" ("Good-bye, fish!") he said, flashing one last smile and a thumbs up before speeding away.

Bouncing up and down, I struggled to keep my head above water. I could see the shore. I looked back again to see how far Juan had traveled. What I saw instead terrified me. My eyes tripled in size, my heart pounded in my chest. But I couldn't let it paralyze me with fear. The closer it got, the taller it appeared. I tried not to panic. I tried to run but the undercurrent coupled with my saggy diaper restrained me. Using one hand, I eventually ripped open the sides to rid myself of it.

Before long the massive wave barreling towards me made its impact. It crashed into me. I closed my eyes. I thought for sure it had swallowed me. I closed my eyes as tightly as I could. I felt my bum hit the ocean floor. Too scared to open my eyes I kept them shut tightly. Then I heard what sounded like a wave crashing ashore.

My eyes flew open. There I was, flat on my ass, at the shoreline. As the wave ebbed, it spun me back around facing the ocean. Still sitting, I struggled to not let the backflow drag me into the sea. *Hallelujah!* I rejoiced. The force of the wave had propelled me forward, saving me.

WHAT!

"Oh God, You are awesome!" I proclaimed despite nausea sloshing around in my stomach. As bile leaked into my mouth, I struggled to swallow the bitter liquid. *Bbblllaaaaaaargh!* The ocean inside me escaped rejoining the sea, rendering relief.

With my diary still tucked in my sweater, fanny pack around my waist, and rosary around my neck, I moved further up shore and onto drier sand. Facing my tear-filled eyes towards the heavens and my arms outstretched, I gave thanks to the higher power who without a doubt had saved me. I was alive! I was in America.

In the distance, I saw a canoe drifting, riding the waves. I'm pretty sure it was Juan. The thought of closing my eyes again as tight as possible and yelling back at him crossed my mind. But besides being exhausted and weak, I didn't want to call attention to myself or him.

"Merci, merci, merci mon Dieu! Gracias, gracias, gracias, gracias a Dios! Thank you! Thank You! Thank you, my God." I sobbed and prayed and kissed the sandy beach. "Ugh!" A dollop of sand somehow ended up in my mouth, forcing me to sputter. "San. Sand. SANDY!" I exclaimed. Jumping to my feet, I called out to Juan waving frantically to summon him. But he was too far out in the distance to hear my call or see my wave.

"Oh. Mi. Dios! Oh. My. God!" I cried out raising my hand over my head and falling to my knees a second time, this time in distress. Juan had forgotten to give me Sandy's number and I had forgotten to remind him.

"No! No! No!," I sobbed, punching the sand surrounding me as I cried out. "Now, what am I going to do?"

I had nowhere to stay.

"The dream is free. The hustle is sold separately."

— Tyrese Gibson

Chapter 3

"I'm in America. What now? Where am I going? What do I do?" I pondered, walking along the seashore. "I know no one here."

It was still early, 6 p.m. or so. It was cold, eerily quiet. The beach was barren with no one in sight. Well, that was until a guy emerged from the bushes that lined the seashore a few minutes later, activating my fight or flight response.

"Oh!" I gasped, unsure whether I should take off running or play it cool. I chose the latter. Amid the struggle to catch my breath and lower my heart rate, I stood, still contemplating my options. *Could he be Sandy's friend? Did Sandy send him?*

"Sup, ma'am?" he greeted me.

"Hi," I acknowledged the gentleman with a smile and a nod.

"It's not particularly a beach day, huh," he added, looking up at the sky and about him. No older than 35-years-old, his deep and raspy voice stunned me. "Be careful with this weather, you don't want to get sick," he cautioned me.

"Neither do you, sir," I smiled, repeating timidly, "Neither do you."

"Ah! See I'm used to the weather. Rain or shine, hot or cold, I'm in it. I'm Marco by the way."

Marco! I chuckled in my head, remembering the little creole my mom taught me that 'marco' means Peeping Tom.

"So what are you doing here, ti marco?" My tongue slipped.

"Huh?" Marco looked at me puzzled.

"Marco. I mean Marco, Marco, what are you doing here?"

"Just wandering like I always do," he replied nonchalantly.

Oh, un ti marco for real. I squirmed subtly.

"What did you say your name was?" Marco asked, forging through a cough.

"I didn't. But I'm Gloria. Gloria Estevez," I hesitated but gave him my real name, perchance he was Sandy's stand-in. Marco extended a hand to grab mine.

"Gloria Este who? Nah..." Marco stepped back to size me up.

"Estevez, Gloria ES-TE-VEZ," I replied with a slow and deliberate annunciation.

"Oh! My bad! I thought you were um, um that singer, that singer from Cuba, what's her name again?" He snapped his fingers, trying to recall.

"Gloria Estefan," I interrupted.

"Right, right..." Marco laughed revealing the few teeth he had left in his mouth.

Whoa! Is that a gap or is he missing a couple? Wow! Young guy, eh, missing all these teeth? And he's cu-te too. But, um...

"Gosh it's cold and I'm thirsty," I said, stroking my arms to keep warm. "Where can I get a drink of water around here, Marco?"

"You've never been here before?" He asked, staring at me perplexed.

Oh boy, what did I just reveal?

Letting Marco's question fall on deaf ears, "Water, where can I get a drink of water?" I repeated.

"There's a water fountain over there," he pointed. "Right outside the restrooms. I'm headed that way, I'll show you."

Huh! Restrooms?

Marco's request to accompany me near the restrooms, on a quiet beach, with just the two of us was unsettling.

Do I trust him?

"So where are you from and what's a beautiful young lady like you doing here all alone, on such a cold night? It must be 40 degrees out here today. Although not as cold as it was yesterday."

"Yesterday was colder, huh?"

"Yup 'twas about 25 degrees or so."

"Oh my! It gets that cold in Florida?"

"Strange, huh, for the Sunshine State? I know," Marco laughed. "Where are you from?"

Marco seems to be a real nice guy. Should I tell him? Maybe he can offer me a bunk. But then again, gleaning from what he said earlier about being outside rain or shine and coming from under the bushes over there, it looks like he, himself, is either on some serious marco vibes or homeless, my mind went into overdrive as I prepared to answer Marco.

"Well," I cleared my throat and stuttered, "Cu-Cub-Cuba!"

"Cuba? Just now?" he laughed. "Wow, you must be tired, hungry, and thirsty."

"All of the above," I chuckled. "We left Cuba around this time yesterday. The sandwiches my mom had prepared for us got soaked when the storm suddenly came through and flooded our canoe."

"We? There's more of you?"

"Nope just me. Just me. Juan, the guy who transported me is on his way back."

"Wow! He didn't stay? So where are you staying?"

"Um, um, my boy. Friend. My boyfriend is picking me up. He should be here any minute." By now I had figured that Marco wasn't Sandy's stand-in, so the honesty and accuracy with which I'd responded went out the window.

"Oh! He's a lucky, lucky fella. Pardon me but I just can't stop staring. You are such a beauty, although those lips are a little dry," he cackled. "And those wet clothes and the way your hips sway… Dang girl, you're pretty sexy."

My eyes widened. My heart raced. I hastened my steps. Becoming conscious of the wet clothes clinging to my body, I wished to be transformed into an octopus. It's a pity I only have two hands. I used them to wrap my arms around my chest area. I contemplated forgoing the restrooms but my dry throat and full bladder wouldn't allow me. I had to go.

Protect me, God I pleaded in my head. Sighing silently, I continued walking. "Are these the restrooms over there?" I asked pointing with my left index fingers, my arms still folded.

"Yes."

"Gracias, Marco. Take care now." Flustered, I made my way to the water fountain, positioning myself in such a way to keep an eye on Marco. I needed to make sure that he had truly gone away. Leaning forward, I cupped my mouth to catch the water and pressed the button, making sure to keep my eyes open.

"Mierda!" (Crap!) I screamed. The water totally missed my mouth, landing in my eyes, and on my clothes. I must've pressed too hard. Closing my eyes, I stepped back to escape the spewing water. "Oh!" My eyes flew open remembering that I needed to keep my eyes out for Marco.

Where the heck did he go? "Marco!" I called out terrified. *Where did he go?*

I looked all about me but he was nowhere to be seen. While the pit of my stomach urged me to keep looking for him, my bladder said there were more pressing matters to attend to. Rushing into the bathroom stall, I pulled down my sweatpants and knickers at the nick of time. *Shhhhhhhhhhhhhhhhhhhhhhh…* It was literally the longest piss I ever took. Relieved, I closed my eyes, letting out a long, drawn-out sigh.

Marco! my mind flashed back to him. *Where did he disappear to?*

Pulling up my sweatpants and underwear at once, I rushed outside.

"Oh! Marco!" I almost ran into him right outside the bathroom door. My heart became too powerful for my chest and I struggled to hide my fear, "I was um, I was wondering where you um, where you disappeared to."

"Here!"

"What is it?" I asked. "Oh Henry?"

"A mini chocolate bar. Henry should hold you over until you get some real food," Marco chuckled.

"Oh!" I grinned, still too startled to give much more. "Thank you, Marco. How thoughtful."

"Ah! Enjoy it, young lady. Welcome to America! And ay, if it doesn't work out with your boyfriend, you know where to find me, aiight?" Marco laughed then went on his merry way.

"Whew!"

If Marco had looked back, he'd have seen me breathe a literal sigh of relief.

"Silly girl," I chided myself. *What were you thinking? Oh, you weren't!*

Realizing that this encounter could've gone much differently and thankful that it played out the way it did, I thanked my Protector in heaven as I proceeded to find an exit. I continued walking along the beach, taking in the sights and sounds around me. The whistling trees, the sounds of the waves crashing ashore, the smell of seawater traveling up my nostrils, evoking memories of mom and dad and me at the beach.

As the memories conjured up, thoughts of the parents I had left behind ached my broken heart. Shrugging it off the best I could at the moment, I continued walking.

Oh, God! Hope I find an exit soon.

I'd walked about a quarter-mile already. It was a long stretch of beach. Finally after about another quarter-mile or so I came upon an opening, a track that led to the street.

Relieved, I breathed deeply and took in the scene before me.

"Wow!" I marveled cupping my cheeks. "Oh. My God! I really am in AMERICA!" I rejoiced as it sank in.

The streets were festooned with vendors from one end to the next. Folks having a merry ol' time in the cold at what looked like a festival. It was around 7:30 p.m. by now and men, women, and children were roaming the streets freely, shopping, eating, and having a good time.

People sold goods openly and freely without fear of being imprisoned by the government. A stark contrast from what I had left behind in Cuba. It was clear that I was experiencing my first bout of culture shock. I was in awe.

I had relieved my bladder and quenched my thirst. Now I needed to satiate my hunger. Stopping at the first food truck I came across, I ordered some food.

"How much are your hotdogs sir?"

"The price is right there madam!"

"Oh! Didn't see it."

Wow, a hotdog, soft drink, and chips just $5?

"I'll have the hotdog combo, please." Reaching into my fanny pack, I pulled a seawater-soaked $20 bill.

Eww! I grimaced, shook it open, and handed it to the vendor.

Muttering under his breath, he too grimaced then raised the bill to the light to check its legitimacy. Impatient and inhospitable, I couldn't help but wonder if perhaps that's why his stall was empty. Grabbing my meal and $15 change, I couldn't get out of there fast enough. Upon securing my change in my fanny pack, I longingly sank my teeth into the hotdog.

"Hmm...delicioso!" I closed my eyes, savoring every bite. *Well, either that or I'm just really hungry.*

"Oh, I have to go..." I whispered to myself. *But wait, where? Where do I go?*

Reality began to kick in, quelling the excitement I had just experienced. I had nowhere to stay.

I continued walking and came upon a bench on the side of the road. Plopping on it I exhaled as I sat. Resting my head at the top of it, I stretched out my legs in front of me and closed my eyes before full-blown panic seized me.

I really have nowhere to stay. How am I going to make it in this place? The streets, lined with resorts, reminded me of the touristy parts of Havana. *Bet they're expensive. Check this one out.*

Considering the little money I had in my pocket, I vacillated between crossing the street to check out a hotel that caught my eye or simply admiring it from a distance. Remembering the teaching of my parents to never tell yourself no, I grabbed my belongings and hastened towards it.

"Welcome to the Margaritaville Key West Resort & Marina. I'm Luna. How may I help you?" The front desk attendant's warm and welcoming smile relieved some of my anxieties.

"Um hi, Luna. I have a question. How much does it cost to stay here?"

"Anywhere from $400 to $800 a night."

"Oh!" my eyes widened and my head fell back involuntarily.

"Let's see here," the attendant did a quick search. "Oh, it's only $229 tonight, ma'am. Wow! Haven't seen such a low rate in a long time."

What! Only? She just said only $229! I only have $185 to my name.

"But it looks like we have no available rooms," Luna continued.

"Oh, no worries, no worries at all, ma'am! Thank you," I exhaled, rushing out the door.

Back to square one, mamacita, I shuddered and sighed simultaneously.

Realizing I probably couldn't afford any of the resorts that lined the streets of Key West, I made my way back to the bus stop where I was sitting earlier. I grew increasingly worried but told myself to embrace the challenges. Maintaining a positive disposition, I greeted everyone with a smile. I didn't quite understand why some people ignored my greeting but didn't let it bother me.

I had been sitting at the bus stop bench for a while when I spotted a General Store across the street and decided to go in.

Crackers, crackers, I think I'll get a box or two, a blanket, maybe two, uh a pair of jeans, a t-shirt, backpack, and some toiletries.

That should hold me over for now. I thought, making my way to the cashier.

"Your total is $28.86, ma'am."

My mouth fell open. My brows shot up.

Back home the toothpaste alone would've cost $15.

"Thank you mami." Collecting my shopping bags, I made my way back to that bus stop across the street.

Far in the distance, I could see a bus approaching. Squinting to read the ticker that ran across the top, it looked like it said 'Last bus.'

"Yup, last bus," I confirmed, jumping to my feet. Even though I didn't know where I was going, I grabbed my shopping bag and boarded the bus blindly.

In what seemed like three minutes, the bus driver announced to me and the only other passenger on board, "Last stop before the bus station, last stop before the bus station."

The other rider, an older gentleman got off at the next bus stop, leaving me with the driver.

"Last stop, bus station. Last stop, bus station," the driver continued announcing.

Guess that's where I'm headed, I reckoned in my head, underneath a heavy sigh.

Should I ask the bus driver for a bunk? Nah. That's inviting trouble. I squashed the thought just as quickly as it entered my mind. *Can't believe I forgot to remind Juan to give me Sandy's number. Aargh! I could kick myself. OK, Gloria, what's done is done, no need to go back now. It's a pity you didn't have an alternate plan. It's not too late to think of one though.*

Sighing, I held onto my belongings, hopped off the bus, and made my way to the bus station. From a distance, I spotted someone inside.

Maybe I should ask him if I could stay overnight here? Could I get arrested for just wandering around? Arrested! Oh-god-no! My parents would die if I end up in jail. Although, if I do go to jail at least I'd have a place to spend the night, right? Stop it, Gloria, you don't mean that.

Searching for a silver lining, I shrugged.

Dammit, I'll take a chance. Heck, I just took the ultimate risk of my life.

Taking a deep breath, my mind flashed back to my experience on the water.

I can't believe he threw me overboard. I'll admit I was being a gallina (wuss) though.

I shook my head.

And mom and dad, oh my god! They were so wrong for telling Juan that I swim like a fish. Me, swim like a fish?

I chuckled and then shuddered.

The look on Juan's face when he threw me out of the canoe was terrifying yet priceless. Funny now, but it certainly wasn't at the moment. I could've drowned and Juan suffered a heart attack. Oh my God, I sighed. *Juan, Juan, Juan. Hope he makes it back safely.*

Pulling out the two blankets I had bought earlier, I strategically placed one on the bench right next to the building. And the jeans I had just bought, I rolled up nicely to use as a pillow. Laying down, I threw the other blanket over myself. Exhausted, I gave thanks, then closed my eyes to sleep.

Tap! A hand landed on my shoulder startling me. My eyes flung open. My heart raced and pounded heavily in my chest. Towering over me was a burly, broad-shouldered guy wearing an all-beige outfit twirling a baton.

"Ma'am! What's going on here?" he asked.

"Sir, sir. I I-I-I'm taking the next bus and I really don't want to miss it."

"You do know that the next one is not until tomorrow, right?"

"I know, I know, I just don't want to miss it, sir."

Please don't ask to see the ticket, please don't ask to see the ticket, don't ask to see the ticket.

"So where…"

Oh God! panic seized me.

"I mean, um, what did you say your name was?" The security guard asked.

"I didn't, sir."

"Ma'am I'm asking."

"Gloria Este… I mean, Gloria. Yeah, just Gloria. My name is Gloria."

"You're not Gloria Estefan!" he laughed and quickly added, "then, I'm Emilio."

"Funny, sir."

"Ma'am, are you impersonating a celebrity? Really what's your name?"

"Gloria ESTE-VEZZZZ, sir," I said, deliberately emphasizing the last syllable of my surname.

"Oh…, EsteVEZ!" he repeated stressing on the third syllable.

Chuckling, he walked back into the station leaving me to breathe a sigh of relief. Extremely thankful for the encounter, I repositioned myself for bed feeling I could rest easy now; feeling that I had just gotten indirect permission to spend the night—and with supervision at that.

I really have to break the habit of telling people my full name, I reckoned before drifting to sleep.

Every accomplishment starts with a dream or a thought. Every achievement comes with proactivity. Wake up, get up, go feed your dreams.

CHAPTER 4

A few hours later the sun came out, its rays falling gingerly onto my face, waking me from my slumber. Feeling somewhat refreshed and energized, I was ready—well, sort of ready—to take on the day.

I thanked God for waking me up, for blessing me with a new day. I thanked Him for protecting me, for strength and guidance and favor, for the sleep which had refreshed me, and for the opportunity to start afresh. And I thanked Him for his grace and mercy.

Rapt in reverie, I sat still awhile.

Every accomplishment starts with a dream or a thought. Every achievement comes with proactivity. Visions remain but mere thoughts if they are backed by inactivity; dreams die slowly if they are unnourished. Gotta go feed that dream, Gloria. Nothing in life comes easy, and giving up is not in your DNA.

Breathing in deeply, I counted my money, then devised a plan to get through my day.

With the little money I had leftover—$156.14—I figured I'd spend it on a couple of days meals instead of a motel for a night or two.

But where will I stay, though? If my parents know things didn't work out as planned and that I slept here last night they'd be beside themselves.

Just as quickly as the thought entered my psyche I shook it off and redirected my attention to devising a plan to earn some money. With Key West being a tourist destination, I figured I'd make my way to the beach and offer to braid the tourists' hair for a buck or two.

But how many people would want that and how much money can I make from that? Oh, so you want fast money, huh? Well... Oh-god-no! Prostitution certainly isn't an option. But what's there to do? How will I make money?

Feeling the urge to relieve my bladder, I broke from planning and heeded the need. The last thing I needed was a urinary tract infection. Gathering my things, I made my way to the washroom.

On my way to the stall, I caught a glimpse of myself in the mirror, well someone whom I thought was me. I leaned back for another glance, it was me. Wrapped in a black blanket, messed up hair, black backpack. Homeless. Vagrant. Beggar. Bingo!

I relieved my bladder, brushed my teeth, and freshened up a little. Unraveling my madras headwrap, I messed up my hair a little more than it already was, and rewrapped it, leaving most of my hair exposed. I grabbed my blanket, wrapped it loosely around my neck and shoulders. Throwing my backpack on my back completed the look I was going for. Now, I was ready. Ready to hit the road.

I rehearsed over and over how I'd approach people but no amount of rehearsal could prepare me for this role. It felt unnatural, deceitful, and wrong. But, I needed to survive. It's a means to an end I justified.

I walked up to a grocery store and positioned myself at the door. Pulling down my shirt, adjusting my blanket scarf, clearing my throat, I readied myself to approach the first shopper. I opened my mouth but the words got caught somewhere inside me. Not sure it even made it to my throat. I opened my mouth again. This time, a high-pitched sound escaped.

The woman walked right past me. *Darn it!*

I spotted another coming.

There, there, there, another one is coming, another one is coming, a cheerleader in my head egged me on. *Go, Glo, Go. Ahh, too late. Shit!*

I breathed in.

It's OK, Glo. Next one, next one.

Poking my head inside the store, I saw a woman checking out. *Looks like she paid with cash.* I stepped back, waiting.

There's your chance, girl. Better aaask! the voice in my head wouldn't shut up.

What's the worst that can happen, huh? Well, being ignored or hearing no, I guess. OK, here she comes, here she comes. I can do this.

"Ahem," I fake cleared my throat, looking at the woman's feet, "Ma'am, may...some change please?"

Separating the paper money and the receipt, she handed me the loose change.

Way to go Glo! I rejoiced, feeling proud that I had uttered some decipherable words. Then, it dawned on me that perhaps it was my attire that did the talking. Regardless of what it was, I succeeded, making the second 'ask' easier. By the third, I was a pro. Well, sort of.

At the end of the day, I bought a soda to wash down the chicken sandwich a stranger handed me and retired for the day. Making my way down to the bus station, I could hardly wait to count my money—$7.11!

"Wow!" I rejoiced and prepared to repeat the process the following day. With each passing day, the 'ask' became easier and I collected a little more than the day before. *Progress,* I'd say. No matter how small it is always a motivator.

A DARING PURSUIT OF THE DREAM

Over three days, I collected about $25.47, a few bags of potato chips, sandwiches, sodas, and a loaf of bread. The station was within walking distance from the plaza, so I made it my permanent sleeping residence.

I wonder if Billy, the security guard, knows that I'm homeless. He never said anything though. He probably thinks it's just my routine. Such a nice guy, eh. We disagree on a lot of issues but I enjoy debating him. He looks out for me every night.

Despite my struggles, I tried to maintain a positive disposition. I spoke to everyone I met and smiled through disappointments. In speaking to folks, I found out that New York or California was the mecca for budding actors, actresses, and entertainers. I trusted God and my daily hustle to help me get there.

On some days I panhandled near the bus station and on others I'd walk over to the parking lot of the supermarket, offering to help patrons load groceries into their cars for a buck or two. On other days, I made my way to the beach to beg tourists for spare change or offer to braid their kids' hair in exchange for change.

Some days, I flat out asked for a buck or two. But I preferred loading groceries or braiding hair over begging for money. I always felt like I was offering a service in exchange for money. During those two weeks, I often reminded myself that it's a means to an end, a means to an end, as I struggled to find congruence and restore my dignity.

One day, January 7th, 1994 while standing in the Publix parking lot, a posh silver car pulled up next to me. The driver's black blazer, crisp white shirt, and red tie screamed CEO. "Looking for work, honey?" he asked, stroking his imaginary beard as he spoke.

"Ye-yes," I responded, stuttering over my words.

"Oh great. Meet me at the Hyatt Hotel down the street."

"How far is that?" I asked.

"It's just a 3-5 minute walk." He winked.

O-K! I was taken aback. "What's your name, sir?"

"D... D... Donald."

"Ok Donald, see you soon."

Excited, I unraveled the blanket from around me and tucked my shirt into my jeans. Using the side view mirror of the car closest to me, I fixed my hair as best I could and checked that my teeth had not retained some of the potato chips or gotten stained by the red Hawaiian Punch I just had. Looking somewhat presentable, given the circumstances, I made my way to the Hyatt Hotel.

Upon entering the lobby, a pleasant young lady at the front desk greeted me.

"Hi, I'm here to meet Donald for a job."

"Who?" she asked puzzled.

"The hiring manager—Donald?"

"Hm?" Her eyebrows shot up, her forehead creased. The puzzled look on her face had me thinking perhaps I was at the wrong place.

"This is the Hyatt, right?" I asked, turning my head in all directions, looking for Donald.

"Sure is, but we have no Donald working here, ma'am."

"Clean-shaven, black blazer, heavy—no? Red tie, silver car…"

"Um, no ma'am. The hiring manager is actually on lunch break right now and drives a black SUV if I remember correctly."

"There you are beautiful!" I heard the same voice that approached me earlier emanating from behind me and felt a hand drop around my shoulders.

"Oh! I was beginning to think I was at the wrong hotel."

"Oh no, honey, right hotel, wrong room." He grinned. At Donald's request, I followed him.

"Donald the attendant says there's no one by the name of Donald working here."

"Oh? I just started so she probably doesn't remember my middle name."

"You go by your middle name?"

"Sometimes."

"Why?"

"Because I don't like my first name."

"What is it?"

"Eh?"

"What's your first name?" I pressed.

"Drop it!" he snapped.

My questioning was cut short by the agitation in Donald's voice.

"I really don't like it, honey." Donald softened his tone, reaching for my chin.

"So what openings do you have, sir?"

"Oh, no need for the formalities, honey. Just call me Donald or Don."

What's with the honey? Is this how they do it in America?

Making our way up to the second floor, we came to a stop at room 69.

"Welcome to my office!" he smiled.

"Office?" I asked puzzled.

"Like it? This is where all the action, I mean hiring, hiring happens," he laughed. His cell phone rang, interrupting his sheepish laughter. He held up a finger, "One second…"

"Hi, babe. Is everything OK? How are the kids? Uh, the weather in New York is actually pretty nice today, not too cold, not too hot, just perfect."

"Huh?" I gasped, my eyes widened and my mouth fell open. *Isn't this Key West?*

As if hearing my thoughts, Donald shot me a look that clearly meant to be quiet.

"Conference is going really well. Will be home the day after tomorrow. OK, babe. Talk to you right after this session. Love you more, sugar, sugar."

Bastard just lied to his wife?

As understanding dawned, a lump suddenly got caught in my throat, threatening to choke me. Beads of sweat burst through my pores. Donald inched closer to me. Stroking my hair, he reached for my chin. The potato chips I had eaten earlier clumped at my throat. Feeling the urge to puke, I swallowed hard.

"What are you doing?" I pulled away.

"You're looking for work, right? Aren't you sweetheart?" he whispered in my ear, reaching for the top button of my shirt.

"I am looking for work," I stated matter-of-factly. "But that's, that's…"

"Hold that thought," he motioned with his index finger 'shh,' moving away to take another call.

"Hey, babe," he walked towards the glass window at the other end of the room. "The key to the Range Rover is on my side of the…"

I grabbed my backpack, clutched it against my chest, and bolted. *Fuck!* The door didn't open all the way. I closed it back to undo the swing bar lock latch.

Donald lunged to grab me with his right hand while holding the phone to his ear with his left hand. His fingers grazed me, but I got away. Looking in both directions to see which exit was closest, I turned right and bolted down the hallway, opened the exit door, and ran down the stairway. Without even looking, I dashed across the street, stopping in the lobby of another hotel.

"Ma'am, are you OK?" The concierge asked, her eyebrows contracted and her nose wrinkled. "May I help you?"

Panting, I took a minute to catch my breath.

"Just gotta use. Your. Restroom," I responded, taking breaths between words and closing my eyes to keep the sweat from entering.

"Well these aren't public restrooms, but go ahead. Second door on your right. Right after door 69.

Oh Lord! my eyes widened. *Got a sense of humor, huh, God?*

"Go on, you'll see the sign," she added, pointing in its direction.

"Hey, lady! Gimme your scarf, gimme your scarf gimme your scarf!" I asked the woman washing her hands at the sink. Her blue jeans, black thigh high, high heeled boots, crisp white button-down shirt accessorized with the brightly colored scarf made for a complete look.

"Huh?" She swiftly turned towards me, her brows furrowed.

"Please?" I asked again, activating my puppy eyes.

Placing her hands on her hips, she breathed deeply then proceeded to slowly remove the scarf from around her neck. Sighing, she reached for my hands, both of them then placed the scarf in them. Holding onto my hands with both of hers, the scarf dangling, she told me how much she loved it, how long she's had it, and how sentimental it was to her.

"But here," she said. "Take it if you want it that badly. Take good care of it, now. My grandma gave it to me before she passed last year."

"Aww, um." My moral compass contemplated refusing it, but my life—I thought depended on it at the moment.

"I will," I promised her. "I don't want it. I need it. I just, uh, I just need it to disguise myself."

"But why? You're a beautiful girl."

"I'm running from a man," I sighed.

"Oh! Should I call the cops?"

"No-no," I sighed again before telling her the story of how I was standing in the plaza parking lot begging for spare change when this man approached me and asked if I was looking for work.

"You said yes?" the woman exclaimed leaning in towards me, looking at me with wide eyes.

"What? I am, though," I responded, puzzled.

"Young lady," she whispered, grabbing my hands. "When someone in the streets asks if you're looking for work, what they're really asking is, 'are you a prostitute.'"

"Oh. My. God!" My eyes and jaw widened in synchronization. "A prostitute?"

We locked eyes, then cracked up.

"I know it's no laughing matter. Pardon me," she said. "But, girl..."

"It's OK. Thank you for letting me know. And thank you for the scarf."

"Don't worry about it. Are you OK, though?"

"I will be."

"Good. I'd love to chat longer but I gotta bounce, I have a flight to catch. Be careful out here, ya hear."

"Thank you. Thank you so much."

"Ah, don't mention it," she assured me with a dismissive hand gesture before rushing out the door.

My hands flew to my eyes to cover them. Taking a deep breath, I slid my back against the bathroom wall lowering to the floor.

What just happened?

My mind went into overdrive recounting the day's events.

"I could've gotten raped!" I shivered.

Thank you, Father, for watching over me, for protecting me. All the signs were there but I was too desperate or naive to see them. Thank you, God, for leading Donald's wife, significant other, or whomever she was to call, saving me. Oh Lord, how can I ever repay you?

Still seated on the bathroom floor, trying to calm myself, another woman came rushing in with her hand luggage in tow. I thought for sure she'd question why I was on the floor. But ignoring my presence, she quickly entered the largest bathroom stall and plopped herself onto the seat. The noise startled me. Br. Br. Br. Brrr... What sounded like a muffler or motorboat trying to start resounded in the bathroom.

Oh!

My eyes widened. A laugh threatened to escape. Then brrrrrrrrrrrr the noise started again, only this time for longer and with more bravado.

Wiggling my nose, I jumped to my feet, grabbed my backpack, and ran out the door. I couldn't stay even if I wanted to. Besides disturbing my peace, the stench would have either killed me or left me half dead. And I didn't come all this way to die like this.

Using the reflection from the vending machine in the hotel lobby, I fixed my newly acquired scarf around my neck and head before venturing outside. I figured by then the solicitor was perhaps gone or onto his next girl. To make up for the lost time with Donald, there was one thing I needed to do.

"Have some change to spare, ma'am?" I fleeced the concierge before making an exit. "What's your name?" I asked, leaning forward, squinting to read her name tag.

"I'm Lucy," she responded, reaching for her pocketbook.

"Let's see here," she said wiggling her hand through the contents of her bag to reach the bottom.

Removing everything in the way, she dug and dug and dug. Satisfied that she had checked the entire circumference, she pulled her hand out coming up empty. Well, not entirely empty if you count the debris on her fingers and underneath her nails. Turning her body away from me, she raised her hand to her face, puffed out her cheeks, and blew the dust off.

She reached into her handbag again, this time fetching a brown multi-section wallet.

Well, alright! I cartwheeled in my head.

Going through her papers, her paper dollars, she decided on one and handed it to me.

"A twenty! Oh my God! Thank you! Thank you, Lucy!" I rejoiced, gawking at the twenty-dollar bill like it was a novelty, a million dollar note. In my two weeks of panhandling, I had never grossed $20 in a single day, let alone in one ask. My gratitude for Lucy's generosity was immense and I couldn't hide it. "Thank you so much. May God bless you with an abundance."

"Aw! Thanks, ma'am! It's only twenty though."

"'Only twenty,' she says. That's plenty, plenty, Lucy! You have no idea."

"Glad I could bless you," she said. "What's your name?"

"Gloria."

"Ah! It was my pleasure, Gloria," she smiled and wished me a good evening.

"Oh trust me, Lucy, you just made my day!"

Grateful and exhausted, I decided to retire for the day, making my way home—the bus station. Upon arrival, I recorded the encounter in my diary, said my prayers, and tried to catch some Zs.

Falling asleep was difficult. After tossing and turning a couple of times, the sun came out, and just like that, a new day had dawned.

"Lord, I know you are hearing me and above all else, you know my unspoken words and needs, my capabilities, and my desires. You have given me patience, patience beyond measure and I thank you for this virtue. I trust your judgment and timing, O Lord, hence I know my blessing is coming right on schedule. For your timing, O Lord, has been divinely designed. And at the right appointed time, your plan for my life will unfold just as it should. Knowing and believing that, humbly and patiently I await!"

Still reeling from my encounter with Donald, I asked for a much better day than the last and hoped it was the last hustle in Florida. I remembered Donald saying that he'd be home in two days, so I avoided the plaza at all costs and opted to panhandle at the beach instead. Continuing my daily ritual I entered the bathroom stall, did my business, and got ready for the beach. Ditching the black blanket, I grabbed my madras headwrap, tied it around my head, and made my way over to a tiny beach in Key West.

It was the middle of the week and although the beach was abuzz, there were hardly any kids so I knew my chances of getting heads to braid was highly unlikely. I was right. Sun-beat, after a couple of hours I headed home. Adding the $3.75 I collected to the pot, I headed straight to the ticket window.

"Hey. It's me!" I cheerfully greeted Melody.

"Nothing has changed from yesterday, Gloria," she said without even checking.

Somewhat disappointed, I walked away to my room.

Was that an attitude I sensed from Melody?
Perplexed, I shook my head.
That's unlike her, though. She's always so talkative and bubbly, she was abrupt and didn't even make eye contact. I mean, I know I visit that window every day without fail but heck, how else will I keep track of the damn fare?

You know, maybe she's having a bad day. Everyone deserves the benefit of the doubt and we all have good and bad days. But girl, you'll definitely see me again tomorrow and for as long as I'm here. Bétiz! (*Nonsense!*)

Anyway, the train ticket to New York was still too hot, so it definitely wouldn't be my last day.

Still a little bit early, I sat on my bed and gazed at passengers until the buses stopped running. Billy eventually reported to work and came over to say hello. As usual, we got into a heated debate, about religion and God and whatever else. His belief in God was nonexistent and my entire world and life thrived on His existence.

I believe that God created the heavens and the earth and all things within it and Billy, he believes that the universe began with a tremendous explosion over 13 billion years ago, subscribing to the Big Bang Theory.

Eventually, duty called and Billy's departure put an end to the healthy debate. He returned inside the station and I turned in for the night.

Billy has never once asked about my homelessness, eh? my mind wandered before falling asleep. *I wonder if he knows.*

A little baffled, I tried to drown out the noise in my head and catch some sleep before the next sunrise.

Dreams come true only if we actively pursue them. Break from the shackles of fear and spring forth into action. Expend energy on your dreams and breathe life into your vision.

CHAPTER 5

JANUARY 1994

It had been one week since the incident with Donald. Figuring that he was gone by now, I decided to revisit the plaza parking lot. I seem to always collect a little more money there. When I checked yesterday, the train tickets to New York were $403. With $175.88 to my name and still over $200 shy of the fare, the chances of getting out in a day or two were pretty slim.

Keeping hope alive, I prayed that this week would be my last before moving to New York. Anxiety and the fear of being raped in the streets were exhausting and started taking a toll on my mental health. Quitting wasn't an option, though. The hustle had to go on. I had a dream to fulfill.

So, as I had been doing for the last two weeks, I headed to the washroom, freshened up, garbed up in my vagrant attire, and made my way to the plaza.

And boy, what a dreadful day it was. A dose of reality hit me in that parking lot, harder than it ever did before.

"I can do this. I know I can do this," I reassured myself. Intent on not forgetting my hardest day in Key West thus far, coupled with the cathartic relief I get from journaling, I took a break from begging to record it in my diary.

```
January 15th, 1994
Dear Diary,
     So, today while panhandling at the
Key Plaza Shopping Center in Key West,
I encountered a beautifully clad and
seemingly classy lady coming out of the
supermarket. She seemed pleasant and
approachable. My instincts led me to
approach her.
     "Hello, Ma'am, do you have some change
to spare, please?" I asked politely.
     "Excuse me!" she responded.
     Thinking she really had not heard me,
I reiterated, "Some spare change, please,
ma'am."
     "Oh I heard you the first time," she
said matter-of-factly, staring at me in
what I now perceived as disgust. "Get off
your fucking lazy ass and find a goddamn
job!" she screamed, drawing the attention
of a small crowd. "What makes you think
that I, Beth Jackson-Gray, will get up
from my bed every single day, go to work
just to hand you my hard-earned money?
You must be outta your goddamn mind! You
lazy, entitled little whatever you are,"
```

she screamed, pointing at me, wiggling her index finger in a circular motion. Get the fuck outta here!" She then entered her Mercedes Benz, slammed the door shut, and sped away.

"Whoa!" I blinked. My heart sank to my feet. Frozen, I prayed for the earth to open up and swallow me, just swallow me whole. I wished for my fairy godmother to wave her magic wand and make me disappear. I prayed for a gust of wind to just pick me up and carry me away, far, far away. I prayed for a savior.

Her tone and response stunned me. No one had ever cursed me out like this before. I wanted to explain my struggle, for it was as real as they come. I wanted to explain why I hustled and why I ended up here but she didn't give me a chance and I doubt she would have cared. I don't think I could've done either because for a minute there, I think I had temporarily lost my ability to speak.

My immigration status came to the fore and if I, Gloria Grace, were legal in America, I'm almost certain that the encounter would've convinced me to turn my life around. But I couldn't—yet. I was an illegal alien, and the possibilities of finding a job were limited.

At that moment I had three choices. One, pray that the ground swallows me up. Two, hang my head in shame and never ask for help again. Or three, use that moment as motivation to hustle even harder. Option one was impossible and so was option two.

I could've allowed this encounter to crush my ego and let pride and shame consume me. I could've allowed it to back me into a corner, but I didn't have that luxury. I could've given this lady the power to ruin my day or derail my goal, but I couldn't. Albeit discouraged, I could only afford to grieve for a few seconds. I had a dream to fulfill.

A few moments later, after I had composed myself and restored some dignity, I approached the very next person who pulled into the parking spot that Beth had just pulled out of.

Obnoxiously chewing gum and popping bubbles, leaving the windows down, a woman hopped out of a blue beat-up Ford F-150 pickup truck wearing a kaleidoscope of colors—a red bandana, a pink cropped top, black slacks, and orange flip flops. It didn't look promising but the idiom, 'Never judge a book by its cover,' sounded in my head.

Taking a deep breath, I straightened up my soiled shirt, ran my fingers through my hair, and readied myself to approach her.

You got this, Gloria. Do it, do it, do it. Go! Ya never know, my internal cheerleader encouraged me.

"Cuse, ex," I cleared my throat. "Excuse me, mami, have some change to spare?"

"Um," the woman uttered looking around her. Reaching into her pockets, "Here, take this," she said, chewing away and popping bubbles with the blue gum in her mouth. "My only five bucks but you can have it," she added, popping another. "I'll get sugar and eggs when I get paid next week."

"Oh no, no, mami, that's OK. Get your groceries."

"It's OK, baby girl. I gave it to you," she insisted gently pushing my hand back towards me. "Coffee and tea without sugar and dry bread or crackers with water for a couple of days until payday won't hurt. I'll be alright," she continued chewing and popping away her gum.

"Trust me I have been through worse," she chuckled, shaking her head. "At least now I have the coffee and the tea and the bread and a roof over my head. Some people don't even have that and just until recently, I didn't either. So no worries, baby girl, have it."

"Thank you! Thank you, mami. Que Dios te bendiga!" ("God bless you!") My eyes welled and my heart sank to my feet yet again—only this time from gratitude and guilt.

"Aw... don't cry, baby girl." The woman inched closer towards me to console me, gently rubbing my back. "It takes courage to ask for help, let alone ask strangers. I know," she said, spitting out her gum.

"No one, especially not a beautiful girl like you, just decides 'Oh hey everyone out there, my dream is to become a professional panhandler. No one just ups one day and says OK, today I'll make it my life goal to beg strangers for money.' I know. I've been there. I've walked in your shoes. Up until three months ago, I was you.

"And although things are not back to where it was before I lost everything and ended up on the streets, by the grace of God I'm getting there. Slowly but surely I'm getting there, baby girl. And let me tell you, by the grace of God you will, too."

The more she talked, the more tears formed in my eyes. The longer she went on, the harder my heart beat. Feeling like I was going to explode any minute and alert the entire plaza, the ugly cry—with wailing and all—tempted to show up. But the introvert in me wouldn't allow it. My heart was full, overflowing with thankfulness and grace, on the verge of bursting.

"Listen, I do not know your story," she said. "I do not know what happened to you or what your situation is. But whatever it is, I pray that you get on your feet soon. Ask God for grace, for guidance, for fortitude, and good fortune.

"We all struggle, trust me, we all do. We all fall down but the important thing is that we do not stay down too long. We all fall down but the important thing is not whether we fall, because we will, it's what happens after the fall that matters. Do we stay down or do we rise up? Do we wallow in self-pity or do we rise up and soar?

"We all struggle, baby girl. We all have a story. Some with happier beginnings than others and some with happier endings than others, but trust me, we all go through our season of struggles and triumphs. What happens after the storm, hm?" she asked, patting my arm prompting a response.

"A beautiful rainbow appears," I responded, wiping the mixture of tears and snot streaming down my face.

"Yes, baby girl, yes! Keep your eyes out for your rainbow, it will come, I promise you. Anyways, best of luck to you. May God bless you with an abundance and may He help you get on your feet soon. Remember to not stay in this too long now, or else you become complacent. Use it as a stepping stone, a stepping stone to get to where you want to go. Good luck, baby girl. I keep calling you 'baby girl,'" she chucked. "What's your name?"

"Glo-ria." Overcome with emotion, I struggled to get my name out.

"I will keep you in my prayers, Gloria. Take care of yourself now, baby girl."

With tear-filled eyes, a grateful heart, and a temporary speech impediment, I stood in awe. Beaten but not broken, I gathered my belongings and with the little bit of dignity I had left, made my way home.

Glo wherever you're planted with grace.

* * *

Mid-January and the holiday season was officially over. Fares should be going down soon, if they haven't already, I hoped. With all my fingers and toes crossed, I endeavored to find out.

"Melody! How are you today?" I cheerfully and enthusiastically greeted the attendant at the ticket window.

"Hi! I'm Angel," she responded turning around. "Melody got, uh, Melody got, uh. I'm Melody's replacement."

"Oh!" My eyes widened. Remembering my encounter with Melody yesterday, I was tempted to ask whether she had been fired or quit but I couldn't wait to know the fare. "How much is a one-way ticket to New York?"

"Let's see here. That would be $75.86. That includes the Greyhound bus fare to catch the Amtrak train in Fort Lauderdale."

"What!" My eyes popped, my jaw dropped, my heart sang. *$403 to $76?* "I'll take it, I'll take it!" I responded, doing cartwheels in my head.

"What's the name?"

"Gloria. Gloria Grace Estevez."

"Here you go Gloria, you're all set. The bus leaves in less than an hour."

"Oh! Thank you! Thank you! Thank you, Angel!" Grabbing the ticket, I made my way to my bedroom and sat on the bench.

BOOK ONE

Cleaning out my backpack, the encounter with Melody from the day before reverberated in my head. The idea that Melody may have been bullshitting me all this time hounded me. *And if she were, why? From $403 to $76? Wow!*

She's gone, huh. I wonder if it was because of something she did or was it incompetence, perhaps? Ah, maybe she was simply having a bad day yesterday. I mean, I could ask Angel but, eh, I don't have the energy. I have other things to concentrate on besides getting the scoop.

Climbing out of my stupor and in complete awe, I sighed and shivered. I prayed for traveling mercies once again while repacking my backpack—my rosary, my newly acquired scarf, my fanny pack, my two blankets, two shirts, a pair of jeans, toothbrush, deodorant, undies—folding them neatly and putting them back in. Emotional, I waited for the bus to take me to the train bound for the city that never sleeps.

Within a few minutes, the bus arrived. Taking one last glance at my makeshift bed—the bench I slept on for the past four weeks—my eyes welled up a little. I hoped that Billy would magically appear. He didn't. Waving goodbye to Angel, I made my way to a seat near the window to take in the sights on the journey.

But, the next thing I knew, I was at the Fort Lauderdale Train Station. I had slept the entire seven hours, if not the whole way, most of it. Within an hour of getting there, the Amtrak train came to a screeching halt. Closing my journal, I grabbed my backpack and settled near a window seat—28C. It was happening. I was really leaving the Sunshine State—Florida.

As the train pulled out, my mind journeyed from Cuba to Key West. From the rough seas and to Juan throwing my ass overboard, to being suspicious of Marco—the first person I met in America.

Marco—yeah he was kinda cute. Well, minus the missing teeth. How did such a young guy wind up on the streets? And the hotdog vendor, how rude was he?

A DARING PURSUIT OF THE DREAM

Fighting back the tears my mind flashed on Billy, the big burly security guard who worked the night shift.

Billy, oh Billy. I smiled.

Wish I could've said goodbye. He made sure to look out for me every night. Poor guy had no idea I was homeless, or maybe he knew, I don't know. I wonder what would've happened had I opened up to him.

Oh and that Donald, the bastard! Can't believe I was so naive. I mean I had just gotten to America. I didn't know, but common sense, Gloria, common sense, phew! And the woman who gave me her sentimental scarf, aww. Bless your heart, lady, may your granny rest in peace.

And that lady in the toilet, oh my, haha...! And that woman driving her fancy Mercedes who gave me my business, Beth Jackson-Gray. I will never forget her.

Lord, I pray You shower her with the spirit of understanding, of kindness and love and compassion.

Aww, and that other lady, my goodness, so sweet she gave me her only $5. Wow! May God bless you, lady! I will never forget you. She was so right. No one is exempt from experiencing the harsh realities of life, from being dealt a bad hand.

I really admired her generosity and wisdom. 'Things are still hard' she said, yet she gave me her last five bucks? Wow! If that isn't compassion and selflessness, I don't know what is.

I had so many questions for her. I wanted to know her story, I wanted to know her name. I wanted to know how she ended up on the street, and I wanted to know how she got off it. But by the time I unfroze, she was gone, content with just inspiring and encouraging me.

Keep your eyes on the prize, Gloria. Just a bump in the road. OK, a huge bump in the road, but stay the course and you'll get there. You will get there. Your rainbow will appear at the right appointed time.

What an eye-opening emotionally charged day that was.

It is so true what they say, eh? That we are more inclined to help when we've been in similar situations. I wonder if she'd have offered me a bunk if I had told her I was homeless? Argh! Too late, Gloria, no going back now.

Lord, I pray for continued guidance and support and blessing upon her life. She understood my situation without knowing my story. Continue to bless her, Lord. Continue to use her, Lord! Continue to help her on her journey. Shower her with an abundance, Lord.

Still bugs me that I didn't catch her name.

And Angel. Can't believe her name is Angel!

I see you, Lord. I see your majesty. I adore you. I'm in awe of you and I'm ever so grateful for your grace and mercy.

God, I hope my parents are doing OK without me. I know they miss me terribly. They're probably worried sick and crying every day, but one thing I know for sure is that they're praying for me. Gosh, do I love and miss them.

Don't think I'll ever have children, though. I couldn't possibly go through letting them go, letting them out of the nest, letting them be free and find their way in this sometimes crazy world. I mean...

I sighed, deliberately breaking that train of thought. *Anyway, I am so happy to say adios to Florida, the Sunshine State, and so excited and ready to say hola to New York, the city that never sleeps.*

The city that never sleeps, huh? How ironic. I smiled. *Considering I have nowhere to sleep, it sounded like the perfect place for a destitute like me.*

Out of my daze, I realized how smooth the train ride was. Well, for the most part. Everyone busied themselves with either chatting, reading, or sleeping.

Having a row all to myself, I reminisced. I prayed. I daydreamed. I slept. I journaled, recording everything—the sights, the sounds, and even the smell from the toilets that overpowered the train a few hours in, making it difficult to breathe, focus, and stay asleep.

Finally, twenty-nine hours later, we were in New York!

But, what now? I still have nowhere to stay.

"Let dreams be your wings."

— Unknown

Chapter 6

Ah! New York, New York! I made it!

Throwing my blanket over my head and shoulders this time to absorb the cold, not to fit the profile of a panhandler, I was now ready to brave the weather. Looking about me in amazement, I made my way from Penn Station onto the city street.

"Snow!" I exclaimed, gawking at the bright white blanketed ground. Making my way to the less-trafficked area, I dropped my belongings and scooped up two handfuls. Just as I imagined, it was cold, loose, and powdery.

Before it could all melt away through my fingers, I shaped whatever was left into a tiny ball and flung it a few feet away. Stooping, I gathered some more in front of me and shaped it into a perfect snowball. Repeating the process twice more, each time smaller than the previous and stacking them, I now had a snowman. Well, the semblance of a snowman. A weird-looking snowman with no eyes, no nose, no accessories, but a snowman in my mind.

"Art is arbitrary," I cracked up. "OK, I'll get better at it."

Still on the early side of Thursday afternoon, I decided to roam the city streets a while. Decorated with remnants from the holiday past, the streets were bustling with no signs of dying down anytime soon. Although it was extremely cold, everyone seemed so jolly and warm.

Such freedom here, such diversity. People of all ethnicities—black and brown and white. Such a melting pot.

Gazing in awe, *Freedom! Freedom!* echoed loudly in my heart and head. Being a free spirit, I never allowed my struggles to quell my joy. Without a care in the world, I stretched out my arms and gave thanks.

Walking a few minutes away, about half a mile or so, I stumbled upon a pizzeria—Patsy's Pizzeria! *Oh!* My heart skipped a beat—the name reminding me of Patsy's Pastries & Cake Delights. The place where my parents bought my birthday cake the day I left Cuba.

I ordered a large slice of pizza for $3.50 and a coke for $1.50. Reaching into my fanny pack, I fetched a $5 bill, got my food, and continued on my way. Topped with pepperoni, tomato sauce, and mozzarella cheese, the huge slice, the thin middle crust, and thick crispy edge, made for a perfect fold.

"Hum." That first bite stopped me in my tracks. Closing my eyes, I let out a delighted moan. In record time the slice was done, I had devoured it. I contemplated getting another but besides my shallow pockets, the voice of my parents' echoed in my head 'always save for tomorrow.'

I obeyed and continued walking. Roaming the streets was my only choice. The architecture, the huge triangular buildings that formed the skyline, the bustling of the city, the energy, the vibe, the freedom, awakened everything inside me.

New York is stunning!

Soon darkness covered the city and reality hit again. I had nowhere to stay.

What now? Where do I go from here?

My only option is to go to the nearby train station for the night.

It wouldn't be the first time I've slept at a terminal, would it now? I chuckled.

Making my way to Grand Central Station, I walked down the stairs and found myself near the train tracks. I didn't plan on taking the train but since a kind passenger swiped me in, I entered, occupying a seat on one of the few benches in the area. Albeit tired and cold, I walked around, changing my location every couple of hours to avert interrogation or suspicion.

Before long, the clock struck midnight and with no signs of the traffic slowing down, I decided to lay my head down and rest awhile. But the noise, the chatter, and the constant screeching of trains pulling in and out of the station made staying asleep impossible.

I know it's called the city that never sleeps but dang, it's 2 a.m. and it's still bustling? I griped, waking up from a catnap. *Hope I can get some shuteye. I am really beat.*

Closing my eyes again, I said a little prayer thanking God first and foremost for everything, and asking Him to cover me with His holy mantle. I asked for guidance and protection on my journey and for patience in achieving the dream. "Thank you for granting my plea, O Lord. Amen!"

As if on cue, a deep gruff voice said, "Hello!"

God, is that you? I joked in my head, flashing my eyes open. I blinked letting my eyes adjust to his glaring purple suit, purple hat, purple vest, dangling gold chains over his gold sateen shirt and you guessed it—two-tone purple and gold shoes.

"Mind if I sit here, ma'am?" he asked.

Yes, I do.

"Oh no, not at all," I responded with an inconspicuous eye roll, before thinking how wrong that was. He was polite, older, and this was a public place, not my own.

"I'm Frank. What's your name, young lady?" he asked plopping onto the bench next to me, the smell of his cologne almost knocking me over.

"I'm Gloria Este…" I responded, twitching my nose and mumbling my last name remembering to only reveal my first name. But like a bad habit, it proved hard to break.

"Who? Gloria Estefan?"

"Nah, Estevez but just Gloria, Gloria."

"Oh! My bad!" Frank chuckled, then broke into song, butchering most, if not all of Gloria Estefan's hit songs. From "Rhythm is Gonna Get You" to "Conga" to "Get on Your Feet" he sang, snapping his fingers, rocking his body from side to side, and humming the words he didn't know.

I'm super tired and you're in my bedroom, sir, I grumbled in my head. Under normal circumstances, I'd entertain Frank. But frankly, I was beat and in no mood to talk.

Five long minutes later, Frank's train pulled in. Opening his eyes, still humming, singing, and rocking to Gloria Estefan's 'Get on Your Feet,' he grabbed the cane he clearly didn't need, spun around followed by a toe stand Michael Jackson-style before going on his way.

"Take care, Gloria."

"You too, Frank." I smiled and exhaled, finally breathing musk-free air again.

"Hope no one else comes," I mumbled.

But 'tis New York, and by their standards, the night was young. My only consolation was that I could fly under the radar at the station. People didn't stay long enough to become suspicious of my homelessness and everyone seemed to always be in a hurry.

Ten days of being in the Big Apple had now gone by and I had made Grand Central station my bedroom and my bathroom the train station, public parks, and recreational facilities.

During the day I spent my time sightseeing and panhandling in the city, and at some point made my way to Central Park to meditate and pray. I survived on cheap hotdogs, burgers, and handoffs from the generosity of strangers who'd offer to buy me food instead of handing me money. Albeit not thriving, I was surviving.

Although I was getting tired of living like a bum, I never once regretted leaving Cuba. I often wondered, however, what life would have been like had I returned to my birthplace, Saint Lucia. But my parents left Saint Lucia two days after my first birthday and I had never visited since.

Mom spoke of its beauty all the time, taught me the creole dialect, and introduced me to the cuisine and some aspects of the culture, but we never returned. Mom said not only was money tight, but her latest memories of her childhood home were still traumatic and raw.

She wasn't ready to go back to a house rife with pain and sadness and trauma—the outside kitchen where her mom had collapsed and the room where her father died. She also agreed that Saint Lucia, much like Cuba, wouldn't feed my acting dreams either. So here I am in New York, I have to make it work.

As time went on, my routine became monotonous—get up, pray, clean up, panhandle, repeat. Months passed, until one day I decided that I had had enough of this monotony. Life was fleeting. It was time to deviate a bit.

Three months! It was way too long to be living on the streets. I wasn't a vagrant and I didn't intend on becoming one either. The little money I had was near depletion and I wasn't bringing in much panhandling, partly due to self-sabotage.

When I first got to New York in mid-January, the winter was biting. I couldn't afford frostbite or hospital visits. My pocketbook and status wouldn't allow it. The little money I had leftover from the train ticket, I spent on a winter coat, a pair of gloves, and a knitted hat.

I didn't buy a scarf, though. I couldn't afford it. To improvise, I doubled my black blankets as scarves. Now, with an all-black winter wardrobe, I was even more ready to resume my panhandling hustle. Freezing to death wasn't an option. I had a dream to fulfill.

I knew I had to start small to get there but for me, begging wasn't it. I was a young, able-bodied, fully-functioning human. I hated competing with other panhandlers. People who were obviously in more dire straights than I was—those incapacitated with a missing limb or two, mental health issues, and mothers with babies in their arms. So, I deliberately stayed away from the more lucrative places. My conscience wouldn't allow it.

Not racking in much money panhandling, I was getting tired of begging strangers for their hard-earned money. Getting yelled at or being ignored stole a piece of my soul every single time. My dignity was wearing thin and so was my patience. With frustration and worry mounting in me, I had to find an honest means to survive.

One Sunday afternoon, while sitting in Central Park meditating, a voice instructed me to walk into the nearby church—St. Patrick's Cathedral.

"Instead of making the sign of the cross every time you pass by, why don't you go in, my child? Go inside. Come and pay me a 'real' visit. Go spend some time in the peace and quiet of the church, in the presence of the Blessed Sacrament."

I wasn't sure what had just happened. I knew I was alone and I didn't feel anyone go by. It had to be the voice of my Father in heaven. Gathering my belongings at once, I made my way into the church, walked up to the altar, and fell to my knees in supplication. I surrendered.

Overcome with emotion, I wept and wept and wept. Usually talkative and expressive, I had suddenly lost my ability to speak. I knew that God was listening—listening to my heart, my intentions, my every wish and plea. For He says in Ecclesiastes 3:7, "There is a time to tear and a time to mend, a time to be silent and a time to speak." Kneeling still, I reflected awhile.

A few moments later, I made my way to one of the pew benches and sat there with my eyes fixated on the cross. Keeping watch all night and day and falling asleep in between, for two nights I had gotten a new resting place away from the chatter, train horns, and screeches.

Oh God, oh God, oh God... At the corner of my eyes, I see a Sister coming towards me. *Hope she's not coming to me, hope she is not coming to me, hope she's not coming to me...*

"Hello there," she greeted me.

Oh God! My heart leapt.

"Ha-Hi!"

"I notice you've been here for two days." *Crap! Time's up!* "I'm Mother Mary, Superior of the Sisters of Charity at the nearby convent. Is everything OK?"

Contemplating for a minute whether I should tell her everything, I said, "Not really, Mother. I just need prayers. Lots of prayers."

"I can pray with you if you'd like."

"Yes, yes, Mother. I'd like that very much."

"What's your name?"

"Gloria," I responded, deliberately leaving out my last name.

"Estefan? The Gloria Estefan?" Mother asked, smiling.

Oh, not the nun too! I laughed and rolled my eyes internally before responding.

"Close, but I'm Estevez, Mother. The Gloria Estevez."

We chuckled.

"So you've been here for what, two days now, huh? Usually, people come in here, pray a short while and hurry out or tourists would come in poke around, take pictures, and leave." Mother laughed.

Surprised that the nun had noticed my extended stay, I chuckled sheepishly.

"Is everything OK?" she continued.

"Not really, Mother. I just need prayers, lots and lots and lots of prayers."

"The Sisters and I can lift you up in our daily devotion."

"Appreciate it so much, Mother."

"Any special prayer requests, Gloria?"

"Yes-yes, Mother," I responded in haste.

Where do I start? Should I tell her the full story? This is my last hope, I pondered.

Ok, give it your best shot, Glo. Go! my internal cheerleader cheered me on.

Breathing deeply, I prepared to respond.

"I need prayers for a job so I can provide myself with food and clothes and a place to stay, oh Mother, I'm homeless, I know no one here, I recently came in from Cuba. I haven't spoken to my parents in four months, I miss them terribly, I hope they're OK. My parents used their life savings to help me flee Cuba and to make my dreams of becoming an actress come true. My father always said America is the land of possibilities, of opportunities. It has been anything but. I'm homeless, I'm jobless, I'm hungry, I have no money, and I am tired of living on the streets. Pray for me, Mother. Pray with me, Mother. I am desperate. I need help."

Opening my eyes, I took my first breath, a deep one. My first since I started relaying my story.

"Whoa! I need a breath after this, Gloria," Mother responded, placing one hand over her forehead, and tilting her head back, pretending to be winded.

Although Mother Mary may not have understood all of what I had said, she gathered that I was in dire need.

At Mother's behest, I reiterated my prayer requests in full and complete sentences this time. I told her everything—my parents' determination to make my dreams come true, my trip to the USA, the fact that I'm undocumented, my struggles for money and housing and food, and how I ended up in New York. Everything.

"Oh! I'm so sorry, Gloria." Mother gasped. "Let's turn to God in prayer. The One who knows and sees all things. The One who provides and is privy to all our needs and innermost desires."

Extending both hands to me, I grabbed Mother's, then we bowed our heads in prayer.

"Father in heaven, I lift this young lady up to You. May You provide her the basic necessities of life. May You open doors for her, Lord, doors that only You have the keys to unlock. May You provide for her the sustenance, willpower, and strength to pursue her dreams.

"And may she never lose sight of Your unfailing love, grace, and mercy. For you, O Lord, in 2 Corinthians 5:7 say, 'Walk in faith, not by sight.' May her faith in You increase ten-fold. May she continue to believe in You and Your word, Your wondrous power, might, and promise.

"And may You, O Lord, give Gloria, the strength, the courage, and the vigor that she needs to carry on life's journey. Give her the tools she needs to fulfill her dreams, her calling, her vocation, her purpose here on earth, Lord. Guide and protect her every step of the way.

"Be with her parents back in Cuba. Guide, protect, and comfort them too. This we ask in Your most precious and holy name."

With tear-filled eyes, we both said, "Amen."

"Thank you, Mother," I whispered, wiping away tears with the back of my hands.

"You are very welcome, Gloria. Come, follow me."

Huh!

Picking up my belongings, I followed closely behind Mother. Making our way around a corner and through double doors, we found ourselves at the back of the cathedral.

There stood a two-story house at the center of a beautiful flower garden, with a well-manicured yard. Making our way up a few stairs and through double glass doors, we were now inside.

"Everyone, meet Gloria Estefan, I mean Gloria Estevez," Mother mused.

"Hi, Gloria," the other eleven sisters seated at the dining room table responded with a chuckle.

"Gloria is a refugee from Cuba and has no place to stay. I've decided to let her stay with us and help her find a job."

"Wait! What?" I gasped, clenching my heart. As my jaw fell open in astonishment, my eyes welled up with tears—again.

"Welcome, Gloria!" The Sisters responded almost in unison.

"Gloria, please, join us at the table." Mother motioned me to have her seat at the head of the table. One of the Sisters gave Mother hers and went off to grab a chair from the adjoining room.

"Thank... you, Mother." Overcome with emotion, I struggled to get the words out.

"You're welcome, Gloria. Shall we say grace?"

Oh, Lord! I rolled my eyes playfully in my head. *But we just prayed, Mother. Granted it was for me, not to bless the food but... Alright, alright, go ahead. Make it quick, though.* I chuckled internally.

Tempted by the spread on the table, I struggled to keep my eyes and mouth closed. Before grace was over, I had already eaten the entire meal with my eyes. I was hungry and could hardly wait to indulge.

"Bon appetit, everyone!" Mother ended the prayer just in time, saving me from embarrassing slobber.

"So, Gloria, what's your dream job?" Sister Theresa enquired in Spanish.

"Oooooo" the other Sisters are impressed.

"Showing off again, Sister T?" Mother teased.

Through the chuckling, "Acting!" I responded excitedly, definitively, and confidently.

"That's wonderful, Gloria. You have this beautiful, exotic look."

"Yes," the other Sisters agreed. "A look perfect for television."

"Thank you!" I blushed. "I've always been interested in the Arts. But I can't work here yet. Well, you know, unless I do what most undocumented people do... housekeeping, nannying, landscaping—OK perhaps not landscaping."

"Ah, too bad you scratched out landscaping. We are in dire need of a landscaper, so... just kidding," the Sisters all laughed.

"We'll help you find a job, Gloria." Mother offered again.

"Thank you so much, Mother and Sisters, for giving me a hot, home-cooked meal. I haven't had one in four months. But it feels like four years, honestly. Thank you for your kind hospitality," I added, fighting back tears.

Savoring every bite, the mashed potatoes were fluffy and buttery, the steak was grilled to perfection, and the asparagus—my goodness, yum-my. I contemplated leaving a couple of scrapes on the plate, but my hungry appetite wouldn't allow it. I also didn't want to send the message that I'd had enough because I hadn't. The Sisters offered me more. I'm convinced my extra clean plate had something to do with it.

"No thanks, I'm full," I said, obviously fibbing.

"Sure, Gl–," Mother Mary started to ask.

"OK. If you insist, Mother," I responded before she could even finish my name. We laughed. Much like the first serving, I gobbled the second up at the same speed. I was hungry.

"Dessert, anyone?" Mother offered.

"No, thank you," Sister Delisha Joan passed. "I'll get back in bed."

"Feel better, Sister D," the Sisters responded.

"Thank you. Pleasure meeting you, Gloria," she said with a smile, walking away slowly.

"Likewise you, Sister. Thank you."

I couldn't help notice how pale and weak she looked. Too shy and for fear of being judged intrusive, I didn't ask what was wrong.

"Gloria, would you like coffee or tea?" Mother returned from the kitchen with a coffee pot.

"Coffee, please."

Mother poured me a cup.

"Mmm," my eyes lit up upon my first sip. For a brief moment, my mind traveled back to Cuba. To mom and dad and me enjoying a cup or two at the kitchen table. The laughter and chatter from the Sisters broke my reverie. I shuddered, rerouting to the present moment. "Tastes like Cuban coffee. Café Bustelo."

"Ah, you know your stuff, Gloria. It actually is."

"This tastes heavenly, Mother. Thank you."

Soon dinner was over. So, like any good guest, I offered to do the dishes.

"Oh no worries, Gloria, you are a guest in our home. We'll take care of it, but only this one time." Mother laughed gently rubbing my back. "Follow me," she said. "I'll show you to your room."

Your room? Did she just say 'your room?'

I silently rejoiced. Mother left the Sisters to do the dishes and escorted me upstairs to one of their empty rooms at the convent.

"This one? My room?" I gasped.

"Yep," Mother confirmed shaking her head yes.

"Wow! So immaculate, tranquil, and quaint!" I inhaled looking around. Pink and purple and white, the décor encompassing some of my favorite colors. "Mother this is so exquisite and pristine. I'm scared to touch anything."

"Ah, no worries, Gloria," Mother laughed heartily. "Make yourself at home. Our only requirement is that you keep it tidy."

"I can live with that, Mother," I assured her with a smile.

"Deal!" Mother replied, extending a hand to shake on it. "We gotta seal the deal, Gloria," Mother chuckled. "By the way, we pray at six o'clock in the morning, at noon, and six o'clock in the evening. You are free to join us."

"Noted. Thanks, Mother. Thank you so much."

"Have a good night, young lady. See you at six o'clock in the morning, maybe?"

"Un…" I responded, wiggling my nose, my forehead crinkled, my eyebrows raised. Looking at each other, Mother and I burst out laughing.

"Good night, young lady."

"Good night, Mother. Thank you for everything."

Just as Mother shut the door I fell on my hands to do a cartwheel. Then suddenly the door flung open again.

"Forgot to mention… Um, what are you doing?" Mother tilted her head left to look at me awkwardly looking up from the floor.

"Never mind," she shook her head smiling. "The towels are over there," she continued, pointing to the hidden closet near the bathroom door. "And, over here are nightgowns and robes. Feel free to use them."

"OK. Thanks, Mother," I responded, attempting to unfreeze midway through a cartwheel.

"Carry on," Mother laughed, closing the door behind her.

Attempting my aborted cartwheel again, I obliged.

Boop! I fell on my butt twisting my arm. But that didn't stop me from doing two more. Grabbing a towel and a washcloth I jumped into the shower.

Oh, the things we take for granted, I sighed, reflecting as the water cascaded down my body.

"A warm shower, a bed to rest our tired heads and heavy eyes, a warm smile or greeting, a roof over our head, no matter how big or modest, a warm meal, freshly washed hair. Ah!" I exhaled as the warm water gently massaged my scalp, moving me to pray.

"Thank you ever so much, Lord! Thank you for everything—for life, for grace, and for your mercy upon me. Forgive me for the many times I've offended you, forgive me for any complaints and seeming ingratitude I have displayed or contemplated. I am truly sorry for having offended you.

"Living on the streets these past months has really opened my eyes, my heart, and my mind, I can never take seemingly trivial wonders like these around me for granted again. Have mercy on me, Lord. Into your hands I commend my spirit, into your hands I commend my life. Thank you, Father. Simply—thank you for everything big and small!"

Eventually getting out of the shower, I gave God some more thanks and praise. Sitting in the quiet of my room, everything came running through my mind. My parents, wondering how they were doing, Juan, and everything else I had gone through since leaving Cuba. Borrowing some of the paper sitting on 'my' nightstand, I penned my parents a letter.

Madre! Padre!

We did it! I'm in America! I know you're probably worried sick about me, but I am living and breathing. I am so sorry I haven't gotten in touch with you. Would you believe that Juan forgot to give me the contact number and I forgot to remind him? I feel so silly. By the time I remembered, he was too far out to sea and didn't hear my call. So, I was left stranded. But you know me, I'm a survivor. Just like you taught me, I fended for myself.

Some nuns have taken me in, the Sisters of Charity in New York, and they will help me find a job and all that good stuff. Yup! I left Florida and moved to New York. People say New York or California are the best places for people who want to go into acting and dancing and singing. Now that I have an address, we can communicate back and forth. I am so grateful and so relieved at this point that I feel like my heart will just give way on me.

Anyways, so besides being worried sick about me and my whereabouts and wellbeing, how are you doing? Hope you're OK otherwise. I'm so sorry for the worry, madre y padre. I was just trying to survive. In case you're wondering, I'm not an actress yet but it's coming, it's coming. I can feel it and I claim it in the Mighty name of Jesus. I will get there someday. This is all part of the journey, right? Anyways keep praying for me as I continue to do the same for you two. I love you to the ends of the earth and back.

Hope Fidel doesn't confiscate this communiqué. Love you eternally, mom and dad.

Yours forever, Glo!

XXx

There's no way I'm telling them I lived on the streets for four months. Uh-un. Their little girl is homeless in America? They would die. They don't need that extra guilt and heartbreak. Perhaps they'll find out someday when all is well and good and I've finally achieved my ultimate dream or when we reunite.

Come to think of it, I should've written to them sooner letting them know that I made it and that I'm ok even though I didn't have a return address. Guess I was too busy trying to survive, huh? Anyway, I'm sure Juan told them I was well, provided that he made it back safely.

I sighed.

Getting back to the task at hand, I licked that envelope shut, then slid underneath my pearly white bedsheets around 11 p.m. or so for some much-needed, uninterrupted sleep.

Chapter 7

*"The best way to make your dreams
come true is to wake up."
— Muhammad Ali*

In what seemed like no more than five minutes, a knock at the door startled me, waking me up from one of the sweetest sleeps I've ever had.

"Good morning, Gloria! It's Mother. Rise and shine. Is everything OK?"

"Oh hi, Mother. It's six o'clock already?"

"It depends on which one you're referring to—a.m. or p.m.?" Mother smiled. "It's 11 a.m., my dear."

"Sorry, Mother!" I sat up, wiping the crust from my eyes.

"How did you sleep last night? Ah, never mind. Your drool-crusted mouth says it all." Mother laughed.

Flustered and self-conscious, I wiped my mouth using the back of my hands.

"Let's see," I said, drumming my face with my fingers as I prepared to respond. "For the first time in four months, I was able to get some sleep on a soft bed with my legs outstretched, *without* the horns of trains piercing my eardrums or people tapping on my shoulder. I don't know, Mother..." I looked up at Mother Mary to see her smiling.

"Thank you, Mother!" My laughter turned into grateful, joyful, happy tears. "I'm so incredibly grateful to you and the other Sisters for feeding me and giving me a place to sleep."

"It's our pleasure, Gloria. Father in heaven instructs us to feed the hungry, shelter the homeless."

"Clothe the naked," I added. "Luke 3:11 says, 'Whoever has two tunics is to share with him who has none, and whoever has food is to do likewise.'"

"Very good, Gloria. Look at you quoting scripture." Mother is impressed. "And Matthew 25:35 says 'For I was hungry and you gave me food, I was thirsty and you gave me drink, I was a stranger and you welcomed me. And 1 John 3:17-18 says, 'But if anyone has the world's goods and sees his brother in need, yet closes his heart against him, how does God's love abide in him? Little children, let us not love in word or talk but in deed and in truth.'"

"Ah! So profound," I responded, my hand flying to my heart. "Thank you for heeding the call, Mother."

"You most certainly are welcome, Gloria. The Sisters and I have a meeting in the city. We'll be back in a couple hours. Make yourself at home, your breakfast is on the table or you can go back to sleep if you like. I know you need it."

"Thanks, Mother. I'll sleep awhile."

"Adios, Gloria. Enjoy!" Mother headed towards the door.

"Mother, Mother," I called out. "I penned a letter to my parents. How do I go about mailing it to them and is it ok if I use your address as my return address?"

"Sure, Gloria. We'll get it mailed for you right away."

"I also need an envelope and stamps," I added, planting my face in my palms, embarrassed that I was asking too much.

"Sure, Gloria. We have some here. Whatever you need."

"Ah. Thank you ever-so-much, Mother. Not sure if they'll receive it because of the embargo but I'll try anyway."

"Doesn't hurt to try. Remember, don't ever tell yourself 'no' before trying or give up at the first 'no.' You try and you see for yourself. That goes for everything in life—a job interview, asking for help or a favor, you name it."

"Ah! My philosophy exactly, Mother," I added handing her the letter. Giving me a thumbs up, Mother shut the door behind her and went on her way. And me? Well, I pulled the comforter over my head and went back to sleep.

Two hours later I managed to get out of bed to break my fast. The rumblings in my stomach were loud and annoying; the symphony within wouldn't let me rest. Jumping in the shower, I readied myself and made my way to the kitchen.

"Oh good morning, Sister Delisha," I greeted, stopping in my tracks. "I didn't know you were here."

"I didn't mean to startle you, Gloria," she tittered.

"How are you feeling today, Sister D?"

"Meh," she responded gently swaying her hand from side to side.

"It looks like you have a fever."

"I just checked my temperature and it seemed normal. Why?"

"Your face is all red, your cheeks and the bridge of the nose."

"Oh. That's a rash, a malar rash. It appears every time I get a lupus flare-up."

"Lupus?" I asked, puzzled.

"You've never heard of it, huh? I know."

"Never."

"Although it's very common, especially in Blacks and Hispanics, it's highly unknown. Basically, it's an autoimmune disease where the body attacks itself."

"Oh!" I gasped. "That sounds painful."

"It's horrible. They say it's one of the most pervasive and painful autoimmune diseases that exist. I think they're right because this ain't easy to deal with. One minute I'm OK, the next minute I feel ill, the next minute the symptoms improve and I feel better. I just never know."

"Wow, Sister, I'm so sorry. I see why you call it troublesome. I'd love to know more but I see you're getting breakfast and don't want to bombard you with a ton of questions."

"Would love to chat a bit, I just need to lay down."

"Did you get what you came in here for?"

"Just water, some toast, and fruit to take my prednisone."

"Go, go lay down. I'll bring them to you."

"Thanks, Gloria. The third room on the left."

"Got it."

Sister Delisha exited the kitchen. Her slow and deliberate steps screamed pain and weakness. Soon the toast and fruit bowl were ready. Grabbing both, I made my way down the hallway to deliver them.

"Here you go, Sister."

"Rest them here next to my pharmacy," she chuckled, moving her pill bottles to make room.

"Can I get you anything else?"

"That'll be all, Gloria. Thank you so much."

"Don't mention it, Sister. I'll leave you to rest. Call me if you need anything."

"You don't have to go, you know, Gloria."

"Actually I do," I grinned. "My stomach is growling. My breakfast is waiting."

"How about you grab it and come chat a bit."

"Sure? You look weak—I don't want to zap the little energy you have."

"Ah, no worries. Once I take my medication I'll feel better, at least for a little while."

"OK. Be right back."

Unable to use the microwave and too hungry to try, I grabbed the plate of cold eggs, hash browns, and sausages the Sisters had left me and made my way back to Sister D's room.

"It looks like you haven't touched your fruit, Sister D."

"Not really hungry. I only took a couple bites of the toast to take my meds. One thing lupus does is that it suppresses my appetite. Don't mind my chubbiness or moon face," she smiled. "It's bloating from the prednisone I'm taking."

"What chubbiness?" I pretended not to notice. "Tell me more about this lupus. It sounds like a horrible disease."

"It sure is cruel and troublesome. I could be well today and sick the next. I battle infections constantly, low white blood cell count, and end up at the hospital quite often."

"How long have you had it?"

"Un... 13 months, thereabout."

"Wow! How did you find out, though? What were your symptoms? Pardon my myriad of questions."

"No worries. It's very prevalent in the African and Hispanic races, yet little is known about it. We have to raise awareness. But back to your question. Uh, I actually self-diagnosed."

"What?"

"Yeah, I had not been feeling well. I was always tired and in constant pain, my ankles and feet were puffy and my joints pained me from inflammation. There were days my hands were so white they looked like all the blood had been drained from them. I had a tiny rash in just that one spot near my left eye, tiny bumps hidden beneath my thick hair. So one day I said to the other Sisters, just nonchalantly, 'I think I have lupus.'

"'Lupus? What's that?' they asked. Like you, they had never heard of it either. I remember Mother saying, 'Sister D, the cadence in your voice is so natural, and from the expression on your face, I can't tell whether you're alarmed or not. But you look tired.'

"She was right. I was tired from staying up all night reading this book I had found here in our library when I first got here, what, eight years ago," she said reaching for the book on her nightstand.

"Embracing the Wolf?" Confused, my eyebrows shot up.

"Right? For some reason, the title captured my attention. I grabbed it, got in a few chapters, then put it down. But, when I started feeling ill, my symptoms sort of mirrored those mentioned in here so…"

"Huh?"

"You should see your face, Gloria!" she chuckled.

"How is this related to lupus?"

Sister D laughed, "Lupus is Latin for wolf."

"Oh… I get it. Wait. Did you know that when you grabbed this book?"

"Nope," she chuckled. "I literally thought it was a story about a wolf."

"Me too, me too," we laughed.

"Anyway, remembering some of the contents and the symptoms mentioned, I realized that I was that girl in the book and couldn't put it down."

"Wow!"

"The Sisters convinced me to go to the doctor. The results confirmed that I had Systemic Lupus, the more severe form of the disease."

"Oh my! You must have been devastated."

"You know, I really wasn't at first because I called it. In the ensuing days post-diagnosis, I sprang into action and followed doctor's orders to a T. I stayed out of the sun, exercised, tried to eat well, took my prednisone to keep the inflammation down, and kept all my doctor appointments.

"I seemed to have had it under control. But per the nature of the beast, one minute the lupus would be in remission and I felt OK, the next minute the wolf within me awakened and all hell would break loose. Pardon my language but, my goodness, it sure feels like hell when I flare-up."

"Oh my. Can you tell when you're getting a flare-up and can you stop it?"

"In the beginning, I really couldn't. It seemed as though they came out of nowhere but I've studied my body and now I know when one is coming on—chest pains, shortness of breath, and those pesky incessant coughs are telltale signs. I don't mean to gross you out but there are days when white and foamy saliva accumulates in my mouth, causing me to spit constantly."

"It's OK I'm done with my cold breakfast, anyway."

"You ate it cold?"

"I couldn't figure out the microwave and for fear of breaking anything I decided to just…"

"You should've asked me," Sister D responded through laughter.

"I didn't want to bother you."

"Oh, Gloria!" she rolled her eyes. "It would be no bother at all."

"Next time for sure because those eggs had to have been on ice, woo," I chuckled, making a face.

"Ew! Cold scrambled eggs are the worst," Sister D grimaced. "Anyway, the doctor has said fluid is accumulating around my heart and lungs. This autoimmune disease affects virtually every organ in the body."

"Scary, huh?"

"To say the least. One minute I'm losing weight, the next I'm gaining. There are days when the rims of my fingernails are so black and blue they look like someone had taken a hammer to them. It's a condition called Raynaud's disease. It's actually very common in lupus patients. When they're either cold or stressed out, the blood flow to these areas is reduced.

"My hair began thinning out due to either the tiny bumps in my scalp, stress, or the medication I was taking. Sleeplessness and restlessness are a constant, and getting out of bed is challenging. There are days I lie in bed motionless to avoid the pain that accompanies even the slightest movement. There are times when I just can't join the Sisters at novena or mass or dinner.

"On some days I pretend to be OK just to appease the Sisters, but little do they know how debilitating it can be. It really preys on me, depletes my strength, erodes my courage to go on, and even shakes my faith at times. Music and dance and laughter used to give me life. But in the throes of pain, even my laughter hurts."

"My goodness. I'm so sorry, Sister," I swallowed hard trying not to cry. My heart ached for Sister D. I didn't know much else to say.

"When I first got diagnosed, lupus was stealing my joy," she continued wiping the tears streaming down her face. "But as I got to understand the disease a little more, you know, I decided that I had to take back control of my life. I remember one time I had an anxiety attack."

"Oh my! What happened?"

"It was a Saturday morning and after a three-week hospital stay, I had been released from the hospital the day before with a laundry list of new medications to administer myself.

"I had also found out that my aunt's husband, who was at the hospital during the same time, had passed on. Sitting on the couch in the living room, and before popping any of them, I read all the side effects, one of which was death. Then suddenly something came over me. Getting up from the couch I rushed towards Mother, who was standing a few feet away, holding onto her tightly as if for dear life. One of the Sisters called 9-1-1."

"Oh my!"

"The paramedics came and took me to the hospital. Laying on the hospital bed I was still freaking out as impending gloom and doom consumed my thoughts. I thought I was dying, so I made numerous requests."

"Like what?"

"I said to call everyone, tell them to come so I can say goodbye."

"Oh my!" I took a shaky breath.

"But the doctor reassured me, 'As we all have a day to die, I can assure you, today isn't your day.' And sure enough, it wasn't. Here I am. Still battling the wolf, but breathing."

"Wow, that's a lot to take in," I breathed out. "Glad you have a handle on it now."

"Some days are better than others, you know. Don't think I'll ever be the same. After leaving the hospital, a bout of depression ensued. Consumed with sadness, hopelessness, and uncertainty I tried to carry on with life as a lupie but it was an uphill battle. As the battle continued, my hospital stays became more frequent. Being sick was becoming the norm."

"But you have it under control now, yes?"

"The hardest part is the shortness of breath. It's affecting my lungs and I really don't know how long I have left. Each biopsy shows more deterioration and inflammation in my lungs than the last."

"Aww, Sister D!" I shuddered, tears forming in my eyes once again.

"You know every time I told the doctors I have a new symptom they'd put my hand down and say, 'It's the lupus, it's the lupus.' I often felt like I wasn't being heard. I remember one time I wrote all my symptoms down on paper and handed it to the doctor. He glanced at the list and turned it into this paper boat," Sister D said, pointing to the white-ruled paper boat, with blue writing sitting on her windowpane.

"A few days after that, I was released from the hospital. Ever since then I've been doing better but, you know, the flare-ups are inevitable."

"How long does a flare-up last?"

"From a week to a month."

"That's a mighty long time to not feel well."

"I've had this one for about two weeks now. If I'm lucky, I will be all better, perhaps, in the next two weeks. But this thing is so unpredictable. Ugh!"

"I know, right? Ugh. What about a cure?"

"Unfortunately, there's no cure yet. I'm actually a part of a new drug study."

"Oh wow! How selfless of you, Sister D! I hope a cure is found in your lifetime."

"Hopefully soon, hopefully soon." Sister D responded, closing her eyes and crossing her fingers.

"So, what causes lupus?"

"Some say it's genetic, others say environmental, some say a combination of both. So yeah, who knows? The cause is still a mystery," she sighed.

Just then a knock at the door caught our attention, interrupting the conversation.

"It's Mother!"

"Oh, you're in here too, Gloria."

"Getting to know Sister D and learning all about her illness."

"Yeah. That darn lupus!" Mother responded shaking her head. "How are you feeling, Sister D? Got you some sunflowers."

"Aww thanks, Mother"

"Have you eaten?"

"I had a few bites of toast."

"That's all? Didn't feel like breakfast?"

"Not really. You know how the taste buds are."

"I'll make you some soup."

"I think I'd enjoy that."

"Gloria, I mailed your letter."

"Thank you so much, Mother."

"Ah, don't mention it. I will leave you two alone and get started on dinner."

"I'll help."

"No worries, Gloria—still on day one. Enjoy the time but by tomorrow the novelty wears off," Mother tee-heed, exiting the room.

Sister D was exhausted from all that talking and decided to get some rest before dinner. I retreated up to my room.

Be hungry enough for success that you smell it, you taste it, you feel and embody it every waking hour.

Chapter 8

Two weeks had gone by. I was caught up on sleep and had also assimilated to the way of life of the nuns, never missing daily devotion or mass, and embracing my new role as a caregiver. Sister Delisha Joan had become my patient while the nuns taught at the school and did their charity work.

It was Friday and the nuns were in the middle of what I had come to find out was their Friday ritual—homemade pizza—an ode to Mother's Italian roots. From the dough to the sauce, they made everything themselves, piling on their favorite toppings—spinach, mushrooms, artichokes, olives, tomatoes, cheese you name it. Soon the pizzas were ready and we gathered around the table to indulge.

"Clink, clink, clink." Mother gently clinked her glass with a fork summoning our attention.

"Gloria."

"Sí. I mean, yes, Mother," I responded with a mouthful.

"We have some good and bad news," Mother continued.

I swallowed then took a sip of my water. "I'll take the good first Mother. No wait, I'll take the bad first."

"Are you certain Gloria?" they chuckled.

"Bad first. Bad first."

With no further hesitation, Mother delivered, "You're leaving us on Sunday."

"Huh?" the smile on my face faded. "This Sunday?"

"Yep," Mother confirmed nodding.

The pizza and water I had just ingested threatened to resurface. I swallowed hard. "OK, hit me with the good, Mother."

"After weeding out numerous offers, we've found you a job—the perfect fit!"

"Oh!" I perked up. A scream escaped my mouth and the smile I was wearing earlier reappeared. My heart and my head once again struggled to find congruence.

"A family of five," Mother proceeded with the details. "Your responsibilities include caring for their three children, a dog, and a 7-bedroom house in Tribeca, Manhattan—13 hours a day, seven days a week. Ready for the pay?"

"Let's hear it," I responded with bated breath.

"$300 a week!"

"Wow!" The Sisters and I gasped.

"You'll be living with the family who will also provide food. And, ready for this? Drum roll, please."

"There's more?" I asked, my eyes popping out of my head.

Sister Annie, the youngest nun at the convent did the honors belting out, "Ta-da-da-daaaaaaaaaa!"

"Hit me with it, Mother!"

The Sisters and I all burst out laughing.

"The dad is a movie producer and director, and the wife is an actress."

"No kidding! Who are they? Who are they?" I asked bobbing up and down in my seat, clapping quietly.

"The Berry's."

"No way!" I screamed. The other Sisters gasped.

"Are you sure this isn't an early April Fool's joke, Mother?" I asked with a hint of too-good-to-be-true-ism. Struggling to pick up my jaw, I sought confirmation, "THE Patrick and Monae Berry from Wolves In Sheep's Clothing and Vindictive?"

"Yep!" Mother confirmed. "I think one of them won a Grammy for Wolves In Sheep's Clothing, if not both of them."

"I think it might've been both you know, Mother. Patrick is a terrific actor, director, producer, you name it, he does it all. He and Monae are a powerhouse and truly complement each other on-screen."

"A dynamic duo for sure. You are super lucky, Gloria."

"And I have you to thank for it, Mother, all of you. Thank you, thank you, thank you, thank you. Thank you for making this possible." My eyes welled up and the tears broke free.

Wow! If this isn't a sign of things to come I don't know what is.

"Aw! Congratulations, Gloria." The Sisters took turns wishing me well.

"Gloria," Sister Delisha called out in a shaky voice. "Thank you. Thank you for helping me. I appreciate you. I will never forget…"

Her words trailed off as the tears streamed down her cheeks, and soon everyone at the table had the sniffles. I got up from my seat to hug her. Scared that I'd be hurting her already aching body, I gently kissed her on her head. "I will miss caring for you, Sister D. I will miss our long chats."

"We'll miss you a whole lot, Gloria." Sister Theresa and I shared a hug, too. The other Sisters took turns hugging me.

"Well, she ain't going away forever and ever and ever," Mother interjected with a smile, attempting to lighten the mood. "Don't be a stranger now, Gloria."

"I promise, I won't, Mother. After all, tu casa es mi casa, right?"

"Riiiight, Gloria," Mother responded playfully.

"Thanks again for everything, Sisters. You will never know how much I appreciate you for there truly are no words. Thank you!" I continued choking on tears.

"It was our pleasure, Gloria. You deserve the very best."

"Aw, Mother! How can I ever repay you?"

"You, my dear, owe us nothing. Your gratitude is enough."

Soon dinner was over. Sister D retired for the night and the other Sisters and I proceeded to clean up. My belly and heart were full, I was bursting with excitement and there was one thing I was itching to do.

"I'll be right back," I informed the nuns who were cleaning up the kitchen.

"Be right back for real, Missy," the Sisters teased. "Your share of chores will be waiting."

Intent on keeping my promise to help out, I quickly ran up to my room. Then boom. A loud bang emanated from upstairs startling the Sisters.

"What was that?" I heard them asking, rushing upstairs to see what had happened.

"Gloria!"

"Yes!"

"What was that? Are you OK?" They barged into my room. "Are you OK?"

"I'm OK, I'm OK," I responded bursting into laughter. "I think," I added, twisting my body on the floor.

"How did you end up on the floor?"

"Wait! Lemme guess, lemme guess," Mother answered, raising her right hand.

"Guess," The Sisters said in unison, looking in Mother's direction.

"Cartwheels."

"Huh?" The Sisters are confused.

"She was doing cartwheels."

"Cartwheels in this small space?" Sister T asked through the hysterical laughter.

"How did you know, Mother?"

"Ask, Gloria," Mother responded, struggling to contain herself.

So I told them everything about the fateful day Mother caught me in the middle of a cartwheel.

"She was so stunned that she aborted the cartwheel and froze in place," Sister Theresa laughed.

"Yes, yes." Mother confirmed, laughing. "It was truly a sight to behold. Luckily for Gloria, the conversation lasted only a couple of seconds. I wonder how long she would've stayed in that position had the conversation went on longer, hm?" Mother added, drumming her fingers on her face.

"Haha. Very funny, Mother." I rolled my eyes playfully.

"This girl is something else!" the Sisters walked away laughing. "See you soon, Gloria. Hope you aren't injured. Hope you can walk."

Mother and the Sisters headed downstairs to resume tidying up the kitchen.

Moments later, I emerged, thumping down the stairs and exhaling, "Ah... I'm back!"

"You OK?" the Sisters asked, falling over with laughter again.

"Having fun at my expense, huh?" I smiled. "What do you guys want me to do?"

"Scrub the floors," Mother Mary responded.

"Oh!" I gasped.

"Kidding, Glo, kidding." The shock on my face prompted Mother to qualify it as a joke immediately. "No need to scrub the floors. Help dry and put the dishes away."

"Phew!" I giggled, tilting my head back.

Before long the kitchen was all tidy and everyone retired for the night.

"Dreams don't work unless you do."

— John C. Maxwell

CHAPTER 9

APRIL FOOL'S DAY 1994

Sunday, April 1st was here—a bittersweet day for me. Though I hadn't been with the nuns for a very long time, I had become very fond of the Sisters and taken a liking to their way of life. They were, in many ways, the siblings I never had. But I knew I couldn't get comfortable. I had to do this; I had to have an income. I had a dream to fulfill. All packed, I was ready to embark on a new journey, ready to take up residence at the Berry's.

"Oh, Gloria! It's Moving Day! Ready?" A knock on my bedroom door commanded my attention. My mind quickly flashed back to the knock at my door when my parents came bearing a candle-lit cake the day I left Cuba on my 18th birthday.

"As ready as I'll ever be, Mother," I responded. The sadness in my voice, apparent and palpable. "Don't think I can ever repay you for all you've done for me."

Mother embraced me before heading downstairs to partake of my farewell meal.

"Mm... smells delicioso!" I inhaled the aroma as I approached the kitchen. There were red velvet pancakes, bagels, potatoes, quiche, crepes, bacon and eggs, sausages, coffee, orange juice, fruit—a little bit of this, a little bit of that, the whole enchilada. "Wow! Y'all don't have to be so excited I'm leaving, now. Feasting on all these goodies like it's a fiesta."

"Haha. Sit down, Gloria," Mother commanded playfully.

Laughing, the Sisters and I sat down to eat.

"Attention everyone!" I called out, clearing my throat. "I just want to say thank you for opening your doors to me—an unworthy and total stranger who serendipitously wandered into your space." Swallowing hard, I continued, "Um, anyway everything is in the letter."

Fighting back tears, I handed Mother Mary a handwritten note and some flowers. "Really, thank you, Sisters, for taking a chance on me. I owe you everything. Whoo. These onions won't stop burning my eyes." I deflected fanning my eyes to keep the tears from falling.

Following a brief chuckle, Mother took over and read the letter out loud.

> "Dear *Sisters*,
> Where do I begin? You guys rock!

"We rock?" Mother paused to look at me from above her glasses. "OK, Gloria," they laughed.

> "When I set out on this journey, never in my wildest dreams did I ever imagine I'd end up at a Convent in all places. But here I am. I will forever be grateful to the Holy Spirit for leading me to you. Thank you for taking me—meek ole Gloria,

> the Saint Lucian-Cuban refugee, a homeless exile—into your space. How courageous and empathetic of you. You exemplify everything the Father above instructs us to do and do it admirably, effortlessly, and selflessly.
>
> Each of you taught me something to better and enrich my life. Thank you for being you. May God continue to bless you and may you continue to bless others. With a grateful and full heart, I thank you immeasurably!
>
> A very thankful and humbled,
>
> Gloria Estefan, I mean, Estevez. Gloria Estevez."

"Aw! Thank you, Gloria. How thoughtful and sweet," Mother replied, taking off her glasses and wiping away her tears. It seemed as though the onions had permeated the entire room. The watery eyes and runny noses and sniffles were widespread. "We're gonna miss you around here, kiddo."

With tear-filled eyes, the Sisters took turns embracing me.

"We have a couple of presents for you too, Gloria," Mother said.

"Aw, Sisters, you didn't have to. Having me here was 'present' enough."

"Oh trust me, we had to, Gloria." Mother laughed, whipping out a gold-toned jewelry box from under her seat.

"Here. Please accept this from all of us."

"You went to Jared's?" I asked, poking fun at the Sisters as I excitedly opened the little golden box. "A rosary? I mean a rosary!" I continued smiling. "Thank you, thank you, Sisters."

"Not exactly what you were expecting huh, Gloria?" Mother laughed.

"I plead the fifth. Jokes, jokes, Mother," I quipped. "No seriously though, thank you! I didn't expect anything, nothing more than what you've done for me."

"We couldn't get our eyes off your broken rosary every time we gathered to pray." The Sisters and I burst into laughter.

My heart was glad, my heart was heavy. I had come to love these Sisters so much. The bond that they genuinely shared, the sisterhood, the camaraderie were admirable and something to aspire to. In two weeks they had really grown to embrace me and I them. And best of all, they laughed at my silly jokes and antics.

"Aw... in all seriousness, thank you, Sisters," I said, managing to pull myself together. "The saltwater really did a number on this one. I've been meaning to get a new one but this one is my very first rosary."

"Ah, it has sentimental value..."

"Sure does, Mother. It used to be my late grandmother's, who sadly passed on the same day I was born."

"Oh my!" The Sisters gasped. "We see now, Gloria. So sorry about your grandma."

Through the tears and laughter and tears, the Sisters thanked me and wished me well. But trust Mother to lighten the mood.

"So, Gloria," she cleared her throat. "Did you just gift us our own flowers?"

"Nope," I responded, trying hard to keep a poker face. "I stole them at the park on my early morning walk."

"You stole 'em?" The Sisters erupted in laughter.

"I think that is worse, Gloria," Sister Theresa pointed out.

"Don't be getting arrested for some wildflowers, now," Mother added using a little New York twang. The Sisters erupted in laughter again. "Anyway. Thank you, Gloria, we loved having you here. Our doors are always open. We can't wait to see you on the big screen."

"Yeah, don't be forgetting us little people now," Sister Annie chimed in.

"Never, ever," I assured the nuns. *I mean, how could I?*

"We'll miss having you around here, kiddo," Sister Theresa added.

"Aw, I'll miss you guys too, more than you know."

Breakfast was over. I retreated to my room to tidy up, making sure to leave it as pristine as I had found it. All packed and room spotless, I was ready to enter a new chapter of my life. In the late afternoon, a black stretched car pulled up near the convent.

"Oh Gloria, your ride is here," Mother yelled from downstairs.

"Coming, Mother."

Placing my belongings on my back, I headed outside. So did the Sisters to see me off.

"A hearse?" I whispered to Mother who was standing beside me. "They sent a hearse to pick me up?"

"Oh, Gloria, Gloria, Gloria Grace," Mother chuckled. "It's a limousine," she whispered back. "It's what celebrities and rich folks ride around in."

"Oh!" I laughed, slapping my forehead. "I always thought these were undertakers. Well, just fancier versions of the ones we have in Cuba."

Mother and I looked at each other, bursting into laughter.

Embracing Mother one last time and blowing kisses to the other Sisters watching from a few feet away, I made my way to the limousine.

"Hello, sir." I nodded, greeting the dapperly dressed gentleman who had stepped out to allow me into the hearse—I mean, the limo.

"Hey, Gloria!" Mother called out just as I entered the vehicle, forcing me to immediately poke my head back out to look at her, "make sure you're taken to the Berry home, not the burial home."

Mother died laughing.

With a dismissive wave and a huge grin, I entered the limousine. Upon getting back into his seat, the driver announced that the Berry's had ordered a special beverage for me.

Oh, I can get used to this, I imagined while sipping on the virgin champagne. *I'm on my way to work. Work? Wait, what! Ah! I like the sound of it. I'll be making an honest living. What I always wanted.*

My mind flashed to Cuba turning my smile upside down, losing my appetite for the champagne.

It's Sunday, they're probably having my favorite, our usual Sunday meal—rice and peas, mac and cheese, green fig salad, and baked pollo. Oh, mom and dad. Wish I could just pick up the phone to share the good news. Someday, someday soon, you will be right here, right here with me.

Shaking it off, I sighed then dried my tears with the black napkins at my disposal. A few minutes later, the limo came to a complete stop.

"Oh! What is he doing?" I muttered to myself, attempting to see where we were, but I couldn't see a thing on the outside. Soon enough, the driver announced that we had arrived at my destination.

"Mama, already?" I giggled. "It feels like I could've walked here."

While still gathering my emotions and belongings, the driver slid the door open, announcing that the Berry family is waiting.

"Thank you, sir!" I replied, hopping from the limo.

"You're welcome, madam. Good luck!"

Chapter 10

Visions remain but mere thoughts if they are backed by inactivity; dreams die slowly if they are unnourished. Get up, get out, go feed your dreams.

Assembled at the doorway of a beautiful, three-story house, in a posh neighborhood in Manhattan, were five people and a dog waiting to greet me.

Climbing out of the limo, "Ah!" I breathed deeply, then released. Composing myself, I held my head up, shoulders back, put on a smile—and walked up to 2876 to embark on the next chapter of my life.

"This. Is. Beautiful," I muttered to myself.

I think I'll like it here. In fact, I know I'll like it here, I affirmed then turned to my Father in heaven.

Into your hands, I commend my spirit O Lord! Into your hands, I commit my life. Reveal and direct me to the path which you have cleared for me. Give me the grace to trust you wholly!

"Welcome to our humble abode!" Monae, the matriarch of the family embraced me.

Humble? Ain't nothing humble about this mansion, but alright. I silently judged as I leaned in to hug her.

"Thank you so much for the opportunity!" I cheerfully responded with utmost sincerity.

"This is my husband Patrick," Monae continued with the introductions.

"Ha-hi!" I stammered, extending my hand for a handshake, "Pleased to meet you, sir." Patrick opted for a hug instead.

Oh, a hug!

Starstruck, I can't even tell them how big of a fan I am of their work.

"This is Owen. He's eight. Jayden here is five and baby Emma is two." Following their parents' cue, the kids gave me hugs, too.

"And this furry pal here is Ringo," Monae continued.

Baby Emma embraced me a second time and wouldn't let go. And Ringo wouldn't stop nibbling at my shoe.

"Hi, buddy!" I reluctantly petted the little mutt going in circles at my feet.

Oh Lord, I gotta get used to dogs licking me and to dogs being inside the house. In Cuba, dogs live outside and eat bones and leftover food.

"Aw! Look how Emma is holding onto Gloria," Patrick pointed out.

"An instant connection, huh, hun?" Monae added. "Emma, you love Gloria?"

Emma rested her head on my shoulder in response.

"Hope you haven't eaten, Gloria," Patrick remarked. "Our chef Harry has prepared a lovely meal in your honor."

"Oh, how wonderful!" I smiled, following the family into the dining room.

As we walked down the grand hallway, my eyes wandered all over the place—to the tall cathedral-like ceilings and extravagant glistening chandeliers suspended from it, back down to the spiraling staircase and the fireplace, back up to the tall windows, and down to the polished floors. The brown and gold tones evoked a welcoming feeling of warmth, comfort, and optimism. We then came upon a large mahogany table laid out with main courses, desserts, and fine china, waiting for its guests.

"Who wants to say grace?" Patrick asked.

"I do, I do," Owen enthusiastically volunteered.

"Dear Lord, thank you for, for, for our food. Bless it and may it nourish our bodies. And thank you for our new nanny Gloria. Amen!"

"Aw! Thank you, Owen," I gushed as my heart turned to mush.

"Great job, O!" Patrick high-fived him. "Bon appetit everyone!" Patrick continued as we sat down to eat.

"So, Gloria, we've heard so much about you and how talented you are. You want to be an actress, huh?"

"Yes. Yes someday, Mrs. Berry," I chuckled, looking down at my plate.

"Please, call me Monae or Mon. We're excited you're here and hope that someday soon you'll not only be our help, but an actress working alongside Patrick and myself."

Yay! I rejoiced, clapping in my head.

"Absolutely! I mean look at her. She's gorgeous, gorgeous," Patrick stressed. "I'm sure the camera will love her exquisite and exotic look."

Squirming subtly, I forced a smile.

He's in the casting business. It's probably normal to speak of other women's looks that way, I thought, trying to justify Patrick's remarks.

"Anyway, make yourself at home, Gloria," Monae continued, dismissing her husband's comments.

"Thank you." I nodded.

The kids sat quietly enjoying their dinner, so well-behaved and subdued it seemed unreal.

"Dinner was delicious," I gushed. "Thank you 'Berry' much."

"See what you did there, Gloria." Patrick laughed.

"Glad you enjoyed it. I slaved in the kitchen all day," Monae smiled. "Chef Harry is the real deal. He really outdid himself tonight."

"Aw, don't I feel special," I smiled.

Eager to begin work, or perhaps the polite thing to do, I proceeded to clear the table.

"Thanks, Gloria." Monae walked over to the sink area to help load the dishwasher.

"We run the dishwasher at night so by morning the dishes are ready to be put away," she said, delving right into the housekeeping items. "The kids usually shower after dinner but since you were coming we showered them beforehand."

"What time do they go to bed?" I enquired.

"They're usually in bed by 8 p.m. So right about now," Monae responded glancing at the fancy clock sitting on the wall. "We'll tuck them in together tonight."

"Come on, kids, it's bedtime," Monae summoned. "Let's go brush your teeth and get ready for bed."

Following closely behind Monae, we went from room to room to room putting the kids to bed, turning down their sheets, reading them bedtime stories, and tucking them in.

"Owen tucks himself in, but at 7:45 we turn down his comforter," Monae continued as I made mental notes of all their nightly rituals. By 8:45 the kids were safely tucked in bed.

"Time to tuck you in now, Gloria," Monae joked, walking me over to the help's quarters.

"The boys are in school from 8:30 a.m. until 2:30 p.m. so they have to be ready and out the door by 8, which means, you have to be up at the main house by 7 a.m. to help get them ready," Monae spurted out. Taking a breath, she continued, "Emma stays home."

"7 a.m. OK got it," I noted.

"Here are uniforms—scrubs—they should fit you. Mother gave us an idea of your size. And the pay we spoke about—$300 a week, 7 days a week, 13 hours a day. Um, let's see, let's see, what else?" Monae asked, tapping her chin trying to remember whether she had covered all the bases.

"Oh, the dog gets walked at least three times a day, or else you'll be cleaning up doo-doo all day," Monae continued. "Be sure to pick up after him."

"Even when they crap outside?" I asked to be clear.

"Yes, ma'am. Or else we get fined. The pooper-scooper and bags are on one of the shelves in the garage."

Not exactly what was going through my mind at the moment but, "I can do that," I responded.

"Feel free to eat whatever you want."

Oh, Lawd, from dog poop to food. But carry on, ma'am, I mused in my head.

"You are free to use the phone for local calls. I'll show you the way to the park sometime this week. You can meet up with other nannies and organize playdates, lunch dates, and all that good stuff. Any questions?"

"Um not really. I think you covered everything. Thank you so much for the opportunity."

"No, thank you! Welcome to our family. And I do mean it when I say make yourself at home, Gloria. Have a restful night."

"See you tomorrow at 7 a.m., Mrs. Berry. I mean Mon, Mon." We chuckled. Flashing a thumbs up Monae exited the room.

"Somebody pinch me!" I exclaimed, pivoting on my right heel just as Monae shut the bedroom door behind her. Kicking off my shoes, I fell on my hands to do my excited ritual. After three successful cartwheels, I sat on the floor a while. A flurry of emotions coursing through me.

Wow! It's finally going to happen! Can't believe I'm actually working for the famed Monae Berry and producer, director extraordinaire—the Patrick Berry! What!

I batted my eyes. My jaw fell open.

Three hundred dollars every week! What! I'll be living here, all meals paid for and on top of that, they will help me break into acting. What! What more can I ask for? I mean seven days a week is a little much but I can handle it. Not like I have a life anyway.

What's that verse again—I can do all things through Christ who strengthens me, right?

Of course, you can Gloria, you most certainly can.

The kids are so sweet and charming and well-behaved—oh such a nice bonus! Gosh, they say if it's too good to be true, it probably is. But, there's an exception to every rule, right? Mother was right in saying it's a perfect fit. What a beautiful family. Family!

My mind journeyed to Cuba.

Wish they were here to see this—mi madre y mi padre. Wish I could tell them. Wish I could share this with them. I sighed, *One day at a time. I'm hopeful for tomorrow and ever thankful for the Lord's grace and mercy. For they both endureth forever. Thank you, Lord. Simply, thank you!*

I got off the floor and unpacked my humble belongings before jumping in the shower. I then said my prayers, recorded in my journal, and set my alarm clock for six in the morning.

Before sliding underneath the light blue comforter to catch some Z's, there was one thing I needed to do—call Mother to thank her again and let her know that the hearse had taken me to Berry home, not the burial home. After a hearty laugh, Mother and I both agreed it was probably best to get a good night's sleep for my first full day on the job.

Feeling tired and wired, I tossed and turned before eventually falling asleep.

Do not be afraid of hard work, for when combined with sweat, determination and persistence, it pays off in ways unimaginable.

CHAPTER 11

APRIL 1994

At 6 a.m. my alarm clock went off. Somewhat rested and refreshed, I was ready to take on the day. At 6:45 I made my way up to the main house to begin work.

"Good morning everyone!" The kids rushed into my arms for a warm embrace. Yup, the kids were up and ready to prepare for school. They were decisive in what they wanted for breakfast—chocolate chip waffles, pancakes, fresh fruit, and orange juice—the easiest meal for Chef Harry to prepare. By 7:20 a.m. they were all done eating, so we made our way upstairs to get ready for school. At 7:55 we headed back downstairs and at 8:00 a.m. they were out the door with Monae, right on time for school.

My first day on the job was off to a great start. All that was left to do now was babysit baby Emma and straighten up the house. I started by clearing the table, unloading, and then reloading the dishwasher with the dishes used for breakfast. Emma, who sat patiently in her high chair while I loaded the dishwasher, began fussing a few minutes in.

"One second, Booba. Give Gloria one second."

Remembering how to use the dishwasher from the night before, I reached under the sink, grabbed the bottle of green dishwashing liquid, and filled the soap cup to the brim. Hitting start, I left the dishwasher to do its job.

Yay! I did it! I rejoiced. The grinding and water sloshing around confirmed it.

Walking over to attend to a now crying Emma, I took a seat across from her at the table, my back facing the kitchen area. Playing with her plush white teddy bear, Emma accidentally dropped the stuffed animal on the floor. Picking it up to continue our entertainment session, the perfectly dried teddy bear was now soaking wet. Puzzled, I looked about my feet to see where the water was coming from.

"Oh. My. God!" I screamed, holding my head. Behind me, the kitchen floor was covered with beautiful white foamy suds. My jaw dropped, my hands flew up cupping my face. I was petrified.

"That certainly didn't happen last night when Monae did it," I muttered under my breath.

Oh Lord, there goes my job! What do I do, what do I do?

Fearing that I'd end up on the floor, breaking a body part, I decided against walking into the kitchen to turn off the dishwasher. I rushed instead into the laundry room to grab some towels.

Oh Lord, these people only have white towels! I complained in my head, but not for long. I had a flood to control. I decided to strap Emma into her highchair but she wasn't having it. Reaching for her baby Bjorn, I strapped her onto my back, got on my knees, and proceeded to wipe away. The more I wiped, the more suds the dishwasher dispensed, the more Emma giggled.

The bubbles, the piggyback ride, the back and forth motion while wiping provided entertainment for Emma. As for me, I was freaking out, on the brink of tears, and drenched in sweat. Sweating not only from the physical exertion of having Emma on my back but from fear. Fear that I had ruined the floor of a multimillion-dollar home.

"Oh!" The bang of a closing door startled me. I jolted, prompting a hearty giggle from the very comfortable baby on my back. "Not funny, Em," I jerked, causing Emma to laugh even more.

"She's here. She's here. Mummy's here, Em!" I fake rejoiced, anxiously biting my lip.

"Oh. My. God! What, what's going on here?" Monae asked.

Wiping off the salty rivulets of sweat dripping down my face with my sleeve, I looked up to find Monae.

"I-I-I, um." I stammered, attempting to explain but couldn't get past that one syllable.

"Let me guess," Monae said, closing her gaping mouth and turning away, thinking her suppressed chuckle was invisible. "You, um," she said stifling a laugh. "You used the dishwashing liquid instead of the dishwasher detergent, didn't you?"

"Um…" I swallowed, closing my eyelids. "Bingo!"

Monae's laughter broke free.

Oh, dear! Is this a too-upset-I'm-about-to-fire-you laugh or does she find it genuinely funny?

I didn't know whether to laugh or cry. Heck, I opted for the former. Monae unstrapped Emma off my back. Over Emma's tears, she recounted the time that she too made that mistake and never wished it on anyone.

My mouth dropped open. Then a feeling of relaxation covered me. Surely if it had happened to the owner of the house she'd be compassionate and forgiving. "How did you clean it up? Because uh, all this wiping clearly ain't working."

"Vinegar and salt."

"What?"

"Using a rag, I removed as much of the dish soap in the dishwasher cup as I could. Then I poured about a half cup of distilled white vinegar into the cup and sprinkled some table salt over the vinegar. I ran the dishwasher on a normal setting for a few minutes. To make sure the suds had subsided, I closed the washer door and let it run a full wash cycle. Then just to be on the safe side, I added more vinegar and salt and repeated the process."

"Salt and vinegar, huh? Who would've thought! I'm sorry, Monae."

"No worries, Gloria. We all make mistakes," Monae patted me on the shoulder, leaving me to carry on with my duties.

About an hour later Monae emerged downstairs with Emma to eat lunch.

"It worked, Monae!" I exclaimed.

"Ta-daaaaa!" she responded animatedly.

Relieved, I exhaled. I thought for sure I would've gotten fired. But the easygoing family was understanding and gave me a second chance. Needless to say, I wouldn't make the same mistake again and like Monae, do not wish it on anyone.

In the afternoon, the boys arrived home from school and greeted me with the warmest embrace ever. I helped them with their homework, we played outside for a little while, then went inside for dinner and a bath. By eight o'clock, right on schedule, the kiddos were all tucked into bed. All things considered, my first day went alright.

The week continued without any hiccups and I received my first $300 pay.

"Yes! My first salary in America. What!" I rejoiced.

Splitting my earnings into three equal portions—one envelope for my parents, another for the nuns, and the other for me—I lifted my mattress, my unofficial bank, and placed the three envelopes underneath.

Two weeks in, and it had been smooth sailing—delightful and easy peasy. The kids were angels and the family was as awesome as the day I met them. Monae and Patrick mentioned my interest in acting often, reassuring me that they were serious about helping me break into the business. But first, they would help me file for permanent residency. The plan was music to my ears.

I continued in the same vein of splitting my earnings between my parents, the nuns, and myself, placing the envelopes under the mattress for safekeeping.

Now, two months in and the dynamics of the family and household were beginning to change. The jig was up. Monae and Patrick helped less and less around the house and with the kids.

The kids' bedtime had gone from 8 p.m. to anywhere between 9 and 10 p.m. The once obedient little angels were becoming disrespectful and bratty and rambunctious. And when they weren't on-location shooting, the parents went from going out primarily on weekends to almost every weeknight.

And Patrick? And Patrick? Well, that's a long story that I was dying to talk to someone about.

With Chef Harry's hours cut and the bi-monthly housekeeper fired, the extra duties fell solely on my shoulders. My days no longer started at 7 a.m. but 5 a.m. if I were to accomplish all my daily tasks.

"But I, Gloria Grace Estevez, I'm no quitter. I shall persevere," I often reminded myself. Having a dream to fulfill, I kept my eyes on the prize and pressed on.

It was a Wednesday night and I could hardly wait to give Mother Mary a call to tell her about Patrick. My knockoff time had gone from 9 p.m. to 11 p.m. By the time I got into my room I realized that it was 11:15. I vacillated between calling Mother and going to bed.

"Ah! Mother is an owl, she's always up late," I reckoned, picking up the phone to call her.

"Gloria!"

"Mother! You're up!"

"Been waiting for your call. How have you been, dear? Guess what I got in the mail today?"

"No... they got it! They wrote back?"

"They sure did." Judging from Mother's tone on the phone I knew she was smiling widely. "Mother, can you read Spanish?"

"Italian and French but not Spanish—yet, Gloria," Mother chuckled, "but I have someone here who can. Hold on, my dear."

Who?

"Hey, Gloria, how are you doing?"

"Sister T! I'm doing wonderful. I remember your broken Spanish the night we met but I didn't know you were fluent. Sorry about that Spanish curse word I uttered in your presence, the day I stubbed my toe."

"What curse word?" We laughed, Sister Theresa clearly pretending not to remember. "Well, I wouldn't go as far as saying that I'm fluent but I can read it. I did a little in school. And um, yes, I do know the not-so-nice words."

"Oops. Sorry, Sister."

"It's OK, Gloria," she laughed warmly. "Ready?"

"Can hardly wait, Sister T., I'm all ears."

"Our dearest, dearest Gloria,

We can't begin to tell you how happy we were to have received your letter. Oh my God! When Juan told us you made it safely we were so elated and relieved. But then he told us that he had forgotten to give you Sandy's number to be picked up and our hearts shattered. Although we know you are a fender and survivor, we worried about you every single day and night not knowing your whereabouts. We can't begin to tell you the dark thoughts that crossed our minds.

Juan apologized profusely and reimbursed us the $500 lodging fee. We wondered every day where you were, how you're faring in

America, where you're staying, and if you were...

Anyway, it warms and relieves our hearts so deeply to know that you are OK. Phew! We can breathe and begin to live again. We slept so much better the night we received your letter, and have been ever since knowing that you are in good company at the convent. We cried our eyes out when we received your letter but for different reasons this time. Anyway, our beloved child, we are so happy that you are alive. Please forgive us, Gloria, forgive us, my child. We only wanted the best for you. Not a day goes by without us thinking of you and praying for you.

Please thank the Sisters for us and never stop being grateful to them.

We hope you've gotten that job, princess. Give God the praise and glory without ceasing. Don't worry about us, we're old, we'll be alright. Just take good care of yourself. Our hearts are heavy as we write but we did it all for you, Gloria. The difficult journey will lead to a beautiful destination, rest assured of that, our sweet, sweet Gloria Grace. We love you more than life itself.

We are doing OK. Things are the same over here in Cuba. Fidel is being Fidel.

Many hugs and kisses to you, our beloved Glo. Hope to hear from you again soon.

So are you a nun now?

Haha... I knew that was coming. Bet that was dad.

```
    Your father wants to know. Nothing
wrong with that if you are, our love.
Remember, the world is your oyster. You
can be whatever you want to be.
    Anyway, we love and miss you terribly,
Glo. Endless hugs and kisses and love our
beloved child.
Mom and dad,
XxX"
```

"Gloria. Are you still there, Gloria?"

"Here, Sis-ter," a sob threatened to choke off my voice. "Thank you!"

"Aw… Such a beautiful letter, Gloria." Sister Theresa's voice cracked a little. "Your parents were really worried. Their love for you is palpable. So happy that serendipity led you to us."

"Oh Sister T, you have no idea how happy I am for listening to that inner voice."

"We miss you."

"Aw! Miss you guys too, Sister T. How is Sister D doing?"

"She has been doing really well. No flare-ups in the last month or so."

"Oh, praise God! Please give her my love."

"I will, Gloria. Have a good night."

"You too, Sister T, you too. Thanks again for everything."

"Gloria." Sister Theresa handed the phone back to Mother Mary.

"I'm still here, Mother."

"How beautiful was that letter? I see where you got your grateful attitude and wit from. Happy we were able to help you, kiddo. I'll be sure to keep this in a safe place for you. Have a good night, my dear, you hear?"

"Will try, Mother. Thanks for everything. Have a good night yourself. Oh, Mother, Mother," I stopped short of hanging up the phone. "I have a little something here for you. Please come get it whenever."

"What could it possibly be, Gloria?"

"It's a surprise for you and my parents."

"Hm... OK, Gloria. I have a meeting on that side of town this week. In fact, I think it's Friday. I'll stop by."

"Sounds great, Mother. Can't wait to see you. It's been two months too long.

"Miss you too, Gloria. Have a good night."

Overcome with emotions, I hung up the phone, gave thanks to the Almighty, and grabbed my diary to record in it.

> June 1994
> Dear Diary,
>
> Oh, what a day! A day filled with mixed emotions. Today I called Mother to tell her about my job and Patrick but I was so happy to have received my first letter from my parents, I didn't get around to telling her.
>
> So, here goes.
>
> Today while holding little Emma, her chin resting on my shoulder, Patrick walked up behind me to play with her. Although I felt he was invading my space and standing too close to me, I figured he was only playing with his kid. I attempted to put Emma down but she latched onto me and wouldn't budge.
>
> Then all of a sudden I felt a hand on my butt and a soft squeeze. I jolted

subtlety. I wasn't sure if I had imagined it or not. Too stunned and embarrassed to ask, I let it slide and hoped it was just a figment of my imagination. But I couldn't help flashing back to how strongly he spoke of my looks on day one and couldn't help but think it was deliberate. I pray to God desperately that I'm wrong. But if in fact, he did make a pass at me, I hope he doesn't take my silence as consent. I'm conflicted. I hope to God I'm wrong.

On a much lighter note, Mom and Dad's letter today was timely. I can only imagine the relief they felt when they got my letter. Now with a permanent address, I can communicate with them more frequently. Best of all, I can share my earnings with them.

I will forever be grateful to the Lord Almighty for his grace and mercy and to these nuns for their mission and compassion. Thank you, Lord, for blessing me. And thank you, Lord, for keeping mi madre y mi padre. May you continue to bless them and look upon them with abundant favor, Heavenly Father. Grateful eternally. Eternally grateful.

Glo wherever you're planted with grace.

Overwhelmed, I gently closed my diary and paced around the room a while. With tear-filled eyes, I dropped to my knees and said my prayers before sliding underneath my soft blue comforter to catch some sleep.

Friday came and Mother was here. With Emma on my hip, I made my way down to the help's quarters, lifted my mattress, and handed Mother her envelope.

"Oh, Gloria!" Her jaw dropped agape. "You don't have to. You owe us absolutely nothing, dearest. Your gratitude is enough."

"Please take it, Mother. I want to make sure that you get a portion of my first paycheck."

"But, Gloria, isn't this more than one paycheck?" Mother asked, her brows furrowed.

"Well, I have three envelopes, Mother." Lifting the mattress a second time, I grabbed two more envelopes—mine and my parents. "Every time I get paid I split my earnings into three equal parts—you, my parents, and me."

"Is this your bank?" Mother threw her head back roaring with laughter.

"Yes, ma'am," I admitted in a hushed voice.

"What if the house burns down, Gloria?" Mother asked, her head tilted sideways, her fists on her hips.

"Hm..." I responded, mimicking Mother's posture. "Guess I'll lose my life savings, huh?"

"Perhaps it's best if you open a bank account."

"Can I do that without papers here, Mother?"

"I'm pretty sure you can."

"Oh great! Let's do that then."

"I'll look into it and get back to you."

"OK. Take the money now. If possible, great. If not, you can always hold on to it for me."

"Sure, Gloria."

"Oh, that was a hasty 'Sure,'" I teased. "No fancy vacations now."

"Darn! I was just thinking of taking that long overdue trip to France!"

"Haha, funny. Thank you so much, Mother. Having you open the account will make it easier. Every time I need to send money or something to my parents, you'll have access."

"Ah, sounds great. You can also have Monae deposit your salary directly into your account. That would save me a trip here every so often."

"Oh! Tired of seeing me already, are you?"

"Never!" Mother laughed, playfully rolling her eyes. "And, Gloria, don't worry about us. We're fine. Thank you for the token, but no need to split your earnings with us. Ok, kiddo? Save your money."

"Aww, Mother, it's just that I'm so appreciative of you guys. Thank you ever so much."

"You're most welcome, Gloria."

"Speaking of which, I'd like to send some money to my parents. Please mail them the contents of their envelope."

"Will do. Oh, Gloria, you know, it just dawned on me. You can probably ask the Berry's permission to receive mail here."

"You know, I've thought about that, Mother, but I'm thinking this is a job. Although things are going OK, there's no guarantee that it will last forever, you know what I mean? Plus I don't want to confuse my parents. I'd rather have them sent to a more stable address. You know how long these letters take. I could be out of here while one is in transit and never receive it. Know what I mean?"

"You've got a point there, Gloria. Didn't look at it that way. But you're right, it probably is best to separate your work life from your personal life."

"Yes. I don't want to get the Berry family all up in my business." We chuckled. "Hope I'm not bothering you and Sister T, Mother."

"Oh not at all, just thought you'd get your letters right away and we wouldn't have to be all up in your business," Mother gestured and laughed. "We are happy to assist in whatever way we can. Remember that. Hi...! Hi, Emma-Emma!"

Emma smiled, resting her head on my back as Mother played with her.

"She's so precious and so well behaved huh, Gloria?"

"She sure is, especially if she's attached to me somehow."

"Ah..." Mother threw her head back. "Bye, Emma-Emma. You're so cute, aren't you? So cute, aren't you, Emma-Emma! Look at those cheeks, ou! Adios, Gloria."

"Adios, Mother, I appreciate you!"

"No matter where you're from, your dreams are valid."

— Lupita Nyong'o

Chapter 12

AUGUST 1994

Within two months of receiving my first letter from my parents, I received a response to my second letter. Dramatically clearing her throat, Sister Theresa prepared to read it to me.

> ```
> "Our dearest Gloria,
>     We love and miss you so, so much. Thank
> you for the money you sent us. Your father
> and I treated ourselves to a wonderful
> dinner as you suggested. I had…"
> ```

"Wait, Sister T, let me guess. Dad had ropa vieja."
"What's that?"
"It's, uh, pulled beef with onions, garlic, wine, tomato puree, and whatever else. And mom probably had the same because in Cuba,

beef is a rarity so anytime they go out, they indulge if it's available. They contemplated whether they should have dessert. And if they did, Dad had an arroz con leche with coffee, and Mom had flan."

> "We even had dessert - dad had arroz con leche, I had flan and we both had coffee.

"Do I know my parents or what?" I responded laughing and crying at the same time.

"I'm impressed, Gloria," Sister T laughed then continued reading the letter...

> "Thank you, Glo. But remember what we told you. Don't worry about us, save your money. You are young. Start a life for yourself. We will be OK. The ban on selling produce was lifted recently, so Dad has been bringing home a little money.
> And, speaking of which, I don't know if you've heard what's going on at home, if it's being reported on the news in America, but there are riots and protests going on all over Cuba against the government. So, Castro says whoever wants to leave Cuba can go.

"What!" I gasped. "The Mariel Boatlift, all over again? Wow! Sister T, heard or seen anything on the news?"

"Nope. Didn't hear any of the Sisters say anything either."

> "Lots of people are taking him at his word and fleeing in droves. I heard Manuel

```
                from next door, his wife and two children
                abandon the house and leave."
```

"Oh wow!" I gasped. "Surprised my parents didn't make a run for it."

```
                "Dad and I were thinking of leaving too but
                I haven't been feeling well, no strength,
                no energy, unbearable pain throughout my
                body, I'm not sure my body will be able to
                handle it.
                    I have a doctor's appointment in a
                couple of days but by the time you receive
                this, it will have passed already. Will
                keep you updated. Until then, goodbye, Glo.
                Remember to take good care of yourself. We
                love and miss you more than words can say.
                Eternally yours,
                Madre y Padre
                XxX"
```

"Wow! Another mass exodus, huh? That would've saved me the worry of being intercepted at sea... Anyway, not going back in time, not going back in time. Thank God I got here safely."

"That's right, Gloria, pointless looking backward. I pray God guides and protects all making the journey. Would you have wanted your parents to come?"

"On a reliable boat, of course. I remember the Mariel Boatlift of 1980. My parents contemplated leaving but I was 5 years old and dad didn't want to abandon the last vestiges of his parents— the house and mementos they had left him."

"I think over 100,000 Cubans fled to the U.S. during that time," Sister T remembered. "It was being reported how guards were packing boat after boat, overcrowding them without considering the safety of the refugees. During that period I think there were about twenty-something deaths."

"Yep, fourteen of them were on an overloaded boat that capsized."

"How sad and tragic. All they wanted was a better life, a piece, a taste of the American Dream."

"Indeed Sister T. And we are willing to go to whatever lengths to get it. I hope my people are taking every precaution, not overcrowding boats and makeshift rafts to flee." I shuddered. "I pray they all make it here safely and alive." I sighed. "As for my parents, I mean, they have a path now. So I'm kind of glad they couldn't make it. Once I get my citizenship, I can file for them and we can reunite then."

"I agree, Gloria, and especially she's not feeling well. Being on the water for so long wouldn't be good for her. Just a little patience and all will fall in line. You guys will be reunited before you even know it."

"Ah… I trust that Sister T. Hope she's OK though. I mean mom never complains, so if she's going to the doctor she must be really feeling unwell. You know, I wish I could send her a care package but I don't know how I can go around the embargo. Hm…Oh, wait! I know, I know via Saint Lucia!"

"Saint Lucia?"

"Yes, yes, Sister T. Cuba has good relations with Saint Lucia and, you know, that's where my mom is from."

"Do you think we could try to contact her relatives?"

"Hey, Gloria." Sister Theresa handed Mother Mary the phone. "We can contact the Convent over there. I know Mother Angelica at the Convent in Coubaril. Perhaps she can help us. I'll get working on that ASAP."

"Ah! Thank you, Mother. You guys always come through for me."

"Don't you mean gals?"

"Huh?"

"Never mind. Happy to help you, Gloria," Mother laughed.

"Oh... gals, gals," I responded belatedly, chuckling.

"There's that laugh."

"You always bring it out, Mother, with your incredible sense of humor."

"Have a good night, kiddo. Don't worry—your mom will be fine. We'll continue to intercede for her in our daily novenas."

"Appreciate it, Mother. Give the Sisters my regards."

With a heavy yet grateful heart, I hung up the phone, turning to God for comfort.

Dear God,

I come before You today with all that is within me to praise Your holy name. I come not asking for anything for me but the restoration of health for my mom. I pray that You, lay Your healing hands upon her right now and heal her mind, body, and soul. Just like You did the lady at the well and just like You raised Lazarus from the dead, just like Saint Monica who prayed for her son for forty years, I come on bended knee seeking healing for my mom. Bless my dad; be with them at this uncertain time.

Thank You, Lord. Thank You for the Sisters of Charity. Continue to bless them and their mission. Thank You for planting them in my life. All praise and glory and honor belong to You, Father. Thank You, thank You, oh Lord of hosts. Thank You, Lord, from whom all good things flow!

And dear God please be with all the refugees fleeing Cuba right now. Please

> *guide and protect them all dear Jesus, that they get to the shores of America safely. This I ask in Your precious and Holy name. Amen. Your forever grateful, and humble servant, Gloria Grace.*

Getting off my knees, I rolled into bed. Feeling overwhelmed, tossing and turning, I struggled to fall asleep.

Before long, my alarm clock made certain to remind me that it was time to get out of bed and get ready for my workday. With barely enough sleep, I hit the snooze button. Another hour passed and I was still struggling to get out of bed. Although my agreed starting time was 7 a.m. I always gave myself a head start so as to complete all my daily tasks. But today I was tired and decided to go up to the main house at 6:45 a.m.—15 minutes early, not my usual two hours earlier. And boy, oh boy did I get in trouble for the 15-minute early start.

"Good morning, Monae," I greeted with my usual cheerful disposition.

"What the fuck happened this morning, Gloria? Where have you been?" *Whoa!* Monae's hostility and aggravation shocked me. "The baby has been up since 4 a.m. I barely got any sleep."

The hell! I screamed in my head before attempting to answer. "I-I-I..."

Before I could get another 'I' out, Monae handed me baby Emma and stormed upstairs. Within minutes the other two kids were up for breakfast and school. With a now-crying toddler and two kids to prepare for school, I struggled to get anything done.

"What would you like for breakfast, Owen?" I asked.

"I want mommy to do it."

"She can't, she's sleeping, O."

"No, she's not. I just heard her yelling. Please..." he begged.

"Not today, Owen, let mommy sleep."

I swear this kid's lungs, I sighed.

"What would you like for breakfast, Jayden?" I asked, ignoring Owen's tantrum for a moment.

"Bacon and scrambled eggs and pancakes."

Oh lawd! Of all mornings, bacon and eggs and pancakes?

I breathed deeply, struggling to not lose my cool. "Sure you don't want chocolate chip waffles, Jay?"

"No. Bacon and eggs and pancakes."

"OK, Jayden," I responded, inconspicuously rolling my eyes.

"Thanks, Gloria."

Lucky I love you to bits boy.

Two months into my hire Chef Harry's hours were cut. From being at the Berry's beck and call for three meals a day, and even snacks, he now prepares one meal a day—dinner. *And yours truly gets the morning and afternoon job. But, no worries, Gloria, as my mom often said pwan tjè (take heart), nothing lasts forever. Keep your eyes on the prize.*

About a half-hour later Monae emerged from her room, ready to take the kids to school.

"Come on, kiddos, let's go," she sang and clapped, climbing down the stairs. "You're gonna be late for school."

"I'm still eating, mom," Jayden responded, struggling to eat the breakfast of champions he had to have.

"Mom, can you make me breakfast?" Owen asked on the brink of tears.

"You haven't eaten yet, O?" Monae turned to him stunned.

"Gloria!" Monae huffed, turning to look at me. "Gloria, why aren't the kids all ready and why didn't you make Owen breakfast?"

Eyes on the prize Gloria. Eyes on the prize, the cheerleader in my head reminded me.

"Um well..." I uttered, struggling to find a response that wouldn't get me terminated on the spot.

Before I could respond, Monae muttered under her breath," So friggin' useless."

A DARING PURSUIT OF THE DREAM

"Pardon?" I asked though I had clearly heard what Monae said.

"Come on kids, let's go, let's go, you're gonna be late for school," Monae ordered, dismissing my question.

"But Mom, I haven't had breakfast!" Owen complained.

"Why Mom? I don't wanna be late," Jayden whined.

"Because the help started work late today," Monae responded sharply.

"Now, now, now, I know you're not referring to me, Monae!" I snapped, annoyed, and offended at the same. "First of all, my name is Gloria. Second of all, may I remind you that our agreement was 7 a.m. and I got here at 6:45 a.m., 15 minutes ahead of time? So what's the problem?"

Letting my words fall on deaf ears, Monae grabbed the kids and walked out the door. On her return from dropping the kids off at school, Monae walked straight into her room to get some rest while I carried on with my daily chores. Annoyed with Monae, coupled with tiredness from sleep deprivation and worry about my mom's health, getting through the day was a struggle. But I did. At 11 p.m., two hours after our agreed time to knock off, I made my way down to my room to get some much-needed rest.

"Ahh..." I exhaled, plopping onto the bed. A few moments later I found the strength to shower. But before sliding underneath my comfy blanket, there was one thing I had to do.

> August 1994
> Dear Diary,
> What am I doing here? Oh what a day, what a day! What a dreadful day I had today. It was through the mercy of God that I didn't get fired. Today was trying, but I thank God for patience and understanding, and self-control.

> *But wait, why am I taking the blame? Typical. While it's true that I spoiled the Berry's by starting work two hours earlier than what we agreed upon, no one has the right to speak to anyone in that manner. Today I saw a different side of Monae. She treated me like I was worthless. She even called me useless! Useless? I'll admit, the devil in me came close to coming out. But, OK, strike one. Everyone deserves a second chance, right?*

Continuing my journal entry, I recounted just what had happened.

> *Best believe I will never forget how Monae made me feel today or what she called me. But, c'est la vie, as mom always says, such is life. Nothing in life comes easy. I wonder if they have plans of ever helping me. But I remain positive, patient, and hopeful.*
> *Glo wherever you're planted with grace.*

At midnight, with a heavy heart, I turned off the light, set my alarm clock for 4:45 a.m, and slid underneath my blue blanket in the hopes of falling into a deep sleep.

"Oh! I gotta give Mother a call!" I remembered, hopping out of bed at once.

"Hola, Mother! Did you mail the package to Mom?"

"I'm fine, Gloria. How are you?"

"Pardon my manners, Mother. How are you? Did you mail the package to Mom?"

We laughed.

"A little tired but good."

"You, tired Mother? Shocking!" I teased.

"I do get tired, you know, Gloria. Not often, but it does happen," Mother responded, her smile evident through the phone line. "How are you? How was your day?"

"Well let's just say I survived this day—barely though."

"What happened? You sound defeated. Where's that spunk, that upbeat and optimistic tone in your voice?"

"Had a very very challenging day today."

"What happened, my dear?"

"Ah, long story, Mother, but I'm OK now. I'm really tired and worried about Mom."

"OK, dear. Get some rest, you hear? Don't you worry your little head now, for worrying is always a waste of time. It has never helped anyone. Continue to intercede for your mom. Release her pain and illness at the foot of the cross. Your mom will be OK. I promise."

"Thanks, Mother. You always know how to make me feel better. Have a good night yourself. Oh, and the package, mailed it?"

"I sure did, dear. I mailed it to the Convent in Saint Lucia and the Sisters over there will take care of it and mail it to your parents."

"Ah. Thank you, Mother. How can I ever repay you?"

"No need to, Gloria. I'm happy to help whenever and wherever I can. Get some rest, kiddo. It will be alright in the morning."

"Yes, it will."

With a grateful heart, I hung up the phone and climbed into bed.

Ah! I can always count on the nuns...

My mind wandered.

Such a blessing to have prayer warriors and resourceful people in my corner. How can I ever repay these nuns? They have helped me so much. Getting me off the street, welcoming me into their home, finding me a job, now helping me communicate with my parents. Wow! Lord, I live in infinite gratitude to you and them. Simply, thank you!

Breathing deeply, I turned onto my stomach, pulled my sheets up to my eyes hoping to get some shuteye.

I wasn't sure what time I fell asleep, but before long, my alarm clock signaled that it was time to get up. Hoping for a better day than the last, I went through my morning ritual and made my way up to the main house to get a head start on my duties.

At 6:45 a.m. the kids strolled into the kitchen ready to break their fast. Cooperative, like when I first arrived, they were decisive about what they wanted for breakfast, wanted nothing fancy like the day before, sat and ate nicely, and were ready to get dressed for school. Baby Emma was still asleep, so my morning was off to a great start.

Like clockwork, Monae came strolling into the kitchen, ready to take the boys to school. She greeted me good morning and stroked my back as she walked past me near the kitchen sink. Shocked by her warmth today, I decided not to question my good luck. Needless to say, the day went on incident-free. Monae never addressed the incident and neither did I.

As the days and weeks rolled on, the dynamics in the household remained the same—parents worked a lot and went out a lot, and I worked to appease them a lot. I made it my duty to begin work at 5 a.m. without fail to avoid conflict, while also continuing to blame myself for having started spoiling them in the first place.

Within a couple of weeks, I received word from my mom that she was doing so-so health-wise. Her blood pressure and sugar were a little elevated but she assured me that she was following the doctor's orders to get and keep her numbers down. The doctors also said that the body pain she was experiencing might have been due to depression and inflammation. But she's doing OK otherwise. I penned her a reply.

Dear Mom,

I love you. Always a pleasure hearing from you. How are you and dad holding up? Hope you're OK. As for me, I'm hanging in there. I'm doing alright. Ever since your possible-diagnosis of diabetes and hypertension, I've been doing a lot of reading. According to the encyclopedia, diabetes when left untreated can lead to potential complications such as heart disease, stroke, kidney damage, and nerve damage. And so does high blood pressure, which can affect your heart, brain, and kidneys.

It also says to exercise regularly. You can walk up and down that hill near the house a couple of times a day, eat right, eat healthy, cut your sugar intake, and even coffee, too (I know this one will be hard for you). Cut your salt intake; you don't even need to cook with salt. Your signature blend of homegrown herbs and seasonings should be enough.

Some people say garlic, beets, cayenne pepper and honey, and apple cider vinegar in water also lowers high blood pressure. Ask your doctor about them.

Please promise me you will take every precaution, Mom, and will continue to follow your doctor's orders.

About deciding against fleeing, I think it's best you decided not to come. I know you will miss Manuel and them. They were

> *really nice neighbors. I pray they make it to America safely, hope they all make it ashore safely. As for now, Mom, take care of your health and remain patient. I will file for you guys when I get my citizenship and we can be together again someday soon.*
>
> *Anyways, give Dad my regards. And do take good care. I love you two with all my heart. Be well, Mom.*
> *Yours forever, Glo!*
> *XXx.*

I was worried about Mom, I had no choice but to carry on living and working towards my dream. Life in the Berry household was still the same. I tried hard to not step on anyone's toes and I tried hard not to allow anyone's stepping on my toes to affect and derail my dream. Pushing through the challenges and taking everything one day at a time, I persisted. Within a month or so, I heard back from my beloved parents.

> *Our beloved Gloria,*
>
> *Hope you are doing OK. Dad is great, working hard as usual. I keep telling him to slow down a bit but you know this man is a workaholic. I, too, have been doing some gardening to keep active and healthy.*
>
> *Anyway, thank you so much for the package. Thank you, my love. God will continue to bless you.*
>
> *The doctor said I can try the natural remedies but said to take them in moderation and don't overuse them. Like the vinegar he*

> *said, too much can lower blood pressure. And low blood pressure is just as dangerous as high blood pressure. He even said it helps with other ailments and conditions like indigestion, heartburn, and weight loss.*
>
> *Good news, though. My blood pressure and blood sugar are under control. I really have been monitoring and exercising and eating right. I have even been gardening more often with Dad. It's a great exercise to keep active. Trust me, my child, I'm really committed to keeping these silent killers under control.*
>
> *Anyways, Glo, we love and miss you so much. Everything happens for a reason. Perhaps my being sick right at the moment was God's way of saving me from taking the trip and asking us to be patient. We pray for you every single day and hope you are inching closer to achieving your dreams.*
> *Eternally yours,*
> *Mom and Dad*
> *XxX"*

"Phew. Thank you, Jesus!" I exclaimed, throwing my hands in the air, breathing a sigh of relief. "I pray Mom's health continues to improve. You are the Mighty Physician, Lord, continue to work on her. Thank you, Father, in heaven. Thank you!"

And we both said, "Amen!"

"Thank you, Sister T."

"You are welcome, Gloria Grace. Have a restful night."

Endeavor to be kind to every person you interface with, for they may be fighting battles you can't begin to imagine.

Chapter 13

MAY 1996

I continued communicating with my parents as the months passed. Mom's health fluctuated from time to time. After all, she was getting older. Life was going on. I was still working with the Berry's as the nanny, housekeeper, and whatever else, trying everything to remain in their good graces. Albeit not the ultimate dream I had dreamed up, it was a stepping stone that I was incredibly grateful for.

Owen—who was now 10—was a teenager in his own mind and was too old and too cool to play with his younger siblings. He had also graduated from basic playdates to sleepovers with his friends, all of which took place at the fun house—our house.

Seven-year-old Jayden always found himself in a quandary, feeling that he wasn't old enough to play and hang out with his brother Owen and his friends and too old to play with baby Emma, who was now 4.

Emma was joyous, exuberant, and was becoming increasingly independent—an independence that forced me to pray for even more patience letting her do certain things on her own. Although the kids were now 10, 7, and 4, and baby Emma was now in school half a day, my workload hadn't lightened as a result.

Monae fired Chef Harry once Emma started kindergarten, making me their only help—full-time chef, nanny, housekeeper, tutor, dog walker, you name it.

She and Patrick were traveling more than ever for work. To compensate for their guilt of being away, they'd shower the kids with gifts, bedtime delays, and even weekday sleepovers. As you can imagine, their absence started taking a toll on the kids. Being a non-quitter and an exceptionally patient person, I coped as best I knew how. I had my ultimate dream to fulfill.

Taking every day in strides, I remained hopeful, hopeful that someday, someday soon the Berry's would keep their word and help me realize that dream. I also came to realize that one of my biggest strengths—patience—was also one of my biggest shortcomings. Household chores—ironing, doing laundry, putting dishes away, and wiping down surfaces—always afforded me time to get into my head to reflect, to pray, and to dream.

After two-plus years of employment with the Berry's, I was still the nanny. With each passing season, I hoped that it would be *my* season—the time that they'd finally help me achieve my dreams. The perfect angels I met on that April Fool's Day, my first day on the job, were far from perfect. The parents worked a lot and traveled a lot. The kids had become disrespectful. I tolerated it. My hands were full—three kids, a 7-bedroom house, and a dog to tend to on my own. Thirteen-hour days, seven days a week, 365 days a year.

Regardless, I never skimped or cut corners and never allowed resentment to keep me from giving my very best. My perfectionism—another trait I see both as a strength and weakness—would not allow it.

I grappled with the thought of quitting and disappointing those who had helped me. I feared jeopardizing my chances of fulfilling my childhood dream and of making my parents proud. I knew my workload was too much and it was beginning to manifest in my appearance and energy level. There were days when I would be so weak and tired and overwhelmed that my body struggled to rest. My skin had begun to break out. My eyes were always puffy and I had become the skinniest I had ever been my entire life—105 pounds—even though I ate well. The stress of the job coupled with the uncertainty of my mom's health was taking a toll on me.

But every time I thought of quitting, I talked myself into staying. I hung in there with hope in my heart and a will to achieve despite the odds.

So close, yet so far, I often thought. *I mean, I've invested sweat equity...*

Two and a half years is a mighty long time. Everything came flooding into my mind one day.

What if I quit and next week was the week they were going to help me for real, for real? I mean, I'm no quitter. I don't want to disappoint the nuns or insert myself into their space again. If I leave I'd have to start all over again with a new family, new environment, new this and new that.

Argh! I mean they hired me with no job experience, you know? They took a chance on me. They gave me a place to stay. I feel like I owe them for giving me my first job in America. I don't want to let them down. I don't want to disappoint Mother, who gave me a glowing reference. I feel indebted to the nuns, I feel indebted to the Berry's.

Gosh! What do I do? What do I do?

The inertia overpowering my thoughts while doing the laundry was a powerful force to reckon with.

Yeah, that's all it is—complacency. We, humans, fear leaving our comfort zones, we fear change, we fear the unknown and we fear starting over.

But what good is it staying in a job if you're unhappy, a job where you're stagnant, not thriving and growing and working below your potential? You are truly doing yourself a disservice, Gloria. And, by extension, others too. Others you can bless with your talent and contributions.

And girl, why are you staying in a job where your boss keeps making passes at you? Patrick is always winking at me, always wanting to play with Emma while I'm holding her and brushing up against me. Ugh! Am I reading too much into this? Am I in denial? I mean, I don't want to lose my job, let alone on bad terms. Mom always says don't burn bridges, plus they're my only real reference. I mean, the nuns are too but I'm thinking if I put that out there other families will be reluctant to hire me. You know how fast gossip spreads. Um, don't think I wanna be the talk of the town.

As for Monae, helping me never comes up anymore. I wonder why though. Is she threatened by me? OK, get over yourself, Gloria, hehe. Seriously, though. I mean, she always says 'Gloria, you're so pretty,' 'Gloria, you're so graceful, you're so expressive, you're so this, you're so that.'

Truth-be-told, every now and again Patrick brings up helping me get into the business but that always seems to occur while also making subtle passes at me. Ugh! Girl, what are you doing? Why haven't you said anything to anyone? Yes, the incidents are recorded in your diary, but what good is that? How's that helping you get out of the situation? Great questions! Great freaking questions. OK! It's time! Woy, woy, woy it's time, Gloria! I screamed in my head, throwing my hands in the air.

"But wait!" I sighed, lowering them. Hunching, placing my elbows on the counter and clenched fists under my chin, the reverie continued.

I don't have papers; I'm still undocumented; I'm an illegal alien. I… Argh!" I griped, rolling my eyes in disappointment.

Another thing they promised to help me obtain but never did, my green card. What will I do if I leave, though? It would have to be babysitting, working under the table. But do I want to start all over? Will Mother be upset? Will she put her credibility on the line for me again?

Oh, these kids. They've grown to love me and I love them so much like they're my own. 'Twas so cute yesterday when Jayden out of the blue, said to me, 'Gloria, will you be my babysitter forever? I don't think I can ever live without you.' It turned my heart to mush. And little Emma, the way she latches onto me and gives me the biggest, tightest, sweetest hugs followed by, 'Glowwea, I wove you this much,' outstretching her arms as wide as they can go and melting my heart every single time. Ah! And O, the sweetest kindest kid you'll ever know.

Gosh, I love those kids. They can be stubborn and don't always listen but...

"Pring, pring, pring!" The sound of the house phone ringing interrupted my inner monologue. Breathing deeply, I shook my head, dried my eyes, put on a façade, and continued tackling my other chores.

"Gloria, a call for you," Monae walked into the laundry room, handing me the cordless phone.

"Huh, for me?"

"It's Mother Mary."

A call from Mother in the middle of the day? I questioned. Puzzled and frightened at the same time, I put the phone to my ear.

"Mother?"

"Quick question, Gloria. How long have you been in the states now?"

"Um three, let's see," I responded, counting on my fingers to make sure, "Yep, about three years, Mother."

"Oh good! So you're eligible for permanent residency."

"How so, Mother?"

"There's this thing, um policy, called wet foot, dry foot for Cuban refugees."

"Oh, I've heard about that but don't know how it works."

"Did you register with immigration when you first got here?"

"No, Mother, the person I was supposed to live with would have helped me take care of that, but of course things didn't work out as planned. I guess I was so busy trying to survive that I forgot to find a way to go register, and I don't really know the process."

"The wet foot, dry foot policy is an Act, a Cuban Adjustment Act that essentially says anyone who fled Cuba and made it to shore in America would be allowed to pursue permanent residency a year later and eventually gain U.S. citizenship."

"Oh wow!" I rejoiced, then immediately quelled my joy. "Ugh, but how will they know when I first got here? This may delay or complicate the process, no?"

"I mean you have the bank account that was opened over two years ago so that could be proof, plus the letters from your parents. Tell you what, I'll reach out to our immigration attorney to see what he says and then begin the filing process."

"Sounds like a plan, Mother. Thank you so much. Will call later with all my info."

"Oh, and you've got mail."

"Yay! Two letters in a month!" My heart leaped with joy. "Open it, open it, Mother! Don't think I can wait 'til tonight."

"Hold on a sec, let me get Sister T."

"Gloria. Oh, Gloria." Monae called from upstairs.

"Shucks. Gotta go, Mother. I'll call later." Disappointed, I hung up the phone and exhaled before making my way to Monae.

"Coming, Monae."

There is no way I'm working 'til 10 tonight.

"Gloria, have you seen my gold Cartier watch? I've looked for it everywhere but can't find it," Monae asked, yelling from upstairs.

"Really, Monae?" I mumbled. "It should be in either the top or middle drawer in your jewelry chest," I yelled back, making my way up the stairs to help find it.

Pulling the top drawer of her chest, it wasn't there. So, I did the next logical thing and opened the middle drawer. Voila! There it was in all its fabulousness.

"This one?" I asked, dangling the gold bedazzled watch.

"Oh my God!" her mouth dropped agape, sharply extending her hand to retrieve it.

Didn't she say she looked for it everywhere? I recalled, rolling my eyes in annoyance. *The darn watch was in its usual spot!*

"And it's not in its case? Oh my!" she gasped. "Thank you, Gloria. You're the best!"

"Oh, didn't I tell you I have superpowers?" I responded, my voice dripping sarcasm.

"You do?" Monae looked at me awed. Not sure if it was an act or if she actually believed me.

Aggravated, I chuckled, sighed, then headed downstairs to carry on with my chores. Before long, the kids were home. I went through my after-school ritual of homework, play, bath, bedtime stories, and then bed. Soon enough the clock struck nine. Keeping my promise, I retreated to my room to have mom's letter read to me.

"Motherrrr…."

"You're early tonight, Gloria."

"Funny you should say that. Just said to myself that I hope I don't get in trouble. Anyway, I'm excited and a little anxious about the letter."

"OK but first, good news! Our immigration attorney says you may be eligible, all you need is a sponsor, which we can do, and about $2,000. That includes payment for his services and filing fees."

"Oh, sounds great Mother! I can afford that!" I chuckled, tears forming in my eyes remembering the days I didn't have that and was begging on the streets. "Thank you for sponsoring me, Mother. And, you know where to withdraw the funds."

"Of course, Gloria. It's our pleasure to help in whatever way we can. I will pass on your information tomorrow and will get the ball rolling right away."

"You truly are the best, Mother!"

"I know." Mother chuckled. "Let me get Sister Theresa." In two twos, Mother was back with Sister T in tow.

"Hi, Gloria, ready?"
"Listo, Sister T."

> "Our beloved Gloria,
> How are you, our love? Hope you are well. As for Dad and I, we are doing OK considering I recently got a little health scare. My blood pressure and blood sugar are still under control, as I have been following the doctor's orders to a T. I really have been exercising, eating right and using some of the natural remedies you mentioned.
>
> But, I did a mammogram about a month ago and it came out abnormal.

"What!" I gasped. My heart sank to my feet.

> "The doctor said it might be nothing. So, we're awaiting the results.
>
> Anyways, don't you worry your little head. I will be OK. As for your dad, you know how he is—a caring and sweet gentleman but a chronic worrier. He says to have the nuns pray for me. Have them pray for him, too, so he could be less anxious. I assured him I'll be OK. You know we have the best doctors here in Cuba. I will be fine.
>
> Anyway, hope you are taking care of yourself, my child. I've been asking your dad to go for a general checkup but he refuses. He says he feels great and doesn't

> need to. I keep telling him we go to the doctor to keep us healthy and keep us from getting sick but he doesn't get it."

Of course, because like many, his school of thought is that you go to the doctor to make you well... My mind wandered.

> "Always remember to do your annual checkup. I know you work seven days a week, but you gotta find time to do your physical. As cliché as this is, our health is truly our wealth. You must take care of yourself first before taking care of someone else. OK, Glo? We love and miss you a whole lot.
>
> By the way, any acting gigs yet? If not, keep working towards it, my child. Keep going, Glo, you'll get there someday. You remain in our thoughts and prayers and imprinted in our hearts.
>
> Love you eternally,
> Madre y Padre
> XxX"

"God, I pray the doctor is right and that it's truly nothing," I sighed. "When it's not one thing it's another. Thank you, Sister T."

"I'm sure she'll be OK, Glo." Sister Theresa attempted to console me. "As she said, Cuba has the best doctors. And if anything, at least it will be caught early."

"If anything happens to Mom, it will crush me."

"I know, Glo, but remain positive. Think positively. The universe is listening. Father said 'I will never leave you nor forsake you.' Lay your burdens on His shoulder and your troubles at His feet. He asks that we trust Him and not be afraid. God always answers prayers and still performs miracles. Trust and believe, Glo. Keep the faith and hope alive. Alright, dearest?"

"Alright, Sister T. Mom will be ok. She has to be."

The Holy Spirit impressed upon Sister Theresa to pray.

"May the Spirit of the living God fall afresh on her. May He lay his hands upon your mom, Gloria, and may He heal her mind, body, and soul. Lord, for the sick and suffering all over the world, we also pray. Lay Your hands gingerly upon them, Lord. Take away their pain, sadness, and worries. Touch them with Your miraculous hands. Console and comfort them, O Lord. I pray for healing for all. For I can attest that prayer conquers all. May you be with Gloria and her family right now, Lord. For those who are worried and overwhelmed, we pray. Take away their worry, Lord, and give them a calm spirit. Relieve them of all worry and fear and uncertainty. This we ask in Your most precious and Holy name."

"Yes, Lord, touch my mom GloryAnna with Your healing hands! Remove every disease, every malady, every foreign invasion in her body. Please, please, please, dear Lord, I beg. Ask and you shall receive, You promised. Seek and you shall find. Knock and the door shall be opened unto you. I come before you, Lord, on bended knees with all that I have, with everything within me begging for mercy for my mom. Thank you, Lord! Thank you for granting my plea."

And we both said, "Amen."

"Thank you, Sister T." I exhaled, a calm spirit falling upon me. "Have a good night."

"Sleep tight, Glo."

Hanging up the phone, I readied myself for bed. Sliding underneath my blue blanket, I cried myself to sleep.

Never allow instant gratification to kill a dream that will take time to accomplish. Time is fleeting, you will get there someday as long as you keep working at it. Be patient.

Chapter 14

One month later, I received a communiqué from my parents. As usual, I looked forward to having the letter read to me after work. I needed to know the latest on my mom's health-scare.

It was a Saturday and I had started working at 5 a.m. to complete my duties for the day—breakfast, laundry, the kids, dinner, playdates, the whole lot.

That night, Monae and Patrick went out to dinner, and I couldn't wait to put the kids to bed to get some rest myself. On weekends the kids would usually be in bed by 10:00—or 9 if I was lucky. But that night they had their new friend Brazen over for a sleepover and chose to deviate from the norm. Little Emma had an extra early start that day and was in bed by 7:00. But the boys were another story. Fighting, wrestling, throwing pillows at each other and refusing to stay in bed.

"In bed, right now!" I ordered sternly around 1:00 a.m. after numerous prior requests.

"You're not their mom!" Brazen, the sleepover guest, answered.

"Wh-what did you say, lil' boy?" I needed to make sure that what I heard was, in fact, what he had said.

"You're not their mom and they don't have to listen to you," he reiterated.

"Excuse me?" I asked, shocked by his persistent disrespect. "Perhaps in your house, there are no rules, manners, and respect but in this household, we practice etiquette.

I turned to my charges Owen and Jayden, "Boys, turn off the television and get into bed right now or I'm calling Brazen's parents to come get him."

Once again, my words fell on deaf ears. So, I walked over, turned off the television, and stood directly in front of it, intentionally obstructing their view. The sleepover guest Brazen threw a pillow in my direction then charged at me to push me out of the way. Like real copycats, my two boys followed. Picking up the pillow, I flung it lightly left, right, and center to ward them off.

"No! No! No!" My boys yelled out kicking and screaming and latching onto me.

Brazen backed away then started yelling, "Ow! Ow! Ow! Let me go. Let me go. You're hurting me! Let me go. You're hurting!"

Awed and disgusted I rolled my eyes, ignoring him. Right at that moment, the door flung open.

"What the fuck is going on here? How long have you been abusing my kids, Gloria?" Monae screamed. Her breath reeked of alcohol, forcing my nose to twitch.

"What! Abuse? Oh-god-no, it's not what it looks like. I-I-I, let me explain, Monae." Stunned, perplexed, and horrified I stammered and pleaded to have my voice heard but no one was listening or cared to listen. Monae, immediately grabbed the phone sitting on the dresser to place a call.

"Hello, 9-1-1!" My mouth dropped agape. "I just walked in on the help beating up on my kids. 2876 Tribecca, Manhattan..."

"Seriously, Monae?" Closing my eyelids, I shuddered.

Within minutes sirens were heard blaring in the distance. Soon, there was a knock at the door accompanied by an announcement, "Tribecca Police."

Patrick rushed downstairs to let them in.

"What's going on here? Where is she?"

Patrick led the officers to the third floor where the commotion was taking place.

"Ma'am, you're under arrest. You have a right to remain silent. Anything you say can and will be used against you..."

"What!" That's all I could get out. Dumbfounded, I complied as they read me my Miranda Rights and slapped the cold silver handcuffs onto my wrists. With the parents tucking in the little monsters closely—*kids, kids, I mean*—tucking in the kids closely, they all looked on as the cops escorted me away. My eyes flashed to Brazen standing off to the side smirking. Our eyes met. He winked.

The fuck! Did... Did... I huffed. *Did that lil' boy just wink at me?*

I blinked. My lips pursed. I puffed, shook my head, frustrated I couldn't say a few choice words or two. He was a kid—an uncouth kid—but still a kid.

"Get out! Get the fuck outta my house!" Monae screamed.

Baffled, I turned back in an instant to look at Monae. I really didn't understand why she was so angry. I mean no one wants to know that someone is abusing their kids, but her reaction and behavior towards me tonight was over the top, unbecoming, and outright bizarre. And why wouldn't she listen to my side before calling the cops? What was this really all about? Was she too intoxicated?

"Good luck! Good fucking luck becoming an actress or landing another job after this."

"Really? Um! Um!" I stammered. Confrontation was never my strong suit. Not sure what to say next, I blurted, "Your bright-eyed husband has been sexually harassing me ever since I stepped foot in here. Now check that, salop!"

"What did you say?" she asked, stunned.

"You heard me. But here goes. Your husband Patrick has made numerous passes at me, proclaiming how beautiful I am and promising me an acting job," I reiterated slowly and deliberately. "Oh, and 'salop' is a not-so-nice creole word, depending on the context used."

"Get the fuck outta here!" Patrick spoke up for the very first time that night, his eyes widened, his cheeks reddened.

"Bye, Patrick. Don't forget to explain to wifey."

"No need. I know, idiot." Monae responded.

"Lies!" I yelled back to Monae. The officer roughed me up a little.

"Oh, and Patrick, be sure to also tell your wife what you said about my potential to give her a run for her money on-screen, easily. Easily, you said!"

"Ma'am, if I were you, I'd remain silent…"

"Why do you think I…" Monae replied, stopping mid-sentence.

"Oh! Why do I think what, Monae? Why do I think you're having me arrested? Is it so your husband would stop drooling over me? Why do I think you never kept your word about helping me break into acting, huh?"

Oh ok, I see what this is all about.

I zoned out scanning the mansion as the police officers led me down the stairs and outside. Red and blue and silver lights flashing, bouncing on every house in the neighborhood, reflecting everywhere. There, in the driveway, two white police cars waited, the entire neighborhood and their dogs within the vicinity. Miraculously all the neighbors' dogs had to go at 2 a.m. that day. I glanced up to see blinds drawn, nosy neighbors peeping through their windows to get a glimpse of what was happening. No one had to tell me what the talk of the neighborhood would be in the morning.

The police officer stuffed me in the back of the cruiser and then we were off. *What in the world just happened?* I thought as I tried to wrap my head around the night's events. *They were hitting me. I took all the blows. Yes, I flung the pillow to ward them off, but lightly.*

And this kid Brazen, oh my gosh. Can you believe that lil' boy moved away from me then started yelling, 'You're hurting me, you're hurting me, let me go.' And then he winked at me on my way out? What the fuck! Hope they realize that this kid named Brazen is living up to his name sooner rather than later. Tanto, tanto...

The parents didn't even ask what happened or care to listen. Wow! I always thought we had a good relationship, that things were going OK. I mean there were sporadic misunderstandings, but nothing major. I thought we were good. I am truly, truly dumbfounded. Was I naive in thinking that they'd ever help me? I mean, why wouldn't they?

On and on I rambled in my head, trying to make sense of it all.

I loved those kids as if they were my own. Can't even lie, I will miss those kiddos. I will miss those kiddos. Should've left a long time ago. Should've known that I had already overstayed my welcome. Monae showed me who she was a month into my hire.

I bowed my head for a moment, *I had never laid a hand or even raised my voice at the kids. And there I was, riding in the back of a police cruiser. Arrested in America? And could be charged with child abuse. What!*

I shuddered. *She even cursed my dream. Wow! I really wanted my dreams to come true. But dreams are nothing without sanity, and I was this close to losing mine. Maybe this is God's way of removing me from a toxic situation, of protecting me. Should I have escaped to my homeland Saint Lucia instead?*

I sighed. *Well, at least I won't have to deal with Patrick's advances. I don't know why I didn't tell his wife earlier. I guess I didn't want to cause trouble for their marriage or come between them. Thank God I recorded all the incidents. My diary! Oh God, my diary! Hope I get it back. Hope they don't destroy it.*

Arriving at the county jail a few minutes later and being led out of the cruiser, I knew there was one Man I could always call on, so I did. "Lord, whatever you deem necessary, I accept. Let Your will be done, Lord. I am ready for the next step on my journey and if this is all part of your plan, I graciously accept."

Entering the police station, I breathed deeply, hoping for the best but preparing for the worst.

Chapter 15

*"You can kill the dreamer, but
you can't kill the dream."*
— *Martin Luther King Jr*

Now inside, the yellow line running across the floor caught my attention. Officer Jack stopped at it and asked that I wait there.

"A female colleague will be right with you to pat you down," he said.

"Why, Officer?" I asked puzzled.

"It's a standard part of the booking process, ma'am. We have to make sure you aren't carrying any weapons or illegal items."

"But, Officer, where could I have possibly gotten the illegal items from between the house and here? Oh, I know underneath the seat in the cruiser, with handcuffs on," my voice dripped in sarcasm. Rolling my eyes, I snickered.

Officer Jack, looked at me. His forehead knitted deeply.

"Think it's funny?" he asked, his voice dripping in annoyance.

"Not at all, sir."

Taking a deep breath, Officer Jack heaved a heavy sigh.

Down the hallway, a woman was approaching—her head down, focused on the paper in her hand, belt around her waist adorned with what looked like a gun. She came to a halt right in front of me, her legs spread wider than her broad shoulders, her face stoic, her eyes unblinking.

Oh boy. She looks tough. Tougher than Jack.

"Gloria Grace Estevez?" she asked to verify.

"Yes, ma'am."

"Officer Renee. Follow me, hun."

OK, perhaps not so tough. Her soft and pleasant voice surprised me.

Upon entering her office she announced that we'd start with biometrics. I followed orders to be photographed, fingerprinted, and whatever else. The sight of the black ink on my fingertips cemented the reality and gravity of the situation, sending shockwaves down my spine. Chills covered me. And there, just like that, I had a mugshot in America. My worst fear since leaving Cuba.

"Do you need to call your parents, attorney, or..." Officer Renee asked, unknowingly throwing a wrench in my heart. It was impossible to call my parents. They didn't own a phone, for starters, and even if they did, I'm not sure I would have wanted to even if it was allowed or possible. Besides the bevy of nuns and the Berrys, I knew no one else here. And I wouldn't, I couldn't drag the nuns into this.

As for an attorney, I'm innocent, I refuse to use my savings on one. I can defend myself. I will tell the Judge exactly what happened. I will...

"Ma'am, ma'am!" Officer Renee called out drowning my thoughts. "Would you like to call..."

"Oh! No, no thank you, Officer," I responded, amid the knots in my stomach and thumping of my heart.

The reality of having a record in the great U.S.A. gripped me.

Will I ever get another job in America? Will my dreams ever come true? And oh Mother of God! Will I be deported and, if I do, what will Fidel do to me? rapt in reverie, beads of sweat burst through my forehead. That last thought terrified me the most.

"All done here, ma'am," Officer Renee told me.

Right outside the door, Officer Jack waited to escort me to the next step in the booking process. He ordered me, once again, to extend my arms in front of me so he could slap the cold jointed metal on my wrist. He set off, telling me to follow him.

Why the fuck is he walking so fast? I thought, walking as fast as I could to keep up with him. I didn't realize how much being handcuffed with your hands in front of you slowed you down. *Is he training for a marathon or something? Look at his tight shirt. Can he even breathe?*

The corners of my mouth curled up, forcing my eyes to crinkle and my cheeks to protrude.

As if on cue, Officer Jack turned around to see me smiling. "Hearing voices, ma'am?"

"Huh!" I flinched. "Oh, no-no sir. Just reminiscing," I responded, wiping the smile off my face. I attempted to raise my hand to wipe the tears forming in my eyes but the cuffs around my wrist restrained me.

He stopped long enough to allow me to catch up to him. "Do you realize how much trouble you're in?"

"I really didn't do anything, though."

"Do you realize that the majority of people who walk in here say the same thing?"

"I can only speak for myself, sir. I swear to you, sir."

"Yeah, yeah. And, O.J. is innocent too. The magistrate will see you tomorrow." Officer Jack continued, dismissing my plea of innocence.

A few feet further down the hallway we came upon a room, a holding cell. The guard let us in.

All these people in here? I gasped audibly. *Wonder what they did?*

While getting uncuffed, my mind flashed to Cuba, the Batista regime, to what happened to my dad's parents in the Cuban jail.

Officer Jack went on his way and Guard proceeded to pull the heavy steel door shut. Locking us in, leaving me with my thoughts. Once again, tapping into my faith, I released the situation into my Father's hands for He has never failed me yet. Realizing that there was nothing more I could do, I surrendered, climbed onto the bunk bed, and tried to fall asleep.

Chapter 16

Carry your most authentic self everywhere you roam. People will either love you or hate you. But most importantly, you will be less spent trying to be who you're not.

Finally, Sunday was here. *Funny, it wasn't the worst place I had ever spent the night. It's amazing how every experience in life, good or bad, prepares you for the next.*

At around 8 a.m. an officer came bearing a tray with a granola bar, orange juice, and a freckled banana.

"The magistrate will hear your plea today," she said, reminding me that the dream I had last night about this situation being all a dream was, well, not a dream. "Another officer will come get you in thirty minutes."

After breakfast, I brushed my teeth, washed my face, and waited.

Soon the officer came to pick me up, reintroducing me to the handcuffs. As he helped me into the backseat of the cruiser, butterflies in the pit of my stomach fluttered mercilessly. My plan was to rehearse one last time what I'd say, but the banana I had just eaten seemed to have had other plans. With my stomach grumbling, my mouth watering, and beads of sweat breaking through my pores, my primary goal now was to keep the banana from resurfacing.

In about 20 minutes or so, we were at the courthouse—uneventful. *Whew, thank God for His mercy and small victories.*

Empty church pew-like benches filled the courtroom. At the front of the room, a gentleman stood with his hands crossed in front of him—the bailiff. He directed me to the defendant's stand. A few feet away, a court recorder sat waiting. Within minutes, the magistrate entered the room from the side, taking a seat at her desk.

The bailiff announced the case. The clerk read my charges and asked how I wanted to plead.

"Not guilty," I stated definitively.

The presiding magistrate took it from there.

"Good morning, everyone. I'm Judge Judy. I'll be sitting in for Magistrate Lennard who couldn't be here this morning. If I'm being honest, I'd much rather be in church with my family right now but here I am." Judge Judy chuckled then breathed in deeply, "You young people don't know how to behave yourselves. Anyway, let's get started."

"Gloria Grace Estevez," the Judge called out looking up from the paper in front of her.

"Yes, Your Honor."

"Do you have an attorney, a family lawyer?"

"No, Your Honor. I can defend myself."

"We have court-appointed lawyers you can speak to after your arraignment. Let's proceed. You pleaded not guilty to the charges brought against you. Let's hear your side of what happened."

Confident that I had done nothing wrong, I pleaded my case as eloquently, confidently, and succinctly as I could.

"Your bail will be set at $15,000—that's $5,000 for each battery charge. But..."

"Fifteen what!" I interrupted Judge Judy.

"But, you will only need to come up with..." she continued, but with my mind stuck on $15,000, her words trailed off.

What! $15,000?

"Judge, Judge, I swear to you I did not hit those kids! Never did and never would have, ever."

"It's your word against theirs. Do you understand that, Gloria?"

"But I'm telling the truth, Judge, I swear!"

"Of course, Gloria."

"But, Judge..."

"Eh, eh, eh, young lady," Judge Judy rose from her seat, wiggling her index finger at me, her eyes damn near popping out of the sockets, "you interrupt me one more time and you will be sent straight to..."

"But, Judge. But, Judge, Judge..."

"OK, that's it! Gloria, you're sentenced to three years in jail without bail for battery on three minors."

"What?" I gasped, then winced as the sound of the gavel reverberated in the courtroom, signaling the end of the hearing.

"Take her out of here!" she snapped, continuing as she exited the courtroom, "I will not tolerate disrespect in my..."

"Wh-what does that mean?" I asked, turning to the officer who drove me to court.

"Um, it's over," he said, clearing his throat. "You're off to the slammer."

Everything became a blur. I hung my head low—really low—as I was being led out.

"She can't just, um... You should've... You should've gotten an attorney, Gloria. They would've pleaded on your behalf and explained things to you. Perhaps..." The officer stopped mid-sentence.

"Perhaps what, Officer?"

"Ah, never mind. I'm not at liberty to offer counsel or none of that so it's best that I, uh, stay out of it."

"Hmm?" creasing my forehead I looked at him sideways. My mind wandered a bit trying to decipher what the officer was stifling. Making our way outside, he once again helped me in the back of the cruiser—this time a little gentler—and off to jail he took me to serve a three-year sentence.

My parents will die. The nuns! Oh. My. God! The nuns!

Is this how they do it here? Can she do that? I mean, I know absolutely nothing about the court system but something tells me this is against the law. The law, huh? Well, technically she is the law, isn't she? I sighed.

There was a lump in my throat. I wasn't sure whether it was the near-rotten banana I had eaten earlier making a comeback or the shock of what had just transpired in that courtroom. I think it was both.

Slumped forward, retching, water forming in my mouth, I cried out, "Pull over, Officer. Pull over!"

"Oh shit!" the officer exclaimed, looking in his rearview mirror before veering off the road, parking, and quickly jumping out to open my door.

"I think I'm gonna…blaaaaargh!" Everything inside me escaped landing on the side of the road, the hem of the officer's pants and his polished black shoe.

"Crap!" he blurted out.

"Sor-ry, Of-fi-cer," I apologized, still slumped over, my mouth dripping water.

"It's OK, Gloria," he replied over the stomping to get the chunks of vomit off him. "Done?"

"I hope so, Officer," embarrassed, I smirked, wiping my mouth on my sleeve, avoiding eye contact.

Relieved from vomiting, Officer once again helped my head inside the cruiser, shut the door, and off to jail we continued. The embarrassment from vomiting coupled with the shock and awe from the recent events vyed to consume me. I resisted.

Is this the next step on my journey, Lord? I asked, resuming the internal dialog. *Patience and hope and faith have always carried me through the most difficult situations. I will survive this. I have to. God orders our steps and perhaps this is the next step on the journey. Perhaps it is a test—although I'm yet to understand the purpose.*

I think it was Proverbs chapter 3 verses 5-6 *that says 'Trust in the Lord with all your heart and lean not on your own understanding. In all your ways submit to Him, and He will make your paths straight.' I trust and believe, Lord. I trust and believe.*

And Job? Yeah, Job 19:25 says, 'I know my Redeemer lives.' And no matter how much he was tested, cursed and plotted against, he remained faithful, steadfast, and true to God. In the end, he was rewarded. God gave him back his children, restored his health, and blessed him with a long life.

Rest assured this isn't the end of you, Gloria. Like Job, you will come out of here with a testimony. You will come out of here, undefeated but even more motivated. You will rise. You must rise, Gloria. You have a dream to fulfill.

I'm ready, ready to write the next chapter in my book of life. I have to be. I have to accept that it is what it is, it had to happen this way, I sighed.

Well, at least I have a place to stay for the next three years, I thought, searching for a silver lining. *But someday, someday at the right appointed time, God will open the doors and lead me out. I trust and believe. Looks like we're here. This is it, Gloria, this is it.*

The police car came to a complete stop, interrupting my thoughts. The cop helped me out of the car and led me inside the prison.

"Gloria, a female colleague will be with you to conduct a strip search."

"A strip search?" I asked puzzled. "I have nothing but the clothes on my back, officer."

"It's a standard part of the booking process, Gloria. We have to make sure inmates aren't carrying contraband."

Realizing now that the situation was serious, I responded in a much softer tone than the night I was arrested, "OK, Officer."

Within a few minutes, the other officer came in and asked me to follow her. I undressed. Standing before her in all my nakedness and as timid as ever, I followed her every instruction. The officer proceeded to examine me, depleting any shred of dignity I had left. To make it official, my civilian clothes were traded for black and white overalls that matched to perfection my freshly inked fingers, black Converse-inspired shoes, and a pair of black ankle socks.

"A nurse will now see you," the officer told me.

"A nurse? But I'm not sick."

Well um, truth be told I'm really sick to my stomach right now.

"Ma'am, it's standard protocol," she responded, speed walking ahead of me.

Well, there's that physical that madre has been urging me to get.

The nurse asked whether I was taking any medications, whether I had any mental health issues, was addicted to anything—drugs, alcohol—and whether I had any known medical conditions, low mood, or anxiety.

"No nurse," I responded to all, even though my anxiety was through the roof, and despite the heart palpitations and sweaty palms.

Continuing with the orientation process, they made known to me the rules and regulations of the prison, what's expected of me, how to make my bed, jobs at my disposal, inspection times, and all that stuff—basically, the services, policies, and procedures of the facility.

By the time the booking process was over, the name I had known all my life—Gloria Grace Estevez—was now associated with a nine-digit number—112819760, my inmate number. Certainly not the nine identifiable digits I had hoped for in America—a Social Security number.

At some point, the intake officer asked if there was anyone I'd like to call.

"Ye-yes, please, officer," I stammered. "The nuns."

"Nuns?" The Officer asked, stunned.

"Yes, sir. I lived with them."

Picking up the phone, I paused to gather my thoughts before dialing.

I have to tell them. Hope I won't disappoint them, I thought, biting my nails as I prepared to place a call to the convent.

"County jail?" I heard Mother questioning before saying hello.

"You have a call from, Gloria Estevez, would you like to accept it?"

"O-oh, of course!"

"Hello, Mother!" I greeted cheerfully, pretending to be unbothered by the situation.

"Gloria?"

"It truly is me, Mother. I'm-I'm-I'm in jail."

Oh God, can't believe I just said that.

"Whatever for, my dear?" Her voice filled with astonishment.

"Um," I said, searching for the words. "Uh, it would be easier to explain if you were here."

"Don't think it works that way, Gloria. Visits are usually scheduled."

"Oh! Hold on, Mother." Turning to the officer who was hovering, towering over me, I asked, "Uh, Officer, can the nuns come visit me today?"

"Um..." Officer scratched his head.

My eyebrows drawn together, head tilted sideways and downward, eyes looking upwards at the officer, I begged, "Please, please?"

"Humph," he sighed. "This isn't customary but uh, uh, OK, I'll make an exception only because um...alright, alright yes."

"Thank you, Officer! Yes! You guys can come, Mother!"

"Which jail?"

"Bayview Correctional," I answered. "Right, Officer?"

"I think that's the one at the south corner of West 20th Street and 11th Avenue," Mother continued.

"Officer, is this the prison on 20th Street and 11th Avenue?"

"Yes ma'am," Officer confirmed. "Directly across the avenue from the Chelsea Piers sports complex."

"Yes Mother, across from the sports complex."

"We'll be right there."

"Mother, Mother," I yelled out quickly before she hung up the phone. "Can you please bring me the letter from my mom? I want to know what happened at the doctor's."

"Will do, Gloria. See you soon."

"Gloria, so uh, this isn't customary but because of who they are and because this day has been uh, unconventional in many ways, I'll make an exception. So, here's what we're gonna do. I'll take you to an empty room where you'll wait until they get here."

"Yes, Officer," I responded, water forming in my eyes. "Thank you so much."

"My kids are in your age group and I can't begin to imagine…" he said tilting his head towards the ceiling. "And you share a name with my littlest one—Gloria Louise."

"Aw, such a lovely name, Officer!" I quipped through the grateful tears. I looked up just in time to see the corners of his mouth move upward, his cheeks dimpled, and the corners of his eyes wrinkled. I could tell how much he loved his kids.

"Anyway, follow me, Gloria."

Taking me to an empty room, the Officer asked that I wait and that he'd come get me upon the Sisters' arrival. Locking me inside, he stepped out, leaving me with my thoughts. Afraid to move for fear of alerting the attention of anyone, I stayed put. Not that I could touch anything anyway—my hands were cuffed. To pass the time, I rehearsed, prayed, and rehearsed some more what I'd say to the Sisters.

Before long, Mother and a couple of the other Sisters arrived at the prison to check up on me.

The officer came to get me, leading me to the room where they were waiting.

"Here she comes," Sister Theresa pointed out.

"That's not, Gloria." I heard them debating as I approached them.

"Sure is," I said, putting an end to the debate. "Sister D! You look well."

"Well enough to come check on you, Gloria."

"Aw! Thanks for coming, all of you."

"Gloria, what happened, my dear? You look incredibly thin." Mother Mary seemed more concerned about my health. "I almost didn't recognize you."

"I know, I know. I've aged, too. See all my grays and creases and wrinkles? I even think I went through menopause," I joked, attempting to lighten the mood.

"So what are you in here for? What happened, Gloria Grace?" Although Mother was witty, she was also a no-nonsense type, cutting straight to the point.

So, I told them the whole story. The night with the kids, Monae's rage, how they dumped more work on me, dangling the promise of helping me get started in acting in front of me every chance they got with no follow-throughs. Everything I had wanted to share for the last two and half years just came rushing out and I couldn't stop.

"What?" the nuns were awed.

"So, back to the recent events," Mother prompted, "They asked no questions before calling the cops?"

"Mother, I kid you not. No questions asked. I tried to explain. Instead of a listening ear, what I got instead was, 'Shut up, shut up, shut up! I saw with my own eyes. I heard with my own ears. Don't care what they did. You have absolutely no right to raise your hands to my kids and blah, blah, blah...'"

"Wow! So, what did the husband say?"

"Good question. The salop, I mean he, he just stood there like a cat had eaten his tongue and said absolutely nothing. Not a word."

"The 'what' stood there?" Mother asked.

"He, he, Mother. Um, he stood there," I chuckled.

"When did this happen?"

"Saturday night."

"Why didn't you call us, Gloria?"

"Twas late, Mother."

"We always pick up the phone, Gloria, you know that."

"I didn't want to bother you guys. I did nothing wrong. I really thought this was gonna blow over quickly. Thought I'd walk into court today, tell my side of the story, and that would be it. But here I am."

"Oh, Lord." Mother responded with an eye roll, before asking, "How much is bail?"

"Well..." I said, hanging my head low, really low. "Judge Judy initially set bail at $15,000 and there was no way I was going to burden you guys with this."

"Well, you know we have money in an account for that purpose, just in case one of us Sisters gets, you know, get arrested."

"Really, Mother?" the other Sisters gasped, looking at Mother puzzled.

"Kidding, kidding, guys," Mother chuckled. "But we would've figured this out, Gloria. From the little that I know about these things, you normally don't have to come up with the full amount upfront."

"Really, Mother?"

"Really, Gloria. And if I remember correctly you have a huge chunk of change sitting in the bank."

"I didn't have to come up with the full $15,000?"

"Usually ten to twenty percent will get you out until a hearing—well, depending on the crime. Didn't they tell you?"

"Can't say for sure they didn't. I think I stopped listening after the $15,000."

"Oh, Gloria!" Mother shook her head clearly irritated. "That's why you should've accepted the free legal counsel."

"I would never hurt those kids, though," I said breathing in deeply. "Never!"

"We know, we know, Gloria. You always spoke so lovingly about them. By the grace of God, we'll get you out of here."

"Um, well the Judge decided to send me straight to jail."

"What!" The Sisters gasped.

"She sort of asked me to not interrupt her, I sort of did, so she abruptly ended the hearing, sentencing me to three years."

"This is unheard of," Mother gasped. "Is this legal?"

"Well... she's the judge so..." I said.

"Nonsense!" Mother was irate and understandably so. "She may be the judge but she isn't above the law. There are certain precedents and protocols they must follow that prevent this very thing—abuse of power and violation of judicial duty. This is unjust, Gloria. We've gotta fight this."

"Um..."

"Whatever is this look, Gloria? Don't you think you deserve justice?"

The words to make my mixed feelings known to Mother and the other Sisters were stuck inside me. Mustering the courage and heaving a heavy sigh, I said, "I mean.. Don't bother, Mother. I don't think I want to or have the strength to go through a lengthy and costly legal battle."

I just didn't see putting myself through that—not me, not my parents, not the nuns. I was undocumented, and for some reason I foresaw it causing more legal trouble for me. My instincts, my gut, have always guided me and so has the Holy Spirit. Perhaps it's all part of God's master plan for my life.

"I'll just serve the time."

"Ultimately, it's up to you Gloria but this is pure B.S."

Oh! I gasped in my head. *Nuns curse?*

Still shocked by Mother's choice of words, I continued, "I refuse to spend my earnings or anyone else's on this. I just can't put this burden on you guys. Go back to doing your charity work, to your quiet and drama-free lifestyle. By the grace of God and protection from Him, I'll- I'll get through this. I'll be OK. I promise."

"Looks like your mind's made up, Gloria."

"I just, I just, um, yeah pretty much, I've surrendered. I've been through worse, I think. Anyways…" I shuddered, raising both shoulders and dropping them as hard as I could. "Of course, all my stuff is over there. If nothing else, I'd love to have my diary."

"We'll work on getting it for you, Gloria."

"Thank you so much, Mother. Oh, and if you do speak to them, they might bring up Patrick."

"What about him?"

"I kinda sorta blurted out that he was sexually harassing me."

"Oh!" The Sisters gasped.

"You lied?" Mother asked.

"The incidents with Patrick are recorded in my diary."

"Nothing really happened beyond the sexual harassment, right?"

"Oh no, no, no. Nothing like that. Oh, and you know what his wife said in response? 'I know.'"

"Aha!" Mother is awed.

"Then she said, 'Why do you think…?' then stopped herself."

Mother's hand flew to her chin. A frown drew her brows together. "So, this is what this situation is about."

"Perhaps, Mother, perhaps."

"How come you never told us, Gloria?"

"I actually called one night to tell you, but you had gotten the very first letter from my parents, so that took precedence. Writing in my diary has always been cathartic, so I just did that every single time. Afterwards, I would think that I should just suck it up in order to pursue my dream."

"I'm really sorry that this has happened, Gloria. I put you in their care, so I feel partially responsible."

"Oh, Mother. Please don't feel that way. You promised to find me a job and that you did—that's all. I'll be OK. I promise."

"Sorry things didn't work out, Gloria."

"It is what it is, Mother. I'll serve the time and hopefully come out of here a much better person."

"You're right, Gloria. Prison has a way of making one either bitter or better. I pray the latter prevails for you."

"Think I'll get deported after serving?" I whispered.

"That I don't know. What I do know is that the Cuban Adjustment Act affords some protections, but I'm not sure. And from what I've heard, Cuba hardly accepts refugees from the states."

"Oh!" I perked up. "Wonder what happens after release then?"

"Not sure, Gloria. But if I were you, I'd concentrate on the present. Try to get through this first phase and we'll worry about the rest when we get there. Alright, kiddo?"

"I guess," I agreed, slumping my shoulders.

"Oh, here," reaching into her pocket, Mother handed me the latest letter from my parents.

"Oh! Thanks, Mother."

With bated breath, the Sisters waited as I silently read its contents.

"She's smiling, she's smiling," Sister Theresa muttered under her breath.

"Yes!" Incredibly relieved, I rejoiced, waving the letter in the air, "Thank you, Lord! Mom is fine! Mom is fine! It was a non-malignant lump. The doctors will monitor it for now."

The Sisters and I breathed a collective sigh of relief.

"This is wonderful news. You needed that, Gloria."

"Sure did, Sister T. Can you imagine? Thank you, Jesus!"

"Yes, Gloria! All praise and honor are due to Him. I think our time is up. Officer is coming. Officer is coming."

"Aw, man!" I griped.

"Well, kiddo, we have to go now," Mother sighed. "We'll be praying for you, Glo. Oh! What about your parents? Are you gonna tell them?"

"Oh, no! No, no. They can never know. I'll keep it a secret and continue writing to them as usual. They preach to me all the time about saving my money, so I can cut back on how much and how often I send, but I will continue sending them care packages and such. Well, that's providing you'll help me get the items, of course."

Reality was beginning to set in. Like an angry river, a flood of emotions came rushing over me. Planting my face in my palms, I sobbed for the first time since the incident.

"Aw, Gloria. It'll be OK. You will be OK. We'll help you get through this," Mother assured me. "It'll be alright, kiddo."

"Thank you guys so much. And thank you for helping me cover this up."

"What up?" Mother asked, seeming oblivious.

"Exactly, Mother." I giggled through the tears.

"Time's up, Gloria. Sorry, Sisters." The Officer interrupted, putting an end to the laughter.

"O-K. Bye... guys," I said, all choked up. "Love each and every one of you. Thank you so much for everything."

"Bye, Glo." The Sisters' somber tone was evident, hitting me with a hefty dose of reality. "We love you too. You'll be alright though. You will be alright."

Too choked up to speak, I stared, then waved goodbye to them in one timid swipe.

Saddened, the Sisters headed back to the convent, promising to visit as often as they could and I headed to the cell to begin serving my time.

I should've called these nuns, you know. Argh! You know, on second thought, perhaps it's a good thing I didn't. The money I have saved up will now allow me to cover this up—will allow me to continue sending money and packages to my parents like nothing is going on. Forgive me, Father. It's for their own sanity. Their only child in an American jail? What! Don't think they'll survive it if they know.

"Life, life, life!" I muttered under my breath, shaking my head as I headed to the cell.

This journey called life is so strange and unpredictable. This isn't exactly what I had in mind when I left Cuba, but c'est la vie. What are we gonna do—such is life.

> "Never give up on your dreams."
>
> — Barack Obama

Chapter 17

"Ay! Ay! What's your name?" one of the women called out the minute I stepped foot into the cell.

"Gloria Este..." I responded, looking up at her and her large frame, mumbling the last syllable of my surname.

Damn, she probably can pick me up with her pinky. Easily. Easily.

"Huh! Estefan? Gloria Estefan? Ain't you that famous singer or sumting?" she continued questioning me, flinging a couple of the golden dreads covering her eyes over her shoulders.

"No she ain't!" one of the other women blurted out before I could answer. Laughter erupted throughout the cell.

"So why you lyin'? Whatcha lyin' fo'?" The large woman charged towards me, grabbing me in a chokehold.

It must've been the funniest thing the other women had ever seen.

Through their hearty laughter, another girl stepped forward yelling, "Let her go, Latisha!"

Her request stunned the other women, turning their laughter into gasps.

"Wanna feel it for her, Lisa?" Latisha asked, turning around to look at the woman who'd defended me.

Lisa held the stare. Refusing to back down she asked, "Whatcha gon' do, big mouth?"

"Oh!" the other ladies gasped again, stunned that Lisa was fighting back.

Latisha released me and charged towards Lisa, punching her in the mouth.

"Oh my God!" I screamed. "You busted her lip!"

"I did! So what?" Latisha replied showing no signs of remorse. "Wanted me to smash your beautiful supermodel face instead? Huh, huh?" she screamed in my face.

"Oh my gosh, are you OK?" I rushed to Lisa's aid, ignoring Latisha.

"I'm fine, I'm fine," Lisa responded, wiping away the blood dripping down her chin.

Guard Curtis rushed in to see what all the commotion was about. Medics came. Latisha was reprimanded and wouldn't be allowed outside for the next two weeks.

That afternoon while cleaning the prison grounds, Lisa and I plotted our revenge.

"So how's that lip, Lisa?"

"Throbbing. It feels as though it's the same size as Latisha's head."

"Truth-be-told, she does have a big head."

We giggled.

"Seriously though, it feels really swollen."

"Well, judging by the size of Latisha's head, it must feel really huge."

Lisa let out a hearty laugh, "Ow!" she winced. "Don't make me laugh, Gloria. It hurts."

"Aw, I'm so sorry, Lisa. Thank you for standing up for me. Pretty courageous of you to defend a stranger."

"Ah, no worries, Gloria. Wish I had someone who stood up for me against her when I first got here."

"You met her here?"

"Oh yeah, she's been here since the devil was a lil' boy."

"Haha! Must be a mighty long time."

"So, yeah, I'm sure you've gathered that she is the cell bully. She started picking on me from the day I stepped foot in here. And not just me—she does that to every new inmate. The other women have had their share with her, too. But everyone's scared of her. God! I can't stand her!"

"Truth be told I'm not a fighter, but there's no way I'm letting her get away with this, Lisa. If I allow it just this once, like you, she'll think she can continue bullying me. She yanked my hair so fucking hard, my eyes watered by force. I'm pretty sure she pulled a fist full of my hair out."

"Where?"

"Here." I gently parted my hair so Lisa could examine my scalp.

"Oh my, you're right, Gloria!" Lisa gasped. "It's red and dotted with moisture."

"Burns like hell." Running my hand gently through my thick hair avoiding my scalp, I discovered a hand full of uprooted hair.

"Whoa!" Lisa gasped. "She must've really pulled on your hair, Gloria."

"I'm telling you, it burns so bad. This bully has to be stopped!"

"Totally agree, Gloria! When I first got here she twisted my arm so hard, she dislocated my shoulder."

"What!" I gasped.

"I was scared. No one stood up for me. I never spoke up. She picked on me every single day. It wasn't until the next inmate came that she eased up on me a little and started picking on them. Argh!" Lisa rolled her eyes.

"She's testing the waters. Well, she's gon' learn today."

"Oh! OK, Gloria!" Lisa laughed again, forgetting that her lip pained her every time she did. "But I know. She has bullied us enough. She terrorizes all of us, but me more so for some reason.

"I should've stopped her from day one," Lisa added, shaking her head. "But today I just couldn't let her bully you. Don't know what came over me, Gloria. But girl, let me tell you I was sweating like a stripper and trembling like an unstable pole but I had to say something."

"Haha. I couldn't tell. I was like 'You go, girl, you go on, skinny girl,' in my head." Lisa and I giggled like we had known each other all our lives. From there, I knew I had made a lifelong friend. But I needed to know, "For real though, how long has she been in here?"

"Six years. Every time she gets out, she's back in within a day or two."

"What! Is it an escape for her or a hobby?" I asked puzzled. "What's she in for anyway?"

"Battery."

"Oh dear, same as me. Not surprised, though," I added, rolling my eyes.

"You're in here for battery? I assumed for DUI or petty theft or something, so..."

"Oh!" I let out a sly smile. "Why, though?"

"Your looks. Pretty and young."

"OK," I laughed, making a face. "Well, this woman I babysat for accused me of putting my hands on her kids."

"On kids?" Lisa's eyes widened.

"Girl, that never happened!"

"And, I've never shoplifted either," Lisa smiled crookedly, her comments laced with sarcasm.

"Whatever!" I responded with an eye roll.

"Anyways, back to Latisha, back to Latisha," Lisa clapped. "So, apparently this time it was a classmate she was jealous of and had a crush on."

"Oh, dear!" I jolted, sitting upright. "What do you mean jealous of and had a crush on? A female?"

"Yup."

"She's gay?"

"Yeah, girl. Can't you tell? It's as clear as day."

"What do I know, chile?" I responded with a shrug. "I mean, I notice she acts and walks macho, macho, but I've learned to never assume anything. Things aren't always what they seem, so yeah."

"I think she has a crush on you, though," Lisa laughed, then winced.

"On who, me?" My eyes widened, my hand flew to my chest.

"Yes, you," Lisa confirmed.

"What makes you say that?"

"Heard when she called you beautiful and supermodel?"

"So?"

"She's never called any of us beautiful. And the way she looks at you."

"Girl, you're just saying that. I just got here."

"I swear I'm not!"

"Oh lawd!" I rolled my eyes mortified.

Lisa attempted a deep belly laugh, but again, her burst lip restrained her.

"Aye, aye, Lisa and new girl!" The guard on duty yelled out. "Less talking and laughing more working."

"Sir, yes, sir."

Lisa and I went back to work but with unfinished business. After a five-minute or so break and the disappearance of the guard, we resumed our plotting of the bully takedown.

"But how are we going to get her though, Lisa?"

"Fight her in her sleep?"

"Nah, girl," I disagreed, shaking my head.

"Why not?" Lisa asked.

"Too cowardly."

"Wait, aren't you in here for battery on minors?" Lisa joked.

"At least they were awake, Lisa. That's what started it in the first place. Never mind. But that's not funny. Not funny at all." My mood took a downturn.

"Too soon? OK, no more jokes. I can tell how much this is hurting you. I'm sorry. Sorry, Gloria."

"Apology accepted, Lisa. It is very sensitive for me."

Before long, it was time to head back inside. Latisha was on punishment so she had already fallen asleep. The time was ripe to execute our plan.

"Her grease is right there," Lisa whispered pointing aggressively towards Latisha's belongings.

"Go, go, go!" I egged her on.

"I can't find the shaving cream, the Nair," Lisa whispered back.

"There! Here." Locating the Nair, I handed it to Lisa. The other women stood around pretending to mind their own business.

Even though they looked as light as feathers and as thin as spaghetti, it was widely known that the one thing Latisha treasured most were her golden dreadlocks. So, the next day as she routinely did, Latisha reached for her Loc and Curl. Plastering it all over her hair, she proceeded to brush her teeth and take a shower.

Now out of the shower and dressed, she reached for her oversized brown brush to retwist her thinning locks and lay down her raised strands and edges.

With smirks on our faces, Lisa and I glanced at each other and gave a virtual high five.

"Oh my God!" Latisha screamed, a couple of dreads dangling in her hand. The more she brushed, the more dreads uprooted. "My hair stank. What's that strong smell? Nair? What's going on here? Who did this?" Latisha's questions fell on deaf ears. "Who. The hell. Did this? Lisa? Gloria?"

With targets on our backs, Latisha thumped towards us.

"I know you guys did this!" she continued.

Silence.

Panning the room, in a bold and calculated move, Latisha attacked Lisa.

I rushed in to help my new friend fight the bully, throwing punches with no regard as to where on Latisha's body they landed.

The other women looked on with glee while we pounced on Latisha like a punching bag. Without saying a word, they made hand gestures and occasional eye contact with Lisa and me signaling their approval. They too had had enough of the cell aggressor.

The guard was called in. Lisa and I were reprimanded and separated from the rest of the group and each other for two weeks. We didn't sweat it, though. At least we had stood up to the queen bully.

"Start where you are. Use what you have. Do what you can."

— Arthur Ashe

Chapter 18

Two weeks in solitary confinement. Not bad, not bad after all, I thought, welcoming the peace and quiet.

During that time, I prayed a lot and wrote a lot and had written the first few scenes of a screenplay 'A Daring Pursuit of the Dream.' Because even though I was in jail, the dream that lived deep within my soul wouldn't let me forget it. I knew someday I would walk out of jail, and as uncertain as the future was, I couldn't not prepare.

Lisa and I had not seen each other in two weeks. It seemed to have gone by pretty quickly, for me at least.

With two weeks gone by, it was time to reunite and rejoin the larger group. Guard Curtis escorted us in. The thought of what could happen terrified me.

Did they plan a takedown? Was a prison riot about to ensue? The uncertainty scared me.

"Welcome back, Gloria and Lisa!" Cheers and applause erupted in the block.

"Whoa!" I stepped back, my eyes fixated on the enemy—Latisha.

Is this for real? Is this the calm before the storm? my mind wandered.

"Gloria, um, Lisa," Latisha said, walking towards us. The other cellmates froze in place, uncertain of what was about to happen. "Thank you!"

Gasps reverberated in the room.

"For what, Latisha?" I probed.

"Thank you for standing up to me," she responded, stunning us all.

"No one has ever stood up to me before, and so I always thought I'd get away with my bullying ways. Well, you guys showed me the other day," she chuckled, continuing to walk closer to Lisa and me, "Thank you for challenging me."

What's she gon' do, Lord?

"Truce?" Latisha reached us, extending a hand for a handshake.

Astounded and perplexed, Lisa and I glanced at each other and accepted the handshake.

"Aw, Latisha. You're welcome, I guess," I shrugged. Not sure what to say next, "Nice haircut by the way," I added.

"Oh no, boo-boo. You gotta get your money back," Lisa responded laughing. The swelling on her lip had gone down and the gash healed.

Witnessing the whole thing, the other women looked on nervously. Those who weren't biting their nails were either scratching their arm or some other body part.

I shot Lisa a look.

"What?" she asked, seeming oblivious. "Too soon?"

"Yah!" I nodded. Latisha burst into laughter.

Bemused Lisa and I looked at each other.

"I can fix it for you," Lisa offered.

"You can cut hair?" Latisha asked, puzzled.

"Nope but I sure can make it look better than that."

Running her hand over her head Latisha erupted in laughter, infecting us all.

"Phew!" Lisa breathed an audible sigh of relief.

"I'll have the nurse shave it off for me."

"Yah. It'll look good on you," Lisa added.

"OK whatever, Lisa. What do you think, Gloria?" Latisha really wanted my opinion.

"Oooo!" Lisa teased, throwing a wink my way.

"Um, yah. Yah. I think a skinhead will look good on you," I responded agreeing with her. The other ladies listening fought hard to keep a straight face.

"Gotta tell you, ever since that fight, Latisha has been as docile as a cat being stroked. She hasn't gotten into any fights or arguments since."

"Are you serious, Chantelle?"

"For real."

"Yep!"

"Yep!"

"True," the other ladies concurred.

"Aw!" I responded, inching closer to her. "I'm so very proud of you, Latisha."

"You are, Gloria?" Latisha gasped, turning to look me in the eyes.

"I really am, Latisha."

"No one say this to me before, Gloria. All ma' life I've been hearing, 'You a bad kid, you is stoopid, you a fat bully, you will never come to nuffin.' So I just thought, heck, if everyone is saying it then it must be true."

So it became a self-fulfilling prophecy.

"Aw, Latisha. You're none of those things. You are beautifully and wonderfully created. You have to believe that and keep telling yourself that. Don't know if you're a believer but Proverbs chapter 23, verse 7 says, 'For as he thinketh in his heart, so is he.' Gotta look and think of yourself in a positive way."

"Imma try, Gloria. Will you help me? Will you be my friend?"

"AA!" I replied. Unclear what that meant, the ladies looked on puzzled. "As long as you'll be mine."

Latisha embraced me a little tighter than comfortable. I shot a glance at Lisa just in time to see her puffed cheeks and crinkled eyes—a poor attempt at suffocating a laugh.

"And me, too, and me, too," the other women echoed.

"OK ladies, we all can be friends."

"Yes!" They echoed in applause.

Pounding my chest twice and raising my clenched fist in solidarity I proclaimed, "To the sisterhood!"

The women followed suit coming together in a kumbaya. We were all getting along for the moment and the atmosphere in our unit couldn't be more beautiful or lighter.

"Always knew there was something special about you, Gloria," Latisha added. "I liked you from day one."

"Um, OK!" Lisa muttered under her breath, smiling.

Day one? I gasped in my head. *Girl, are you forgetting why we're having this present conversation? How you welcomed me? So why did you wanna fight me on day one, huh? Is that her way of expressing love? Judging from what she just told me, perhaps it is, OK perhaps it is...*

"Thanks, Latisha. You are special too," I responded.

Darkness came. At 8:55 p.m. the lights flickered, reminding us that we had five minutes to get into bed. At 9:00 p.m. lights went out, forcing us to retire for the night.

At some point in the night after the guard had already conducted the mandated headcount—I'm not sure what time it was but the room was pretty quiet except for a few snores and snorts, grinding of teeth and farts here and there from some of the other ladies—I was awakened by someone calling my name.

"Gloria, Gloria. You awake?" The person asked, navigating the darkened cell in search of my cot.

"Un, I am now," My eyes flickered to adjust to the large silhouette towering over my cot. "Latisha?"

My heart raced as I remembered what Lisa had told me about Latisha having a crush on me. With brave pretense, I asked, "What's up, girl?"

"Um, I have this thing weighing heavy on my heart."

"Oh! What's that, Latisha?"

"Ah, never mind. I'll tell you tomorrow."

"Girl, you gon' woke me up to tell me that you gon' tell me something tomorrow?"

"It's just that I don't know how to say it," Latisha whispered.

"OK, Latisha. Get some rest. I'll be all ears whenever you're ready."

"All mine?" she asked.

"Huh! All ears, all ears. Not all yours."

"Oh, OK," Latisha chuckled. "Gloria."

"Yes, Latisha?"

"Teach me how to pray?"

"Aw!" Latisha's request gently touched my heart, I couldn't resist. "OK, repeat after me, 'Jesus.'"

"Jesus?" she snickered.

"Yes, girl. This is the simplest and most powerful prayer. Call His name throughout the day—during good and bad moments, sad and happy times."

"That's it?"

"We'll start with that for now. Baby steps, Latisha, baby steps."

"OK. Thank you, babes."

Babes? My eyes flickered in the dark.

"My pleasure, Latisha." *Oh boy, gotta choose my words carefully now*, I laughed in my head. "I mean, you're welcome."

"Gloria."

"Yes, Latisha?"

"Can I tell you something?"

Oh lawd, don't say it, don't say it, don't say it. Fearing that Latisha was about to go there, I closed my eyes tightly, holding my breath. "Go ahead, Latisha."

"How do I ask…oh, never mind."

"Ask what? Whom?" I asked, curious and scared at the same time.

"How do, um, how do I ask God to forgive me and help me let go of the hurt and resentment in my heart?"

"Phew!" I opened my eyes, silently breathing out. "You just ask with utmost sincerity. You have to surrender. Ask Him and mean it."

"I want to ask God to forgive me for trying to kill someone."

"Oh!" I jolted, my eyes widened in the dark. "Just, um…Just, um… Just talk to Him like you're talking to me now," I said stammering in shock at what I'd just heard.

"Really?" Latisha asked, stunned.

"Really!"

"You see my step- my step- my stepdad… never mind." Latisha struggled to tell her story.

"It's OK, Latisha. Talk to me."

"My stepdad abused me from when I was eight till I was about twelve. I dealt with it. But when I found out that he was doing it to my little sister too, that was it. One day while he was lying on the sofa, drunk as a skunk, I pulled out a knife to lunge at his throat."

Oh, dear!

"The S.O.B. must've felt my presence. He opened his eyes and caught the knife at the nick of time. Even after telling my mom what he did, she did nothing and stayed with him. Eventually, we told our grandma, who reported it to the authorities. My sister and I were taken from them and ended up in the foster care system. Don't think I will ever feel good unless I do away with that, that… And my mom, I don't ever want to see her again, ever," Latisha sighed and growled.

"Oh my! I am so sorry, Latisha. I can't even begin to imagine." My heart sank as I became sad for Latisha. It was now becoming clear why she was the way she was. "Is that what you're in here for now?"

"Nah, I was in juvie. It was the very first time I got locked up. I was 15. Ever since then it's been a downward spiral. I have numerous records and finding a job is challenging. So, I end up back here, you know—free food, free rent, you know what I mean?"

"I know what you mean. So uh, um, how come you guys didn't go live with your grandmother?"

"Grandma would've taken us in but her health was failing and she was deemed unfit to adopt us."

Swallowing hard I continued the questioning. "So, where's your little sis?"

"In L.A."

"How's she doing?"

"She's a nurse over there. She's married and has two kids of her own."

"Good for her. I'm so so sorry, Latisha. Forgiving someone who has hurt you is no easy feat. But, my girl, in order to move forward—to heal, to grow, to live to your fullest potential—you have to let go. You can't fully live if you're constantly trying to seek revenge. While we try to seek revenge all we're doing is hurting ourselves in the process.

"You're gonna have to find a way to forgive them. You have to surrender. I'm not saying to forget, now, because you never will. But, holding on like this is unhealthy both physically and psychologically. Holding on just gives them power over you.

"I once had a friend who betrayed my trust. And this is in no way comparing the horrible, horrible thing that happened to you, but hear me out. I was upset and blindsided and I vouched never to talk to this friend again. I avoided her and her social circles at all costs.

"But guess what? All I was doing was punishing myself. She was going out and having a good time without a care in the world, well, seemingly without a care in the world, while I stayed home binging on ice cream and worrying. But then one day I had an epiphany. I realized I don't have to be friends with that person, but I couldn't allow her to live in my heart and head anymore. In order to feel good, I realized that I had to forgive her. Not for her sake, but for my own.

"No one can make you happy but you. So, in order to be truly happy, I had to make space in my heart for forgiveness. As soon as I made a conscious effort to get over the hurt and resentment, I felt a weight lifted off me—the liberation, I began to feel was inexplicable. You gotta surrender and let God have His way. Try it—you will discover that it's not a powerless act at all but an all-powerful, powerful one. Because you, my friend, deserve it. You deserve to live."

"I never looked at it that way, Gloria. But yeah, you're right. That monster probably doesn't even think about me. Yet, here I am wasting my life in and out of jail because of him."

"Ah! Exactly, Latisha."

"Thank you, Gloria," Latisha responded, wiping the tears streaming down her face. "Thank you for listening to me."

"Anytime, Latisha. You see these tears, it's the last that you will cry. These are healing tears. Let it out, cry it out, and from this day forward, endeavor to live. Drop the weight, drop the excess baggage, and break free. Give yourself permission, give your permission to truly live," I encouraged Latisha, rubbing her back as she broke down in tears. "Endeavor to live, my girl. Endeavor to live fully and free."

"Hey, Gloria," she called out through the tears.

"Yes, my girl?"

Oops. Noo, not my girl. Too late.

"I, I, I…" Latisha stammered.

"Un-huh, Latisha?" I flinched.

Don't say it, don't say it, don't say it…

"I love you."

Oh, God! My eyes flung open. *What does that mean? How does she mean it? Should I, should I, should I...?*

"Love," I choked, fake clearing my throat, then starting over in one breath, "LoveYouTooLatisha."

"Sorry about the fight."

"Ah! Don't mention it, Latisha, it was meant to happen. Look where we're at right now, huh?"

"You know, I think you're right, Gloria. It was meant to happen this way." Latisha and I sighed in synch. "Anyway, thanks for listening, Gloria. Thanks for enlighten, for enlightning, enlighten..."

"Enlightening?" I asked, helping her out.

"Yeh, that!" Latisha laughed out loud. "Goodnight, Gloria."

"Good morning, Latisha."

"Huh?"

"Sun's out, girl."

"Oh!" Latisha's jaw dropped. "Imma be cranky today."

"Eh, eh! Don't be picking no fights today now. Better uncrank yo' ass." Latisha fell over me letting out one of the deepest belly laughs I had ever heard. I couldn't let her laugh alone. I also couldn't pass up the opportunity to remind her of the promise of a new day. "It's a new dawn, Latisha. A new day to begin living."

"Well, as soon as I get out of here," she giggled and sighed. "Thanks for listening, Gloria. You know, you're wise beyond your years."

"Thank you. And, by the way, you don't have to wait until you get out of here. Start working on a better you today, yes?"

"Sounds good, Gloria. Let's see if we can rest our eyes before they come yelling in our ears. Argh! Why do they have to be so damn loud, geez!"

"To remind us that we're in jail, not a slumber party!"

"Haha... Goodnight, Gloria."

"Yes, let's get some shuteye."

"Every great dream begins with a dreamer. Always remember, you have within you the strength, the patience, and the passion to reach for the stars, to change the world."

— Harriet Tubman

CHAPTER 19

No more than fifteen minutes later, the voice of the guard and the sound of the metal door grazing the concrete launched an assault on our eardrums.

Argh, I moaned in my head. It was time to go to Chow Hall to partake of our gourmet breakfast. *Yeah gourmet, right...*

"So, Gloria..." Lisa approached me laughing.

"What?" I asked, curious as to what was so funny.

"So, uh, you and your girl stayed up all night last night, huh? Ouu...," Lisa teased, scrubbing her hands together. "And by the way, what the fuck was so funny this morning? Girl, I was in a deep sleep when I heard the heifer burst out laughing."

"Oh, Lisa..." I snickered. "That's not very nice."

"OK, the bully, the bully. Was in a deep sleep when I heard the bully burst out laughing."

"Hopefully dethroned Queen Bully," I laughed. "Must've been when I told her to uncrank her ass."

"Context, context. I need context, Gloria," Lisa snapped her fingers.

Amid the laughter and snort, I continued, "She said she'd be cranky today because of sleep deprivation, so..."

"How, how do you uncrank, Gloria?" Lisa died laughing. "Is that even a word?"

"Dunno, but it sprang to mind in the moment."

"Girl, you're something else. So..." Lisa scrubbed her hands staring at me, her grin as huge as ever, "did she try a ting?"

"What?" I frowned in bewilderment.

"You know, a ting," Lisa winked.

"Girl, talk to the hand!" I gestured, finally catching on to what Lisa was asking. We laughed and continued eating what was deemed breakfast food.

Feeling a tad jealous that Latisha and I had stayed up all night talking, the other women, too, thirsted for some words of encouragement. So, upon completion of our tasks for the day, we gathered under the Flamboyant Tree in the courtyard for a chat. And I, the newly appointed motivational speaker and spiritual leader seized the opportunity to pass on some of my knowledge. Thirsting for the Word and eager to learn, the women listened intently, hanging on to my every word.

"Gloria, how do you keep your faith up in the midst of all you've been through?"

"Ah, Lisa. Through the darkest, darkest days of my life, scripture has helped me the most. I believe it was in Matthew chapter 5 that Jesus said, 'Blessed are the poor in spirit, for theirs is the kingdom of heaven. Blessed are they who mourn, for they will be comforted. Blessed are the meek, for they will inherit the land. Blessed are they who hunger and thirst for righteousness, for they will be satisfied. Blessed are the merciful, for they will be shown mercy. Blessed are the clean of heart, for they will see God. Blessed are the peacemakers, for they will be called children of God. Blessed are they who are persecuted for the sake of righteousness, for theirs is the kingdom of heaven.'"

Taking a pause, I surveyed the women gathered before me—each of them beautiful in their own way, full of promise and potential. Yet, each of them slowly withering, wasting their lives away behind bars.

Feeling moved to help and nurture them, I continued, "What does this teach us? What are the resounding themes here? Humility, huh? Comfort and strength to endure trials and tribulations in life; compassion and altruism and selflessness; gentleness and kindness, patience and tolerance, obedience, forgiveness and mercifulness, purity of heart, and a heart free from malice and wickedness and grudges."

"Talk to me, Gloria," Latisha yelled out, smacking her hands together in a single clap.

"God was such a merciful and forgiving God that even while hanging on the cross facing death, persecution, and crucifixion, He said in Luke Chapter 23 verse 34, 'Father, forgive them; for they know not what they do.' God wants us to love, love each other, and to live in peace and harmony with each other—and that includes our enemies."

"I hear you, Gloria, but it's just so hard for me, you know?" Chantelle said, becoming choked up. "I guess I'm a little mad at God. He took my little sister Dana away from us. She was such a good girl, you know? She had the purest heart. She treated everyone right, she was an angel on earth really.

"To see her suffer before her passing was just unfair. We pleaded and begged God to spare her life and make her well again, to have mercy on her, but He took her away instead…"

With tears running down her face, Chantelle continued. "I have tried to get over it but every time I try, something reminds me of her—a scent or a song, something, and my heart bleeds a little. I see her in everything. She's everywhere."

"Aww..." my heart ached for her. Taking a deep breath, I continued, "I'm so, so sorry about your sister, Chantelle. What was wrong with her?"

"Lupus."

"Oh, lupus."

"You've heard of it?" Chantelle asked, surprised.

"One of the nuns I lived with has it really badly."

"Speaking of nuns?" Lisa butted in, smiling nervously. "We've been talking behind your back."

The ladies gasped.

"Are you a nun?" Lisa asked.

They chuckled.

"Yah, Gloria, are you?" Latisha asked again.

"Your only visitors are nuns," Chantelle added.

"Mee! A nun? Nah..."

"Yes, you are! Everything about you screams nun, nun, nun!" Lisa teased.

"I'm very spiritual and a staunch Catholic, but I'm so not a nun," I stressed looking up.

"OK. Whatever you say, Gloria," Lisa said rolling her eyes. "She's a nun you guys," she whispered to the other ladies from the side of her mouth.

"I mean my dad was a monk, a dropout monk but, uh..."

"See I knew it!" Latisha jumped to her feet.

"...becoming a nun has never crossed my mind," I continued through their giggles. "Anyway back to the discussion. Back to the discussion ladies.

"Chantelle, my heart really goes out to you. I'm so sorry. May you take comfort in knowing that your sister is now resting in the arms of our Lord. In a place devoid of pain and sadness and lupus. You lost your beloved sister but gained an angel. An angel guiding you through despair. May the wonderful memories you created together comfort you."

"Yeah, she gave her all in all that she did and wouldn't rest until it was done. So, I know she will carry her angelic role and will not tire until we're all OK."

"Ah, Chantelle. You got it. There may be no end to grief, but know that love endures forever. When you find yourself inconsolable, conjure up the fond memories of Dana to help you cope. I am so, so sorry. May you continue to honor your sister's memory and may she continue to rest in the bosom spirit."

"Yes. We are so sorry, Chantelle," a girl named Jordan added.

"It sounds like a horrible disease," said Lisa, heaving a heavy sigh.

"I hate lupus, too," Latisha added. The women rallying around their hurting sister was beautiful to witness.

We're onto something here, I silently rejoiced.

"I grappled with why God punished her. I was the rebellious one, always getting into trouble and skipping school, yet I was healthy. I asked many times to be taken instead. But…"

"Oh, Chantelle. I know what you mean. God spared you for a reason. Your life is not over. You are here for a purpose, you have not completed your earthly mission. He needed Dana for a greater purpose in heaven."

"I should've been a role model for my little sis—I was anything but. After her death, I became angrier. I became angry with God. I begged for Him to make her well again, I begged for Him to restore her health and take away her pain, but no, He took her life away instead." Chantelle broke down in tears.

I broke a silent sob.

"Aw, Chantelle. You know, sometimes God grants our wishes on His time and not on ours. He also answers our prayers—perhaps not in the manner that we expect—but He grants them anyway when and how He sees fit, sometimes in unconventional ways. See," inching closer to Chantelle, I readied myself to tell her something that perhaps would be uncomfortable and hard to hear, "see, you asked God to relieve your sister of her pain, right?"

"Every waking hour," she responded.

"Right. And He did. Perhaps not in the way you wanted, but He did. She's no longer suffering and in pain. Lupus is no longer controlling her life and making her miserable, stealing her joy and strength. Often for our own selfish reasons we want our loved ones to stay around even through immense pain and suffering, to make us feel good, to shield us from the pain and agony of grief, of mourning, but I know you've heard the saying quality over quantity, huh?"

"Ah... you have a point there, Gloria." With raised eyebrows Chantelle continued, "I never looked at it this way. We did pray for deliverance. And that He did."

"'I will never leave you nor forsake you,' God promised. It is so easy to lose sight of God in the midst of the storm. It's easy to lose sight of God and to relent on your relationship with Him when things aren't going the way you think they ought to go.

"But thankfully our God is a forgiving God, a comforting God, a loyal God. 'Come back to me with all your heart,' He says, 'Don't let fear keep us apart.' Though we may wander and stray, God always, always takes us back. But first, we have to seek Him to find Him, trust Him and love Him. He always makes good on His promises. Muster the courage, Chantelle, and seek Him. Go back to your Father in heaven."

"Oh, Gloria, Gloria, Gloria! Thank you! Thank you for listening."

"Of course, Chantelle. Your sister is watching over you."

"Well, I know she ain't too proud of me right now," Chantelle muttered under her breath, eliciting a chuckle from the group.

Seizing the opportunity to minister to Chantelle and the other women, I carried on. Where did the words come from? I don't know, but somehow they came flooding and flowing. It had to be God. Chantelle softened and I could see in her eyes that I was reaching her. Her next words made my heart glad.

"I am tired of coming in and out of here and hurting my parents. They've lost Dana and they've technically lost me, too. Difference is that I can change that, Dana can't." Chantelle sighed. "It's time to turn my life around. I know I owe my parents an apology. They do not deserve to be treated the way I do. They gave us everything.

"I cannot begin to imagine the pain and hurt they must feel. I always felt they loved Dana more than me, but I'm beginning to see that I was the one with the problem. They tried so hard to direct me on the right path, but I always thought they were too controlling. I now realize that they were simply doing their job as parents," Chantelle breathed deeply. The look of remorse reflecting in her eyes.

"Ah, Chantelle. Perhaps you can start by writing them a letter."

"As soon as I get inside."

"Wonderful! Do they ever visit you here?"

"The last time they came, it didn't go well. I told them don't ever step foot here again and removed them from my visitors' list. They were preaching to me and I didn't want to hear it."

"I'm sure they will be happy to hear from you. I applaud you, Chantelle."

With tears in her eyes, too choked up to speak, she nodded.

"Gloria."

"Yes, Quanda?"

"You know how much I've prayed to God asking for this one wish and it never came to fruition? But I still thank Him every day for life, because his grace and mercy are perfectly sufficient for me."

"That's wonderful, Quanda. Perhaps whatever it is you're asking for isn't meant to be, or you're not ready to receive it yet. You know, God answers prayers but not on our time—on His.

"God is privy to our every need and He is always on time. At the right appointed time, Quanda, your blessing will be revealed. Father knows best. Keep trusting and believing."

"Thanks for reassuring me, Gloria."

"Glo!"

"Yes, Lis!"

"Um," Lisa cleared her throat. "You know, I'm always scared that I cannot function in society, so I keep up my stealing sprees so I can keep coming back here. I feel like here, it's less responsibility and I don't have to try as hard not to get into trouble, you know what I mean? I think I'm getting tired of this cycle. But what can I do?" Lisa shrugged, her palms facing upward. "I have no skills, no formal education, no experience," she continued, counting on her fingers. "What will I do out there?"

"Ah, Lisa! 'Take up your cross and follow me.' Jesus said. It's not easy to break habits, but in order to conquer our demons and enemies we have to fight, fight hard with all our might and vigor, everything we've got, you know?

"You can do it, Lis. Often we can't go it alone, so what do we do? We seek help. Alcoholics have Alcoholics Anonymous, AA. I'm sure there are tons of free programs, mentors, counselors, available to help you re-acclimate into society.

"Fortunately you live in the greatest nation on earth—America, the land of opportunity, where you have everything at your disposal. The land where you can be whatever you want to be, but only if you work hard at it. People die trying to get to America for a reason—to enjoy the freedoms that you guys are blessed with, to take advantage of the innumerable opportunities here, to get a piece of the American pie, to live the dream that your forefathers fought so hard to create. You're looking at one of these refugees who risked her life on the open seas to live the American Dream."

"You?"

"You?"

"You, Gloria?"

The women asked in quick succession, gasping.

"Oh my! From where?" Lisa asked.

"Cuba to Key West. Now you'll argue that I'm in jail too, but trust me, it's the last place I ever wanted to land. One of my biggest fears was to end up in jail, be it in America or Cuba. So, I tried everything in my power to live by the rules and do right by others, you know? Unfortunately, one little misunderstanding—*or was it jealousy*—landed me here. Heaven knows I'm innocent."

"Yeah, Gloria. I'm convinced you wouldn't hurt an ant, let alone someone else's kids. There is definitely more behind this."

"For sure, Lis. Am I upset? Of course! Am I angry and disappointed? Without a doubt. But I, me, Gloria, I have chosen to not let this bitterness and anger consume and control me. I thank my faith every day for this mindset, for helping me through.

"So, yeah, I look at it as a stepping stone to my ultimate destination. This right here is a hiccup and best believe when I get out of here—if I'm not deported, that piece of the American pie that I'm hungry for will be satiated. I truly believe that I'm in here for a reason not known to me yet.

"But, someday I will look back and say 'Hmm, so that's why I ended up in jail. I get it now.' So yeah, Lis, as long as you have the breath of life in you, there is hope. You know, life throws curve balls at us that we are forced to deal with, some just deal better than others.

"But, we can all decide to not settle and to claim the freedom that we deserve. Gotta work hard at it, though, and seek the help you need to get there. For no man is an island. It truly takes a village."

"Geez, Gloria. Why are you doing this to me?" an emotional Lisa responded.

Silently, I rejoiced. I was reaching the women. "This is good, Lisa. Breaking down means that a breakthrough is imminent."

"Well, we know why you're here, Gloria"

"Oh! Do tell, Chantelle." I couldn't wait to hear this.

"To do just what you're doing right here, right now. Ministering to us and motivating us, helping us turn our lives around."

The women erupted in applause, echoing Chantelle's sentiments.

"Aw. Thanks, guys. Does this mean I'm reaching you?"

"Without a doubt and we want more," Chantelle responded.

"Aw! You got it, guys. As long as my words aren't falling on deaf ears."

"Yah, Gloria. Since you been here, I'm really trying. I haven't been in any fights."

"I'm super proud of you, Latisha."

"Thank you, Gloria. I have to turn my life around. I want better for myself. I know I can do better."

"It warms my heart to hear that, Latisha. I want better for you, too—for all of you, for all of us. We all deserve the very best in life."

"Deal, Glo! Deal!" Lisa said.

"So Lis, lemme ask you. What did you wanna be when you were a little girl?"

"An actress."

"Oh!" My eyes widened. "There's something we have in common—the same dream."

"Who was the first African-American woman to be nominated for an Academy Award for Best Actress?"

"Dorothy Dandridge!"

"Right! And you know what she said? 'There is no force more powerful than a woman determined to rise.' Can we get working on that and help each other rise?"

The ladies all responded with a resounding, "Yes!"

"What about you, Nikki? What's your dream job, what's your vision?"

"Um, um…"

"Don't be shy. Claim it, Nikki."

"Always wanted to be a rapper or poet," Nikki said, burying her head in her hands.

"Drop something for us, nah?"

The women laughed at my attempt at slang.

"Uh. Next time."

The ladies started beatboxing but Nikki was too shy to show off her talent.

"That's OK. She will when she's ready. What about you, Latisha?"

"Let's see, a teacher, nurse, model, writer..." Latisha started counting on her fingers.

The ladies broke into peals of laughter.

"A police officer—ironic, huh? I know. And an actress."

"OK!" I responded, raising one eyebrow, smiling. "We're gonna work on narrowing it down. Actually, if you were to choose just one right now, what would it be?"

"Um, um, um," she stammered a little. "Actress!"

"Are you sure?" Lisa teased.

"Positive."

"OK, my girl, we'll get working on that. What about you, Jordan?"

"A singer."

"Oh, wonderful! Sing something for us?"

"Nah... I'm shy, I'm shy," she refused, shaking her head violently.

"Well you're gonna have to get over that. Come on, girl, give us a little sample. You're among friends. Right, ladies?"

"Sing, sing, sing, sing..." we chanted, cheering Jordan on.

Then suddenly, drowning out our chants, she belted out "Amazing Grace."

Gasping at the sound of the first note, my mind flashed to Cuba. To the casket draped in white being carried gracefully into the church to the hymn "Amazing Grace." Colors of black and white and purple everywhere in the overcrowded cathedral flashed before my eyes. I closed them as tightly as humanly possible.

The sniffles, screams, and wails on that day echoed resoundingly in my mind's eye. My heart pounded and ached like that mournful day—the day a young and promising student of mine, hit by a drunk driver, was being laid to rest. Overcome with emotion, covered with chills, I fought hard to remain composed.

"Oh, Jordan, you just took Gloria's breath away," Nikki remarked.

"You have no idea, Nikki," I said flashing my eyes open. "That was aaaaaamazing, Jordan, amazing! You are super-talented and blessed."

Blown away, touched, and impressed at the same time, there were no dry eyes in the circle.

"See how much talent is in this place? Just as I suspected—you ladies are amazing. All of you are blessed with talent and potential. All we have to do is tap into it, work on it, and bring it to life. We can't suppress it or waste it away in jail.

"There is greatness in all of you, each of us has a vocation in life, we just have to find time to discover it, to nurture it, use it, and fulfill it. Yes?"

"Ah. You're so right, Gloria. This reminds me of the 'Parable of the Talents.'"

"Sure does, Jordan."

"What's it about? Tell us, tell us, Gloria. We want to hear it," Latisha said, intrigued as ever.

"How about tomorrow?"

"Today, today!" the ladies chanted. They were hungry, thirsting for knowledge, motivation, and inspiration.

"Where's Guard Curtis?" It felt like it was way past our two-hour evening break. He was nowhere to be seen, so I continued, "So Matthew recorded The Parable of the Talents. Jordan I've seen you with one of those pocket bibles, happen to …"

"Here. It's the English Standard Version (ESV). I walk with it everywhere."

"And Jordan saves the day! Thanks, Jordan!" Turning to the Gospel of Matthew, chapter 25:14-30, I start reading, "For it will be like a man going on a journey, who called his servants and entrusted to them his property. To one he gave five talents, to another two, to another one, to each according to his ability. Then he went away.

"He who had received the five talents went at once and traded with them, and he made five talents more. So also he who had the two talents made two talents more. But he who had received the one talent went and dug in the ground and hid his master's money. Now after a long time, the master of those servants came and settled accounts with them.

"And he who had received the five talents came forward, bringing five talents more, saying, 'Master, you delivered to me five talents; here, I have made five talents more.' His master said to him, 'Well done, good and faithful servant. You have been faithful over a little; I will set you over much. Enter into the joy of your master.'

"And he also who had the two talents came forward, saying, 'Master, you delivered to me two talents; here, I have made two talents more.' His master said to him, 'Well done, good and faithful servant. You have been faithful over a little; I will set you over much. Enter into the joy of your master.'

"He also who had received the one talent came forward, saying, 'Master, I knew you to be a hard man, reaping where you did not sow, and gathering where you scattered no seed, so I was afraid, and I went and hid your talent in the ground. Here, you have what is yours.' But his master answered him, 'You wicked and slothful servant! You knew that I reap where I have not sown and gather where I scattered no seed? Then you ought to have invested my money with the bankers, and at my coming, I should have received what was my own with interest.

"So take the talent from him and give it to him who has the ten talents. For to everyone who has will more be given, and he will have an abundance. But from the one who has not, even what he has will be taken away. And cast the worthless servant into the outer darkness. In that place, there will be weeping and gnashing of teeth."

"Wow, this is powerful! It's sort of like with your brain cells where if you don't use it you lose it."

"Spot on, Lisa."

"It's sort of like the saying that the rich get richer and the poor get poorer."

"Exactly, Latisha. Why is that? Perhaps the rich invest the little that they started with and the poor always play it safe afraid of risking the little that they have, so they hold onto it tightly."

"Yes, under the mattress," Latisha laughed. "It's true. They hide it under the mattress while the rich put theirs in the bank where it accrues interest." The ladies laughed. "Or they invest it."

"You can't bury your talents or else you risk losing them. Whatever talents God has blessed you with, it's yours to use and to multiply and to bless others with. On Judgment Day at the end of life's journey, do you want to be like that one who buried his talents? Or do you want to hear, 'Well done my good and faithful servant?' Hmm? Go out there and multiply your talents, work towards your dreams, ladies. Put it on display for the world to see.

"Remember, if you didn't have the ability, God wouldn't bless you or entrust you to fulfill it. He never gives us more than we can carry or more than we can bear."

"We're afraid, Gloria. I know I am," Nikki buried her head in her hands.

"Ah, that enemy called fear. Fear is the most crippling emotion of all. When we feel most fearful is when we must allow courage to take precedence. For without courage, fear weighs us down like sandbags. Our dreams fade away like stars as morning breaks and we become mere beings just breathing, existing, and not fully living.

"But we have the power within us. We can do this, you can do this! We're going to work on getting out of here empowered and armed with the coping mechanisms we need to become fully-functioning citizens, yes? We gotta rise up and soar, my friends. It's faith over fear. We gotta rise up and soar."

"Time to head in, ladies," Guard Curtis appeared twirling his baton, "except you, Gloria."

"Oh!" My jaw dropped, my eyes widened, my right hand flew to my chest. "Am I in trouble, Guard?"

"You know here you're not allowed to stay out this late. Uh..."

"I know I know, Guard Curtis. Sorry about that." *Mehn last thing I need is an extended stay here.* "I'm really, really sorry, Guard, it won't happen again. I promise."

"Are you done?"

"Yes, Guard."

"Sure?"

"Sure."

"As I was saying, but uh, I really like your message and the way you're helping the other women, so I made an exception and allowed you to stay out a little later than usual."

"Phew!" I exhaled. "Thanks, Guard Curtis," I responded, breathing a sigh of relief. "For a minute there I thought my sentence was about to lengthen."

"Keep up the good work, Gloria. You're a good kid. Have a good night."

Relieved, I made my way back to my cell to join the ladies.

"Are you in trouble, Gloria?" the other women couldn't wait to know.

"Yep," I stifled a smirk. I recovered, attempting to activate my acting chops. "Our evening break has been taken away."

"What?"

"What?"

"What?" the ladies gasped and echoed in quick succession.

"Psych!" I butted in before they all suffered a heart attack.

"For real?" Latisha asked, puzzled.

"For real, for real," I reassured them.

"Ah! You just don't want us to feel bad, Gloria," Lisa added.

"Are you serious, it's all a joke?" Quanda wanted reassurance.

"Seriously, it's all good ladies, it's all good. Guard just wanted to commend our little session."

"Gloria, you're a damn fool!" Latisha blurted in a serious tone. The ladies looked at each other then came barreling towards me,

Latisha leading the pack. Their eyes fixed on my face unwavering, their stare unflinching.

Oh, God! I trembled and screamed in my head. *We're all in jail. There's no telling when these ladies can flip. None of them are in here for good behavior.*

Fear and panic rose in me. I tried to conceal it, but with every step that they took forward, I took several backward. With nowhere else to go, my back made contact with the wall.

I know we've become 'friends' but this is jail. Jail, yo? Latisha told me how she attempted to kill her stepdad. I think they're joking but what if they're not? Latisha is a bully. OK, maybe was, was a bully—but I'm sure the urge to revert is still in her. God help me! I screamed in my head.

The thought of running crossed my mind, but where to? My back was against the wall, literally. My knees buckled. The strength ran out of my legs. I didn't fall, but I was forced into a sitting position. *No don't sit, Gloria!* a voice in my head screamed. Forcing myself up, I braced and stiffened anticipating contact.

In what seemed like an eternity, they reached me, crowding my space.

Oh God! I screamed and squirmed internally.

"Psych! Psych! Psych!" they accosted me yelling, smothering me with hugs and kisses. Latisha capitalized on the opportunity to land one smack dab on the lips.

Oh God! I rolled my eyes in my head.

"We love you, Gloria," they laughed roaringly.

Grinning nervously, I fought hard to lower my heart rate. My sudden urge to urinate disappeared, my eyes slipped back into their sockets, and my legs regained stability.

"Don't you ever play us like that again!" Latisha said, amused as ever.

Oh, trust me, never!

Too psyched to laugh out loud, I tittered.

Two hours later and my heart still pounded in my chest.

The ladies got me real good, I tee-heed in my head. *What if the women had jumped me for real?*

Realizing that it could've turned out differently, I shivered a little. But for some reason, I was glad. When I first got here it was every man for himself against the bully. But that day the ladies had united to work towards a goal, highlighting the strength and power of the sisterhood, proving the success of my teachings.

The purpose of being in jail started unfolding right before my eyes. I had now become the ladies' confidant, psychologist, motivator, teacher, preacher, peacemaker, you name it. There were remarkable changes in Latisha, the dethroned cell bully, and in fact, in most—if not all—the other ladies.

The goals I had set for myself were becoming less and less significant for the moment as I had now found a bigger purpose—to mold, to educate, to motivate, and help these women become good stewards outside of prison.

It became clear that regardless of the plans that we set for ourselves, it is God who has the final say. It also became abundantly clear that life isn't all about achieving our own dreams, but also about helping others along their journey.

Intent on blossoming even within the prison walls, I embraced my new mission with passion. From dance and drama classes to catechism, Spanish, and Patois, I taught the ladies on a daily basis. The soullessness once reflected in their eyes was beginning to be replaced with hope. They, too, taught me poignant lessons about life and living, about America, the American culture, and so much more. I knew my life had forever changed and become more meaningful having met these women. My signature closing for every diary entry—Glo where you're planted with grace—was becoming our mantra and was manifesting.

"Sometimes the dreams that come true are the dreams you never even knew you had."

— Alice Sebold

Chapter 20

MARCH 1997

About a year into my sentence and I couldn't imagine the next two years being tougher than the uncertainty and fear I experienced during my first few days of prison. Jordan, who was in jail for possession of marijuana, had served her 4-year sentence and was released.

Within one week of her departure, Claudia was booked to serve a two-year sentence for prostitution. Because the other ladies and I had become sisters, creating a more civilized environment, Claudia's welcome was a stark contrast from my experience on day one. The queen bully, Latisha, had been dethroned.

Life behind bars was going on—albeit in ways unconventional—but it was jail. Limited freedoms, dictations of when to rise and when to retire, when to eat and when to work, the daily assault on our eardrums in the morning as the guards yelled in concert with the opening and closing of the prison door—reminding us of our whereabouts.

Although I had learned to drown out the sound of the metal door grazing the concrete, the clank it made at closing sent chills down my spine every single time.

The initial shock of little-to-no privacy while showering, number two-ing, and number one-ing were slowly getting easier. I was no longer starving myself in an attempt to not use the bathroom often. *The discomfort from that was out of this world.*

And my palette had somehow adjusted to the bland and sometimes questionable food we were served. On the days when I didn't feel for the menu choice of fake mashed potatoes and meatloaf, *Ew!* I opted for a honeybun or muffin from my stash of snacks.

Part One of my screenplay "A Daring Pursuit of the American Dream" was halfway done and there were plenty more ideas in the pipeline that I needed to get on paper.

Communication between my parents and I never ceased and they still had no idea that the letters they received were being written from behind bars. Their letters and the monthly visits from my other Sisters—the nuns, who visited once a month without fail, alternating who'd make the trip with Mother—sustained me greatly.

Life was going on until it wasn't.

It was a Thursday afternoon in 1997 when Guard Curtis came to tell me that Mother Mary and the Sisters were coming to visit.

Yay! Two visits in one month, I rejoiced in my head. Within three hours—but in what seemed like an eternity—the Sisters were here.

Oh my! Looks like they all came except one. She must be having a lupus flare-up, I assumed.

"Sisters!" I exclaimed.

"Gloria," they responded dryly. The excitement was not reciprocated.

"What a nice surprise!" I exclaimed. "Two visits in one month and all of you came! Well, except Sister D. Where is she? Is she having a flare-up?" Mother lowered her head, Sister Theresa adjusted her veil, Sister Annie scratched her arm—those who weren't staring at their nails were staring at the ceiling. The silence, the silence was deafening.

"Um, Sister D is OK, right?" I asked again, breaking the silence.

"Hope she is now," Mother responded. The other Sisters nodded.

"What do you mean now, Mother, I don't understand?"

"She's, she's um…"

"What? What? What guys?" I panned the circle, looking at every Sister in horror.

Silence.

"Is she, is she, is she, um?" Arms crossed on my stomach, one hand gathered the extra fabric from my jumpsuit against my chest, head tilted, forehead creased, I awaited an answer.

"S-adly, Gloria," Mother swallowed hard, her voice suffused with melancholy.

"What!" My mouth dropped agape. I froze in place for a split second unable to move or speak. My blood vessels constricted, my hair follicles contracted. Goosebumps covered me, my hair stood on end.

Lightheaded, I swayed on the verge of collapsing. A few of the Sisters caught me.

"Come, let's sit," Mother led me to the visitors' table.

My heart racing, my lips quivering, tears began flowing.

"Keep fanning her," Mother instructed Sister Annie as I raised my head from the table.

"Are you OK now, Gloria?"

"I'm just, I'm just…"

"We know, Glo, we know. We are, too." The Sisters echoed, some rubbing my back to console me.

When I first got to the convent, Sister D was ill and was having a lupus flare-up. She had only recently been diagnosed with lupus. It was new to her and she hadn't mastered yet what triggered her flare-ups or the symptoms so she could stop it in its tracks.

While the Sisters worked and did their missionary work, for the two weeks I was at the Convent, my primary responsibility was taking care of Sister D. Bonding over some of her worst moments, I had never met a person more optimistic in the midst of a battle.

I had never seen such suffering. I had never seen someone be OK today and not the next. I also had never seen someone just swell up and then deflate. The lupus had put her through the wringer. But through it all, she'd remained faithful and calm. Her grace and gumption were admirable.

"I just didn't see this coming," I said upon regaining my ability to speak. "I mean, I know she had recently been released from the hospital, but I thought she was doing well."

"Neither did we," Mother replied. "It all happened so fast."

"Did she, um. Did she pass at the Con-vent?"

"Uh-uh. Hos-pital." Mother too is all choked up.

"What happened, though? I thought she had this thing under control."

"It was a struggle, eh. With this last hospital stay, it appeared that she just wasn't getting better. That morning she tried to get out of bed, but she was so sick that she could barely stand on her own. We called 9-1-1. In no time the paramedics arrived. They checked her out then wheeled her away. We hopped into the car and drove to the hospital.

"When we got there, rubbing her leg endearingly the doctor said, 'This is a very sick girl. Her numbers are sicker than she looks. We'll take her to the Intensive Care Unit, ICU.'"

"Oh my! Had she ever been admitted to ICU before?"

"Of her innumerable hospital stays, never in the ICU. As the doctor's words hit my ears, it felt like someone had just poured a bucket of ice water down the nape of my neck. We all were in complete shock. I just..." Mother heaved a heavy sigh.

"What broke our hearts even more was what she said in response to her numbers being sicker than she looks. She said, 'I always tell people it's not how I look, it's how I feel.' That was heartbreaking," Sister Theresa added.

"Why was she unable to walk?"

"The doctor said she had an infection—septic shock. We're convinced that it's possibly because the doctors had not adequately treated her previous infection and discharged her from the hospital too soon."

"Septic shock?"

"It's a blood infection, Gloria—a life-threatening condition that happens when one's blood pressure drops to a dangerously low level after an infection. As a result, your internal organs simply receive too little blood, causing them to fail."

"Oh my God, Mother!" My eyes welled up again.

"After a couple of days in ICU, she was transferred to rehab. We thought she was out of the woods, learning to walk again and, you know, doing OK. But, in less than a week, she had to be rushed to the ER."

"Oh that night, that night, that night," Sister Annie added, shaking her head. "I'll never forget the frantic calls over the intercom, 'CHF! CHF! CHF!'—code for congestive heart failure—it still sends chills up my spine. She was then taken to the ER in a nearby hospital. While in the ER, staring at us she whispered, 'I'm scared, what can the doctors do for me?'"

"Oh my God! This is too much!" I screamed, resting my head on the table. My eyes engorged with tears, my heart about to pump out of my chest.

"With tears in my eyes and hope in my heart, I reassured her that the doctors would do everything they can to make her well again. But…" Sister Theresa's voice cracked even more as she wiped the tears streaming down her face. "The doctors couldn't save her."

"My God!" My heart broke again into millions of pieces. The Sisters were also in tears, so utterly filled with sadness. I swallowed hard.

"The last few weeks of Sister D's life were traumatizing, heartbreaking, and nail-bitingly brutal," Mother picked up the recounting where Sister T left off. "And the last three days, my goodness."

Mother lowered her head in a quiet sob but she mustered the strength to go on. "D often said, 'I feel like everything inside me is dead except my brain. It refuses to die.' She was convinced that the problem was with her head and had been asking for an MRI for the longest time. So, the Saturday night before she passed, the doctors honored her wishes.

"Turns out her head was fine. It was the cruel lupus and its complications messing with her head. She thanked everyone, her nurses and doctors, and was unusually talkative that night. We were hopeful she was bouncing back.

"But on Sunday morning a call came in from the hospital. The very content D from the night before was now intubated, on life support, and unable to speak," Mother stifled an audible cry. Fighting the tears, she continued, "We were baffled. The doctors said her lungs had collapsed. A machine was now responsible for her breathing."

Mother paused, wiping the tears streaming down her face.

"Seeing her on the ventilator was so traumatizing," Sister Theresa added, pushing through tears.

"I can only imagine, my God!" I breathed deeply, attempting to compose myself. Failing, the sobs intensified.

"Then Monday came. She held on as long as she could but around 1:15 p.m… Our hearts are so broken." Mother broke down again.

"I'm so sor-ry, Sisters. I am so sorry," I wept. "I only lived with her for two weeks and she impacted my life so greatly. I can only imagine the loss and immense grief that you feel. I'm sorry. I'm so sorry..."

"I pray that God gives us the strength we desperately need to cope."

"Amen, Mother. This lupus really did a number on her."

"For sure. Some people live with lupus for many, many years, but just within four years of being diagnosed, she passed on. Well, that's when she found out, but she probably had it a long time already. Lupus is very difficult to diagnose, you know. Often when detected, it's already affecting organs and such. For Sister D, it was her lungs."

"Did you see it coming, Mother? Did you think she was gonna die? I mean when you hear ICU you know it's pretty serious, but people do get out."

"I mean we knew she was really sick but didn't think, you know, she was going to die. Perhaps we were in denial," Mother shrugged, wiping the tears in her eyes. "She was a very selfless person and remained so 'til the end. We're convinced that D knew she was dying, but in an attempt to save us from the agony of her impending demise, she bore the burden alone."

"She sure was," Sister T echoed Mother's sentiments. "During her sickness, D participated in a drug trial study to help find a cure."

"Yah, she told me. She said even though it may not help her, it will help others. Though there's still no cure, her efforts were not in vain.

I only got to spend two weeks with her but during that time we bonded so much.

"Sister D taught me what it meant to be resilient, patient, and faithful in the midst of the storm, how important it was to take every day in stride. Even through her immense pain, she was incredibly kind and inspired me to appreciate life and health and people, to be true to myself, and to have faith. She was such an inspiration.

"You know, you mentioned she might've hidden her impending demise. She probably did. She once told me that she'd downplay her pain because she didn't want to be a burden. She said she was tired of saying she doesn't feel well when asked, so she'd say she's better today even though she wasn't."

"Oh my!" Mother's hands flew to her chest. The other Sisters gasped. "Hope she never felt she was a burden to us. Hope we never made her feel that way because she certainly wasn't. D was a good patient."

"You know, one of the women in here had shared that one of her sisters passed with lupus. She was only 21."

"Wow! Ten years younger than Sister D. It's very prevalent among blacks and Hispanics. It's a terrible, terrible disease," Mother sighed.

"It sure is," I sighed. "So, when's the funeral?"

"Saturday."

"This Saturday?"

Mother nodded to confirm.

"Wow, I wonder if I can get special permission to attend. Doesn't hurt to ask, right?"

"Um, about that, Gloria. I actually called and asked, but was told they make these special provisions for inmates' parents and maybe their siblings. Other instances, if approved, would require an inmate to be accompanied by a police officer and possibly handcuffed."

"Whoa!" As much as I wanted to be there, the idea of showing up handcuffed was out of the question. But the possibility of not attending broke my already-broken heart into even tinier pieces. Becoming angry at the situation—angry at being in jail, angry at the Berry's, just angry. "Dammit. Gosh, this is hard Mother. Just isn't fair!" I cursed and I cried.

"I know, Glo. Trust me, I know. I'm sure Sister D will understand. I'm sure she will," Mother sighed. "But don't be too hard on yourself. No one can predict the future and things happen out of our control all the time. We can't control God's work. You'll be OK. We'll give Sister D a nice sendoff and lay a wreath on your behalf. In the meantime, remain focused, keep up the good work—the ministry you're doing here—and soon freedom will be yours in every sense of the word. We love you and although we miss you a whole lot, we are patient and remain hopeful that you will be out soon. OK, kiddo?"

"OK, Mother," I responded, understanding exactly what she meant. Mother always had a way of making me feel better.

"Oh, and that swear word you just used, Gloria, didn't go unnoticed."

The Sisters burst out laughing. Trust Mother to lighten the mood.

"Oh sorry, sorry Sisters," I giggled, embarrassed. "Thought I censored myself by not using the other word—you know the stronger one—out of respect."

Mother and the Sisters laughed again.

"It's OK, Gloria. Only this one time, though."

"Well, since we're at it, pardon me for the other couple of times too."

"What other couple times?" Mother shot me a look over her glasses.

"Oh! Never mind." We giggled.

"So, how were you doing before all this, kiddo?"

"You know, Mother, the best I know how. Sister D's death just added another layer, you know?"

"Yeah, we're all deeply saddened. But we'll be OK. We have to be."

"It's what Sister D would want. But, uh. Life in here—uh, you know—it's an interesting place, I'll tell you that. There's a whole group of women here depending on me, looking up to me for strength and courage to go on in life—to improve themselves—and to help them re-acclimate to society. I have to be strong. I mean, I'm upset now that I can't attend Sister D's funeral, but in a weird way, I'm OK with not making bail. Mentoring the other women here has really been therapeutic and purposeful if you know what I mean."

"Ah, of course I do. Still baffled that you didn't reach out for help and refused to use your money on attorneys, but I'm beginning to see and understand your purpose and reasoning against it. I admire your strength and the sacrifice you made to protect your parents' mental health and all the positives coming out of you being here. The bond, the sisterhood that you guys have formed is so refreshing. It really offers peace of mind that you and the other women are getting along."

"Aw, thanks, Mother."

"You're a good kid, Gloria," Sister T chimed in.

"We're proud of you, Gloria," Sister Annie added.

"Aww thanks, Sisters. Although…" I tee-heed, shaking my head.

"Although what, Gloria? What's so funny? Did something happen?"

"You mean what almost happened or what silly me thought was about to happen?" I rolled my eyes and shuddered.

"Oh, dear. What, Gloria?" Mother asked again nervously, staring at me.

I told the Sisters all about the incident when I thought the ladies were about to jump me, how my legs almost gave out, and how it affected my sleep.

"You play too much," Mother responded, earning a laugh from the Sisters who shared her sentiments.

"You said you had just had a very powerful session, why didn't you think they were joking right off the bat?"

"Because prison, Mother. Prison—where people who commit crimes end up, where repeat offenders end up, and there are several repeat offenders in here. One who, by the way, confessed to the attempted murder of her stepdad, so yeah. No telling if or when they could flip. Although," I chuckled, shaking my head, "looking back, I definitely overreacted, but dang was I scared."

The Sisters died laughing, forgetting—at least for a little while—the grief of losing their beloved Sister D.

"Guard Curtis is coming," I sighed.

"Time's up, ladies."

Time's up, ladies, I mocked him in my head.

"Anyway, glad it turned out the way it did and not the other way around, Glo."

"Oh me too, Mother, trust me."

"We've overstayed our welcome so, uh, yeah. Sorry for being the bearers of bad news."

"Ah…" I sighed. "It's OK Mother. C'est la vie, right?"

"Indeed Gloria, c'est la vie. Adios, kiddo."

"Bye, beloveds. I will be sure to whisper a prayer for the peaceful repose of her soul. May God give you the strength and comfort to endure this. Stay strong."

"You too, Gloria Grace, you too."

Grief-stricken, I made my way to the cell with a reminder that no one is immune to grief, dying, heartache, sadness, and pain. I could hardly believe that Sister D had gone to meet her Maker and all that was left were the beautiful memories of her.

Shattered, I curled onto my cot, hoping to sleep it off. I didn't. My interactions with her and the way she impacted my life reverberated in my head.

My evening session with the ladies was preempted with comforting words and acts of kindness and love from them. I couldn't have asked for better shoulders to cry on.

In the ensuing days, when grief threatened to paralyze me, my newly found sisters were there to keep me from slipping. I had to go on—they needed me. I had a mission to complete. I had a dream to fulfill.

"Do not follow where the path may lead. Go instead where there is no path and leave a trail."

— Ralph Waldo Emerson

Chapter 21

NOVEMBER 1999

It was Thanksgiving Day. Barely awoken, I heard a voice say, "Gloria today may be your last day."

"Huh?" I awoke from my slumber, looking about me petrified. The other ladies and I were getting along really well, but I still couldn't let my guard down completely. We were in jail and any one of the ladies flipping at any time was not impossible.

"So, Gloria, you have a hearing tomorrow," the voice added.

"Oh, Guard Curtis, it's you!" I smiled wiping the crust from my eyes and mouth.

"Except for that one fight, your leadership and behavior in here have been exemplary," he continued smiling. "We've arranged for the Judge to see you tomorrow at 10 a.m. Be ready to be transported by 9:30 a.m. Best of luck, young lady. Happy Thanksgiving!"

"Thanks, Guard Curtis!" My eyes brightened, my smile widened, and my heart lightened with gladness.

What about the girls? the thought of leaving them quelled my joy.

Friday, the day after Thanksgiving, finally came. At 10 a.m, the gavel hit the mantle of the courtroom summoning the start of the hearing.

"Gloria," the Judge nodded.

"Judge Judy," I, too, responded with a nod.

"Gloria Grace Estevez?" she gasped, seeming surprised.

"Yes, Judge."

"I thought the name sounded familiar. So, we meet again, huh?"

"Yes, Judge."

"Last time you were here, things didn't go so well. Hope you let me speak this time— uninterrupted."

"Oh! You remember this, Judge?" I gasped.

"There are some cases and some people you just never forget, Gloria."

"I see, Judge."

Sallay! Your conscience was beating you. It wouldn't allow you to forget me, would it? You knew you did me wrong. You knew you abused your power by sending me straight to prison. Anyway, carry on.

"So, you were here for battery on three minors. I have two statements here from the Berry family. One from the night of the incident—with very graphic, emotionally charged language—and another from a couple of weeks ago citing that you are a good person, with good temperament, hardworking, and that they now believe that you wouldn't hit their kids and that they overreacted basically."

Oh! And so did you, Judge! I thought, rolling my eyes internally. *What caused that change? Hm? Did they read my diary? Did they find out that their kids' new friend Brazen was bad news? Did the kids fess up? Did Monae and Patrick break up? Did...*

"So, Gloria. Gloria. GlOria!"

"Uh? Yes, Judge. Yes, Judge!"

"Looks like you zoned out there for a little bit, didn't you?"

"Sorry, Judge. Sorry, Judge."

"Like I was saying, even without their statements, I've heard you've redeemed yourself during your time in prison, that your behavior has really been exemplary, and that you've gained the respect and admiration of not only your fellow inmates but that of the guards and wardens, too. I heard you held Spanish and creole classes—I hope you taught them proper English, too," Judge Judy joked, "and bible study and acting classes. Impressive, Gloria! So you want to become an actress, huh?"

"Yes, Judge," I blushed.

"I have no doubt that I'll be seeing you again—on the big screen, on the big screen that is," she laughed. "Best of luck, Gloria. You have a good head on your shoulders."

"Can I talk now, Judge?"

"Go ahead," Judge Judy responded with laughter.

"Just checking, Judge. I certainly do not want history to repeat itself."

"Understood," Judge Judy responded, still laughing.

"Thanks, Judge," I smiled. "My time here has been productive, I must admit. I could allow myself to be bitter with the Berry's, but thanks to them I've met some really good women here. Women who, I'm sure, will become lifelong friends.

"And yes, I hope you get to see me in movie theaters someday or in your home soon," I chuckled.

"Ah! Enjoy your freedom, Gloria. You're free to come back here anytime."

Laughter once again erupted in the courtroom.

"Putting my foot in my mouth again, huh?" Judge Judy joked again. "You folks know what I mean. The ladies would be happy to have you continue mentoring them."

"I'm sure they would, Judge. Thank you."

"Come on up here, let me give you a hug."

"Oh!" I gasped, fighting back the tears.

"I'm so sorry, Gloria," Judge Judy whispered in my ear.

"For what, exactly?" I whispered back.

"Everything!" she said hugging me tighter.

"Everything?" I asked, puzzled.

"We'll be in touch," Judge Judy said, releasing me from her embrace and adding before she walked back to the bench, "Take care of yourself now, Gloria. You're a good kid. You're free to go tomorrow, young lady."

The sound of the gavel hitting the mantle, signaling the end of the hearing, was a symphony to my ears this time.

"Phew!" I blinked, relieved, and overwhelmed at the same time. "It's truly happening. I'm going home!"

In about 20 minutes I was back at the prison after an uneventful trip—no throw-ups, no screw-ups. No embarrassment, no confusion. Just pure excitement and gratitude coursing through me.

"Guys, guys! The Judge says I'm free to go!" I announced, rejoicing.

"What! When?" they asked one after the other, in quick succession.

"Tomorrow!"

The ladies gasped.

"Tomorrow? No!" Latisha yelled.

The ladies' reactions forced me to curb my enthusiasm.

"Oh, Lisa!" I said as she walked into my arms for a warm embrace. "I'm so sorry to be leaving you all."

"It's OK, Gloria. I don't know where life will take me from here, but one thing I know for sure is that I will come out of here a better person because of you. Thank you!"

"Aw! That's the spirit, Lis!" Lisa's words touched my heart so deeply they reduced me to tears.

"I will miss you, Gloria. Thank you for teaching me how to pray."

"Aw! Latisha, Latisha, Latisha. I will never forget you and how far you've come, my friend. I am so proud of you. Keep up the good work, keep working on you. You have incredible potential and I have no doubt that you will come out of here and venture into the world and make your dreams a reality. Remain focused, my friend. I believe in you. I believe in all of you."

An emotional Latisha lowered her head. It was the first time I had ever seen her cry. It became apparent that underneath that tough exterior was a soft and sweet but broken little girl.

"Gloria, I love you so much and will miss you," she continued. "Had you not been here, I'd probably be in trouble every single day, possibly lengthening my sentence. So, thank you! Thank you for giving me a new lease on life."

Somber, the women took turns thanking and embracing me.

"Hearing your testimonies warmed my heart a great deal. Know that I will never ever forget you," I assured them resting my right hand on my heart. I meant every word.

"Can you come visit every day?"

"Well, I dunno 'bout every day now, Latisha." The ladies laughed. "But as often as I possibly can—if permitted that is."

Before long, Guard Curtis came to get me to do the exit paperwork, interrupting our talks.

"So you're going home, huh?"

"Yep, Guard!"

"These women will miss you. Have never seen anything like this here. And I've worked in the prison system for over 20 years. Young lady, you're a miracle worker," he chortled. "Don't you have some people to call?"

"Yes, yes!"

Guard Curtis handed me the phone.

"Mother! Mother Mary. I'm free!"

"What? This is wonderful news, Gloria!"

"But I wanted to ask…"

"You're welcome back here anytime!" Mother butted in before I could get the words out.

"Yes yes, yes, Mother,' I said, doing a million cartwheels in my head, before calming myself to continue in a much lower tone, "I mean, I'd love to, Mother, if it won't be any trouble at all."

"Gloria! You are so silly!" Mother snorted. "At what time should we get there?"

"10 a.m. right, Guard Curtis?"

He nodded to confirm.

"10 a.m. Thank you so much, Mother!"

"Don't mention it, Gloria. See you tomorrow."

Smiling harder than I'd ever seen him, Guard Curtis handed me a bunch of paperwork to sign.

Now, around 4:30 pm, dinner time was over, which meant the start of our leisure time. So we made our way to our usual spot—the Flamboyant Tree in the yard.

"Where is everybody?" I asked looking around. "Where are Lisa and Latisha? They just upped and disappeared from chow hall right before dinner was over."

Quanda stifled a laugh. No matter how hard she tried, Claudia couldn't hide the smirk on her face. Nikki picked at her nails. Chantelle suddenly fixated her eyes upon the tree.

"OK... Why y'all acting so strange?" I asked, my forehead creased. "Hope they're not in trouble?" My hand flew to my chest, my heart sank to my feet as the thought of that prospect entered my psyche.

"Oh my! Look, look, look at this bird, look at this bird, Gloria," Chantelle pointed up at the beautiful tree shading us. "Look how yellow the tail is. Look how the bright yellow is complimenting the beautiful orange leaves."

"Where? I don't see it. Where, Chantelle?" I asked, bobbing my head and squinting, peering through the branches. "Girl, all I see is the noisy black one right there."

"Look between those branches right there..." Chantelle pointed, drawing closer to look up from my point of view.

"Surprise!" the women yelled in unison.

"What?" I asked, turning around to see Lisa and Latisha standing behind me holding a duffle bag. "Is that the body?"

"Huh! Who?" they reacted, looking horrified.

"Oh… I get it," Lisa laughed. Some of the ladies followed suit, except one.

"Whatcha mean?" Latisha asked, lost.

"We'll tell you later," the ladies laughed.

"Gloria, these are your party snacks!" Lisa exclaimed.

"Huh?" I shot a confused look.

"We thought we'd throw you a farewell party, so we pooled all our snacks together and voila!"

"Aww, you guys. How thoughtful and sweet."

"We love you, Gloria, and will miss you a whole lot," an emotional Lisa added.

"This warms my heart greatly, guys," I continued, pushing through the tears. "You just threw me my first-ever surprise party! You, ladies, are truly special. Thank you. I love you guys so much."

"We love you too, Gloria. Let's eat!" Latisha broke the sobbing party. "I'm hungry."

"Didn't you just eat?" Lisa asked, rolling her eyes and chuckling.

"Girl, what was that they served tonight?" Nikki asked, forcing us to burst out laughing because we knew exactly what she meant.

"It looked like mashed potatoes and meatloaf. I didn't have any of it, but looks can be deceiving so…" I added.

"Girl, not in this case. It tasted exactly how it looked," Quanda laughed infectiously.

"Listen, I didn't touch it. I just drank the juice," I admitted, "or maybe y'all didn't eat to save room for all these snacks."

"Um, no girl. It was pretty bad." Quanda was adamant.

Upon blessing the snacks, we dove in. From chips to crackers to biscuits to sodas, they had thrown everything in.

"Wow, y'all know how to hoard snacks. You mean all this came from the unit?"

"Who would've thought, right?" Lisa laughed.

"Oh and Gloria you never would've spotted that yellow-tailed bird," Chantelle died laughing.

"Of course! You lil' fibber, you!" I smiled, rolling my eyes.

Joking and snacking and laughing and crying and reminiscing, my farewell party was perfect. For some reason, the day went by quicker than any other day of my being locked up. In no time darkness fell, signaling that the end of our leisure time was near. But before then, I had one last thing to share.

"Ladies, I just want to say thank you—thank you for making my time in here worthwhile. I am truly indebted to all of you. I love you and will honestly miss each and every one of you."

Tears, not now, not now! Let me at least get through this, I thought, fighting hard to keep the tears in my eyes from falling. I lost. The tears began to flow.

Somber, the ladies and I gathered in one embrace, sobbing.

"This being our last session..." I said, eventually pulling myself together and away. "I want to share a beautiful poem I came across with you. I think it was written by Mother Teresa.

"It captures the story of life so eloquently and beautifully that I feel compelled to share it with you. Why? Because it has helped me get through many moments of despair. It is my go-to for inspiration and motivation every time I feel down, discouraged, or afraid."

"Can't wait to hear it, Gloria."

"Here goes, Lis. Hope it ministers to all of you like it does me."

Dramatically clearing my throat, I began...

```
"Life is an opportunity, benefit from it.
Life is a beauty, admire it.
Life is bliss, taste it.
Life is a dream, realize it.
```

```
Life is a challenge, meet it.
Life is a duty, complete it.
Life is a game, play it.
Life is costly, care for it.
Life is wealth, keep it.
Life is love, enjoy it.
Life is a mystery, know it.
Life is a promise, fulfill it.
Life is a sorrow, overcome it.
Life is a song, sing it.
Life is a struggle, accept it.
Life is a tragedy, confront it.
Life is an adventure, dare it.
Life is luck, make it.
Life is too precious, do not destroy it.
Life is life, fight for it!."
```

"Wow! Gloria, that was beautiful. I see why you love it so much," Lisa said, wiping the tears in her eyes.

The tears accumulating in my eyes escaped, spotting my overalls. The sniffles and tear wiping movements among the group spoke volumes. They, too, had been touched.

"Wow! 'Life is a dream, realize it.'" Latisha repeated.

"Ah! Absolutely, Latisha. Go out there and live it. You have the power within you."

"Life is a song, sing it." Nikki chimed in.

"Yes, Nikki. Do not be afraid to use your voice, to share your singing talent with the world. Work on overcoming shyness. Go forth and realize your dream."

"Life is a tragedy, confront it. Life is a sorrow, overcome it."

"Indeed, Chantelle. May your Sister Dana continue to rest peacefully and may peace between you and your parents prevail."

"Life is a challenge, meet it."

"Indeed, Lisa, go after it with all your might. You can do it. Do not be afraid. 'Take up your cross and follow me.' He says. May God be your guide every step of the way."

"Yes! I hear you, Glo!"

"And to all of you, I say, 'Life is too precious, do not destroy it. Life is life, fight for it!'"

"Ah! I love it. Can you write it down for me?"

"Sure, Latisha."

"And me too, Glo."

"You got it, Lis."

"And me too, and me too," the women echoed one after the other.

"OK ladies, I'll tell you what, how about I write it down, put it up on the wall and you copy it from there, deal?"

"Sounds good, Glo. Thank you so much for everything."

"Ah, don't mention it, guys. We are going to help each other every step of the way, right?"

"Right!" they agreed.

"Until then remember to always 'Glo where you're planted with grace.' Remember to always do what?"

"Glo where you're planted with grace," they echoed resoundingly.

"Right on."

Sharing high fives and hugs, we proceeded inside.

Soon the lights flickered, signaling we had five minutes to get into bed. The sound of the gate closing and clanking of the door sent chills down my spine one last time. It was the one thing I knew for sure I wouldn't miss here.

"Good night, everyone!" I said one last time.

Climbing onto my cot for the last time was surreal, but my day wasn't over just yet. Turning on my tiny night lamp, I sat up on my cot to write the poem for the ladies and personalized letters with words of encouragement for each one of them. I then parceled out my humble belongings, said my prayers, and went to bed right before the sun's rising.

A dream can never be undreamed no matter how long it takes to achieve.

Chapter 22

THREE DAYS AFTER THANKSGIVING 1999

"Rise and shine, Gloria! It's freedom day!"

"I'm up, Guard Curtis, I'm up!" I sat up, wiping the crust from my eyes.

"Take care of yourself, young lady. Go out there, follow your dreams, and try not to get in trouble again."

"But, Guard!"

"Yeah, I know, you didn't do it. I believe you, Gloria. Take care of yourself. You are free to go."

"Yes!" I rejoiced, but in a hush-hush manner deep down in my heart. Although the ladies were happy for me, they were deeply saddened that their mentor and anchor was leaving. I felt the need to curb my enthusiasm, at least in their presence.

"Good morning, Gloria," the ladies greeted me somberly.

"Aw... guys. I, too, am sad to leave you. But I'm also glad that I can begin to live my li-fe and follow my..." I stopped, too choked up to continue.

"Gloria, were you too happy to sleep last night?"

"Why? Did my light keep you up, Latisha?"

"Girl, I was so ti'ed I was out like a light. Was just curious."

"Good," I chuckled. "Thought I heard you snoring."

"And farting," Lisa added laughing, earning a laugh from all of us.

She was right.

"Whatever, Lisa!" Latisha replied.

"I stayed up all night working on these, Latisha," I smiled, handing each of the ladies the note that I had written them.

"Aw! How thoughtful and sweet, Gloria," Chantelle said.

Each of the ladies was special in their own way and had taught me something different. Having one generic letter just wouldn't cut it—wouldn't allow me to express how special they each were and how they had impacted my life.

"So, ladies, I wanted to give you guys my humble belongings. But to keep favoritism, jealousy, and animosity at bay I've decided to raffle them off instead. Who's ready to play?"

"Me, me, me," they all replied.

"Here's the deal. Whatever you get, you don't get upset. You are free to trade amongst yourselves. Deal?"

"Deal, Glo, deal," they agreed.

"Alright, let's play! Who wants to dip first?"

"I'll go!" Latisha wasted no time in opting to go first.

"I'll go last," Lisa raised her hands.

"OK, ladies, form a line between Latisha and Lisa."

They rushed to get in line.

"Let's have some fun! You're up, Latisha."

"Shake, shake, shake the bag, Gloria," Latisha laughed.

"I did," I retorted.

"More, more, more. Lemme shake it," she insisted, grabbing the paper bag from me, shaking it with all her might.

"Now dip girl!" I ordered, taking it back from her. The ladies laughed. "Open it, open it. What does it say?"

"Watch! Aww, mehn!"

"Be grateful, Latisha," the ladies quickly scolded her.

"It's just that I don't think it'll fit my elephant wrist but that's OK," she responded sighing. "Whoever wants to trade—no offense, Gloria."

"None taken, Latisha. You're up, Nikki!"

"Toiletries—deodorant, soap, sanitary napkins, razors, toothpaste. Yay! Thank you, Gloria!" Nikki rejoiced.

"Want to trade, Nik?" Latisha asked. "Please? Please? Please?"

"OK, I'll trade you, Latisha, but only because the watch doesn't fit you."

"Aw! Thanks, my girl," Latisha rejoiced, picking Nikki up effortlessly and spinning her around before putting her back down. "You can keep the deodorant, Nik."

"No!" the other ladies yelled out in unison.

I stifled a laugh.

"Why?" Latisha asked puzzled.

"It's what you need the most," Lisa answered pointedly. The other ladies looked uncomfortable.

"Whatever, Lisa!" Latisha replied with an eye roll and talk-to-the-hand gesture.

"Claudia, you're up!" I continued, breaking the tension.

"Bible, sweatshirt, sweatpants, socks. Thanks, Gloria! I always wanted a bible. Now I can lounge in my sweatsuit and read up."

"There you go, Claudia. Love it. Quanda, you're next!"

"Night light, notepad, pens. Yay! Thanks, Gloria!"

"Chantelle, you're up!"

"Coffee cup, bowls, snacks. Yay!"

"And last but not least, Lisa!"

"Walkman, gospel cassette, headphones. Yes, yes, yes!" Lisa rejoiced. "Thanks, Gloria. That's exactly what I wanted!"

"Really? I thought perhaps you'd want the watch."

"Nah, girl, who needs time in here?" she laughed. "They dictate when we do everything, so yeah. Thank you very much!"

"You got a point there, Lis." We laughed.

"I should've waited to trade," Latisha moaned.

"No!" the ladies echoed resoundingly again, snickering.

"You got exactly what you needed, Latisha."

"You're right, Lisa, my toiletries are almost done."

"That's not why, but OK Latisha," Lisa replied.

With the applause of thanksgiving, the raffle was over.

"Oh, how thoughtful you are, Gloria. We'll miss you," Lisa embraced me. "Thank you, thank you, thank you for everything. For giving me my life back."

"I love you, Gloria." Latisha embraced me a little longer than comfortable.

"Take care of yourself, Latisha. I am so incredibly proud of you and you and you—all of you. Promise me you'll keep the sisterhood strong. Be there for each other and help each other grow. Remember to pray without ceasing. What's the simplest and most powerful prayer?"

"Jesus!" they all said in unison.

"And remember to always endeavor to do what?"

"Glo wherever you're planted with grace!" they echoed.

"With what?"

"Grace!"

"With what?"

"Grace!"

"Ah! My work here is done," I smiled.

The gratitude reflected in their eyes and the tears that they shared told me how appreciative they were. The time to leave was approaching. I contemplated whether I should take a shower one last time. I did. Changing into the brand new sweats and T-shirt I had recently bought from the commissary store, I was ready.

"Time to go, Gloria." The warden came to get me.

"Adios, mis amigas!" I said blowing kisses to the women who gathered to see me off. "Will be in touch."

"Promise?"

"I promise, my loves."

Grabbing my recently purchased bag containing my diary, paperwork, and screenplay, I followed closely behind the warden as we made our way to Receiving and Departures.

"Bye, superstar, see you on the big screen," one of the ladies yelled out. I think it was Latisha.

"Amen!" I said, turning around to see Lisa and Latisha in a tight embrace comforting each other. It was a much different dynamic than what I encountered when I first debuted on the scene two and a half years ago. Wiping the tears in my eyes, with a broken yet hopeful heart, I turned back around and continued walking.

Warden first led me to the nurse's station to pick up my medical records. Then he asked if I needed to go to processing to retrieve the clothes and shoes and whatever else I was wearing the night of my arrest.

"No, thank you," I said. "I was first at County and then transferred straight from my arraignment. If anything, my stuff is probably still over there, unless it was transferred."

"How long were you in here for?" Warden asked.

"Two and a half years."

"Ah! That's probably gone by now and if still there, there's a good chance that it's covered in mold or has rotted. We can go check to be sure."

"Ah, don't bother, Warden. I think I'll survive without them."

"Alrighty then. Let's put these on."

"Oh!" My eyes popped.

I thought my cuffing and uncuffing days were over. But Warden slapped those cold, uncomfortable, and restraining things on my wrist one last time before we headed outside. My heart thumped in my chest this time with a mixture of gladness and anticipation. I could hardly believe that I was free, free to begin a new chapter in my life.

Knowing that I had made an indelible impact, I walked out of jail with my head held high. As I sat outside waiting for my ride, once again with my thoughts, I could hardly take my mind off the ladies I had left behind. Something told me they'd be aiight.

Just then the tripping of a young girl being taken into jail broke my reverie. No older than 22-years-old, her head hung low, seemingly too drunk or drugged up to hold herself up. My heart ached for her.

As this was happening, a white SUV which I thought looked familiar came to a stop. Heads poking out, veils flying in the wind, the Sisters were here. The warden, who waited with me the entire time, checked out the nuns to verify that they were who I said would be picking me up.

With that being cleared, he proceeded to remove the cold silver jointed bracelets from my wrists—the handcuffs—freeing me.

Ahh! I breathed out internally and prayed to God that I would never have to wear them involuntarily ever again. In a swift swoop, I grabbed my little bag and bolted.

In a swift pivot, the warden turned around, his right hand drawn to the gun on his duty belt. Realizing that I was fooling around, he shook his head, drew a crooked smile then proceeded inside.

"Yes!" I rejoiced. My deliberate attempt to scare him had worked.

"Gloria!" the Sisters yelled out.

"Gloria! You play too much, Gloria!" Sister Theresa and the other nuns laughed. "You should've seen the expression on the warden's face."

"Oh my! You made it out, Gloria!" Sister Annie couldn't conceal her excitement.

"Sure did, Sisters! Now step on it! Step on it, Mother, before they change their minds."

"Huh! Step on what?" Mother glanced at me over her spectacles, her brows drawn together.

"The gas pedal, Mother," Sister Annie answered laughing out loud.

"Good to see you haven't lost your sense of humor, Gloria," Sister Theresa laughed.

What a surreal moment, mixed with all sorts of emotions. As Mother drove away, obeying the speed limit, I looked back to see the prison getting smaller and smaller in the background. Prison was now behind me, the rest of my life ahead of me. As sad as I was to leave the ladies behind, I looked forward to beginning a new chapter in my life.

Achieving your dream is motivation for those whose dreams are killed by lack of courage, self-doubt, and Imposter Syndrome.

Chapter 23

"So, Gloria, how does it feel to be free?" Sister Theresa asked with utmost sincerity, her eyes resting on me.

Swallowing hard, I attempted to answer.

But before I could say anything Mother had another question, "Ay, what's that look?"

"Nothing, nothing, Mother," I lied. My heart was full. I was happy. I was sad. I was glad. I was overwhelmed. My emotions were having a battle that I couldn't quite control or put into words.

"There's a sparkle in your eyes even though it looks like you've been crying," she continued, "but underneath I also see a reflection of sadness. Gonna miss those women, huh?"

"More than words can tell, Mother. I sure hope they keep exhibiting good behavior so they, too, can get out sooner. Those are good women in there with so much potential."

"Something tells me they'll be alright, they'll keep it up."

"Hope so, Mother, sincerely hope so. Mother, can you drive with the windows down for a bit?" I asked.

"Why?"

"I want people to see me," I chuckled. "Kidding, kidding. I just want to feel the wind against my face. Just for a moment."

Throwing a quick glance my way and smiling, Mother honored my request.

Poking my head out the window, the wind blowing my tears away and my eyes shut, it was just what I needed to cement my freedom.

"Remember this place?" Sister Theresa asked, pointing to the church, the park, whatever else along the route, and then the convent.

The two and half years I worked for Monae and the two and a half I spent in jail, away from this place, had taken a toll on my memory. Or perhaps I was too wrapped up in thought to notice familiar territory.

"Oh, we're home?"

The car came to a complete stop, taking me back to the place I wandered into five years ago. Thanking Mother, I climbed out of the vehicle, holding the little bag that contained all my belongings.

"Welcome home, Gloria!" The other Sisters who didn't make the trip to pick me up greeted me at the door—except one. Sister Delisha Joan, Sister D. The same pain and shock I felt the day I learned of her passing made an appearance in my heart and the tears threatened to flow.

But I also couldn't miss the welcome home banner and the table of mementos laid out below it in the living room. Although I felt incredibly blessed, honored, and lucky, the sadness that lurked in my heart was hard to ignore.

Deep down I felt sad. Incredibly sad that Sister D was gone. A teardrop escaped my eye. As if on cue, Mother pointed out a white envelope with blue type and seal on the table.

"Immigration and Naturalization Services? Oh! Did I get it?" My heart skipped a beat with excitement, then sank just as quickly, "Wait! Is this a deportation order?"

"Open it, open it." Mother ordered. I wasn't sure if she was excited or scared.

"When did this come in?" I asked carefully, opening the envelope.

"About two weeks ago," Mother replied. "We planned on taking it to you on our next visit, but here you are!"

```
Dear Gloria,
```

Please report to the Immigration and Naturalization office on December 13th..." On my birthday?

"What, what on your birthday?" Mother asked, curiosity killing her.

I continued reading.

The Sisters huddled together, waiting with bated breath to hear its contents.

"Oh. My. God!" My eyes widened, my jaw dropped. Closing my eyes and taking a deep breath, my hand on my heart, I exhaled. "Phew! It's to have my biometrics taken!"

The Sisters also exhaled in concert, releasing each other.

"On your birthday, Gloria?" Mother asked, awestruck.

"Ye-Yes!" I repeated, totally floored. "My 24th birthday!"

"Talk about timing, my God!"

"Yes indeed, Mother. WOW! Look, I'm shaking," breathing deeply, I shook my head in gratitude and awe of God's timing.

In the pit of my stomach there was an intense feeling—not sure if it was nausea, butterflies, or anxiety. But the feeling was a familiar one and reminded me of the day Judge Judy sentenced me straight to prison, causing me to puke on the officer's shoe. I hadn't eaten much that day and I certainly didn't have any rotten bananas. I didn't vomit, though, but I came close.

"To think had I stayed in jail two weeks longer I would've missed this appointment, my God! I wonder…"

"Wonder what, Gloria?" Mother asked.

"I always worried that I might've gotten deported after serving my sentence. Think that can still happen?"

"I hope not, Gloria. Like I said, the Cuban government is very reluctant to accept deportees and this was your first encounter with the law. I think if anything were to happen, you probably wouldn't have received this letter in the first place. And right out of jail, you would've been handed over to Immigration."

"Hm. You got a point there, Mother," I sighed a little, praying that Mother was right. "I wonder how long after fingerprinting I will get my green card."

"I think it usually takes anywhere from six weeks to six months. And then you can go visit your parents."

"Definitely first order of business, Sister T!" taking a deep breath as the thoughts of my parents in Cuba sprang to mind. "But wait, refugees are barred from returning to Cuba, aren't they?"

"That's right, Gloria," Mother confirmed.

"Oh! I know what we can do."

"What?" Mother asked.

"Saint Lucia!"

"What about Saint Lucia?"

"Follow, follow, Mother," I chortled, snapping my fingers twice. "That's where Mom is from and I'm sure she'd love to visit."

"I'm sure she would, too, Gloria. When last was she there?"

"She left a few days after my first birthday and has never returned. That was what, almost 23 years ago."

"Oh my, that's an eternity."

"Not calling me old, are you, Mother?" I shot her a look. Then, we burst out laughing.

"How come she never went back?"

"You know, financial constraints, the painful memories of losing her parents. But she speaks of it all the time—how breathtaking and majestic Saint Lucia is, her wondrous and adventurous upbringing, the foods she ate.

"She often reminisced about taking baths in the river, cooking on open fires, hunting for snacks—fresh fruits from the garden and yard. She'd talk about the ring games they played, how they used their imagination to create toys from items around the house and yard, the wakes and funerals and how they celebrated the life of the deceased, the festivals they celebrated like carnival and festival of lights, and the big fuss they made around Christmas time, the folklore stories told by the elders to scare the bejesus out of them.

"I'm sure things have changed quite a bit but, I can't wait to visit and hopefully experience some of those activities."

"I'm sure she'd love to relive those memories and create new ones with you, Glo."

"And then, I can bring them here!" I rejoiced. "OK, I might be getting ahead of myself. First things first right, Mother?"

"Right. But it doesn't hurt to be hopeful and to plan ahead. We have one more surprise for you. Ready for it?"

"Sure! What? Hope my heart can take it," I giggled in anticipation.

"Look to your right."

"Where?" I asked pivoting 360.

"Gloria!" Mother and Sister T cracked up. Mother slapped her forehead, "You're back facing the same way."

"Oh!" I giggled.

"To the right, Glo, to the right." Sister T laughed.

"My diary! You retrieved my diary? Wait! That's not a replica, is it?" I asked, staring at Mother intently.

"Get it."

"Oh my God!" I screamed, reaching for the blue diary covered in confetti.

"Thank you, Mother! How did you get it?" I asked, holding onto it tightly against my chest.

"I hunted them down day and night for it," Mother laughed. "Nah, but after numerous attempts, your former employer finally mailed it with the rest of your stuff a couple of weeks ago."

"Hm, well that's interesting…"

"How so?" Mother asked, curious.

"Either they were really remorseful or they needed more time to get through reading it and decoding my handwriting." My theory earned a laugh from the Sisters. "Know what the Judge told me? She said they made another statement not too long ago stating that I'm a good person and how, looking back, they might have overreacted."

"Oh? And costing you close to three years of your life?" Mother responded, shaking her head, clearly agitated.

"Think they read it, Gloria?" Sister T asked.

"I hope they did. I mean, I recorded everything in there. The good times, the bad, and the husband's wandering eyes and hands. Monae probably read it and realized that I truly loved her kids. I wrote lovingly about them often. Anyhow, so happy to have it back. Thank you guys so very much."

"Anytime, Gloria."

"Is my room still my room?" I asked, planting my face in my hands. I needed to make sure.

"Sure is, Gloria. Just as you left it."

"Awesome! Thanks, Mother. I think I need a long shower and good hair washing. If you don't see me for a while, no worries. I'm just reacquainting myself with a bed and shower and toilet and doors and a closet, oh my, all these luxuries."

"And cartwheels?"

"Yes, that too, that too, Mother," I cackled.

"Enjoy, Gloria, enjoy!"

"My plan exactly, Sisters, thank you!"

While the Sisters made their way to the kitchen to finish cooking dinner, I headed upstairs to my room, once again feeling like I was in heaven. Undressing and praying, I got into the shower. My life was about to become normal again, and I couldn't be happier.

After my half-hour-or-so shower, I threw myself onto the bed to rest awhile, but the thoughts of the women I had left behind in prison and Sister D couldn't escape my mind. I mustered the courage to pay Sister D's room a visit.

The minute I entered her room, a spirit of calmness befell upon me. Unfolding my arms, relaxing my shoulders and my jaw, I looked around the room. It was about a year and six months since her passing and her things were still there, unmoved. The Sisters have made a shrine in her memory.

Tears ran down my cheeks as I touched the candle, her rosary, fresh flowers, bible, and whatever else was laid out in her honor. My eyes then diverted to the picture frame hanging on her bedroom wall below the cross. Walking closer to it, I apologized for my inability to be there for her in her last moments.

"I'm sorry I couldn't attend your funeral," I said, fidgeting with the rosary beads. "I'm sure you understand, but I feel guilty. Intercede for me that these feelings of guilt go away. I appreciate meeting you and I'm so grateful I was able to care for you that time. I'm a much better person because of you. Thank you, Sister D. Rest in peace, beautiful soul. Rest in perfect peace."

Blowing kisses towards the picture frame hanging on the wall, I proceeded to exit the room.

"What was that?" Startled, I quickly turned my head to see where the noise came from. The picture frame had shifted and Sister D was no longer standing upright in it. Albeit spooked, I walked back closer to examine it. Before I could straighten the frame, boom, it fell to the floor forcing me to jolt and step back.

"Oh you're in here," the Sisters came rushing in. "Are you OK? What was that bang?"

Arms crossed clenching my shirt against my chest with my right hand, left hand around my waist I attempted to respond, "This, this, um, this picture frame just fell as I turned my back."

"I told you!" Sister Theresa blurted looking at the other Sisters.

"Told what? What?" I asked, puzzled and frightened at the same time.

"We think Sister D is here."

"Oh!" still clenching my shirt with my arms crossed, my forehead creased, my jaw dropped in horror, I slid closer to Mother. "What makes you think that?"

"The lights flicker occasionally. It has happened a couple times," Sister T said.

"What? Maybe there's a power trip."

"An electrician has debunked the notion. He even changed the circuit to be sure, but it happened again about a week ago around her birthday."

"What!" I'm officially spooked. "This place is haunted?"

"I think there's paranormal activity here but nothing to be scared about. Spirits, souls are harmless energies," Mother confirmed.

"Does this mean she isn't resting in peace, Mother? Does it mean that she has not made peace with her death?"

"I think it means she's watching over us and walking us through our sorrows and despair."

"OK. And they're not harmful. Whew, I'll go with this explanation."

The clock chimed, telling us that it was six o'clock, time for evening prayers. The Sisters and I made our way to the chapel. I prayed for me and my sisters in prison, my parents, the nuns, and for the peaceful repose of Sister D's soul. Within an hour, prayers were over and we headed to the kitchen to partake of the special dinner they had prepared to celebrate my release from prison.

"Oh you guys outdid yourselves, didn't you?" The spread was so inviting.

"All your favorite things, Gloria."

"I see that, Mother. I was just thinking how much I'm about to pig-out, taking me back to when I first got here," I laughed, planting my face in my palms. "I remember eating everything in sight. Well, except the napkins, dishes, and cutlery."

The Sisters laughed as if it was the funniest joke they had ever heard.

Something tells me they might have talked about my overindulgence behind my back, I thought, giggling in my head. "What a wonderfully, thoughtfully sweet family you are."

"Sure right, we are family, Gloria. We want you to know that you can call on us anytime. Operative word, any-time." Mother looked at me from above her glasses, "even when you get arrested."

"Duly noted, Mother, duly noted. Mm, mm mmm! Everything tastes oh so heavenly. I think you guys mastered the pumpkin soup and green fig salad in my absence."

"It's probably because you haven't had it in a while, so everything tastes oh-so heavenly." The Sisters mused.

"I can't begin to tell you how egregious everything inside there tastes."

"Well, Glo, it's jail, eh? Not a 5-star hotel," Mother quickly reminded me.

"I will tell you, my homeless days definitely prepared me for life behind bars."

"See how every step in your journey prepares you for the next, Gloria? Everything comes full circle. Everything definitely happens for a reason."

"That I believe, Sister T, without a doubt!"

"Welcome home, Gloria!" the Sisters raised their glasses. "Hear, hear!"

"Thank you so very much, family. Thank you for helping me survive prison, for helping me on this whirlwind journey called life."

My eyes welled up, a crying spell threatened to ensue—the reality of what I had just gone through was hitting hard in my heart and gut. I just wanted to release it.

"Thank you from the depths of my heart, Sisters," I said, on the brink of tears.

"Anytime, Gloria. Any time. Got that?" Mother responded, taking a sip of her tea. Still hung up on the fact that I didn't reach out for help the night I got arrested.

The Sisters laughed at Mother's emphasis.

Soon dinner was over. Upon cleaning the kitchen, the Sisters and I retreated to our respective rooms. As tempting as it was to reacquaint myself in earnest with that well-made bed, thick mattress, plush comforter and pillows, and heavenly scent, upon brushing my teeth, I had one last thing to do...

November 28, 1999 (Day I got released from prison)
Dear Diary,

Today is the first day of the rest of my life. Out of prison and ready to embark on the next chapter. I'm free! I'm excited and I'm ready.

Today I received a letter that would chart the course for the rest of my life and that of my parents, too. It says, Dear Ms. Estevez, please report to have your biometrics taken at the USCIS District Office in New York, New York on Friday, December 13, 1999, at 10 a.m. My 24th birthday! How surreal is that?

The word 'biometrics' sure brought back the night I got booked into jail to the fore. But this one right here from Immigration and Naturalization Services is the biometrics I ever looked forward to taking in America, but God had other plans. All I can say is wow! I am in complete awe of God's plan and His impeccable timing. Hope my time in prison does not affect or delay the process. Although Judge Judy promised that she'd have it expunged off my record, I still worry about it from time to time. Fingers crossed she does.

I can hardly wait to have my green card in hand. But as they say, patience is a virtue. I've waited over five years. What's a couple months more, huh? I can do this. It will all be worth it in the end and I have my parents, The Sisters of Charity, and all the wonderful people I met along the way to thank for it. I am eternally grateful to Mother, who called me on that fateful day at work inquiring about my status, doing all the paperwork on my behalf. Gosh, am I grateful! So, with patience and a grateful and hopeful heart, I humbly await. Because I know that God is always on time. God, I thank thee!

Glo wherever you're planted with Grace.

Closing my diary, I grabbed some of the beautifully decorated paper sitting on my nightstand and penned my parents a letter. I told them about the letter to have my fingerprints taken, how long it may take to receive my green card, and asked about their thoughts on reuniting in mom's homeland Saint Lucia, all expenses paid.

I turned off the lights, slid underneath my plush comforter, and outstretched my body as far as it could go onto the white bedding that dressed my full-sized bed. Resting my head gently onto the pillow, I closed my eyes hoping to catch some much-needed uninterrupted Zz's.

"That which is dreamed can never be lost, can never be undreamed"

— Neil Gaiman

Chapter 24

Clank! My eyes flung open in the dark. My breathing stopped.

Touching everything around me, I exhaled, "Oh!"

My soft bed, plush pillows, and the fresh scent of lavender hitting my nostrils reminded me that I was no longer locked up.

Freaking out, my heart hammering, I grabbed a pillow. Tugging it tightly against my chest, I sat upright, my back leaning against the mahogany headboard. Still very-much tired, after ten minutes or so, I attempted to fall back asleep. Closing my eyes tightly, I slid forward, slowly lowering my back onto the bed. Because laying on my back was never my falling asleep position, I released the pillow and rolled over onto my stomach.

The noises and sounds that had assaulted and infiltrated my eardrums every day for the past two and a half years resounded in my ears, keeping me from sleep.

"Lord, I lay this overwhelming feeling of panic and anxiety at Your feet," I prayed, pressing the pillow tightly over my ear to drown the echoes of prison. "You are a true source of peace, Lord. Please grant me peace of mind and a calm spirit, Lord. I'm exhausted. Please help me fall asleep. Please help me fall asleep. Please Lord, please Lord, please Lord please...."

Not sure how long after my begging and pleading that my prayers were answered, but eventually I must have fallen into a slumber.

"Latisha! Stop it! Stop it! Let Lisa go. Let her go right now! You promised that you had changed your bullying ways. You promised me, Latisha! YOU PROMISED! Let Lisa go! Let Lisa go! Let Lisa go! Let Lisa go..."

I heard a loud bang then felt someone shaking me, yelling, "Gloria! Gloria! Gloria...'

"Latisha stop it!" I snapped, firing a punch.

"Gloria, wake up!" someone screamed.

Opening my eyes, I found three people hovering over me, one sitting next to me on the bed.

"Wait! What are you guys doing in prison, Mother?" I asked, my voice shaking, my heart palpitating. I sat up, shaking the pain from my right knuckles.

"We're not, Gloria. You're not either," Mother answered.

"I'm not?" I asked, confused.

"You're free, Gloria. You are free, Glo," Mother sat next to me cradling my head to her chest, rocking me "It's OK, Glo, it's OK. Looks like you were having a dream, a very bad dream."

My body was trembling, my right hand throbbing. Sister Theresa inched closer to wipe the tears streaming down my face.

"It's alright, Gloria, it's alright," Sister Annie reassured me, handing me a bag with ice. "Here. Put it on your hand. This will soothe the pain."

"So that bang wasn't Latisha banging Lisa's head against the wall, huh?"

"Nah, it was probably the moment we barged into the room."

"And all the violent shaking wasn't Latisha beating the crap out of me either, huh."

"Nah, it was Mother shaking you awake. We heard you screaming in your sleep."

"And that punch, oh my God!" my jaw dropped, my brows furrowed, my heart pounded, embarrassment rising in me. I pulled away from Mother's embrace to look at her, "Did I hit you, Mother?" I asked, horrified.

"Nah, the headboard."

"Oh," I relaxed my face muscles, relieved I had not hurt Mother.

"Mother ducked so fast, eh?" Sister Annie stifled a laugh.

"My knuckles hurt like …"

"I'm sure they do, Gloria. Had that punch landed on Latisha, I can assure you that she'd never lay a hand on you, Lisa, or anyone else for that matter, ever again in her life," Sister T snickered.

"I'm so so sorry," I breathed deeply, burying my face in my hands. Drenched in sweat and embarrassment, I sat upright, my knees pulled to my chest, my back against the headboard.

"It's alright, Glo. It's alright! I think you're traumatized from being in prison, post-traumatic stress. It's common among people who have gone through or witnessed some sort of trauma. It's OK. It will get better with time."

Knowing the Sisters were losing their sleep to comfort me guilted me. I convinced them I'd be OK and that they should go back to sleep.

I'll be alright, I have to be.

Upon their exit, I got out of bed to relieve my bladder and change into dry pajamas. Scared to go back to sleep, I sat in the rocking chair that occupied one corner of the room. Pleading with God, I asked for a calm spirit and to replace the tumult within me with peace. With sleep evading me, I grabbed my notepad and turned to the last lines of my screenplay.

For many nights, thoughts of prison terrorized me. Nightmares, noises, and night sweats were a constant. Often out of nowhere, regardless of where I was or what I was doing, without discretion or warning, anxiety would hit like a ton of bricks, stopping me in my tracks.

Evening devotion was dedicated to laying hands over me and meditation became routine. Mother assured me that they'd help me get through it and that the frequency of attacks would lessen with time. She was right. With intense therapy, prayers, and meditation, my sleep patterns eventually improved and life started getting back to some semblance of normalcy. Although I was not completely the same, I was coping the best I know-how.

Feeling ready to enter the workforce, I posted my resume on numerous nanny and housekeeping agencies, but employers were not biting. Hitting wall after wall, I wondered, *Why?*

Although Judge Judy promised that she'd work her magic and have my records expunged, the thought that perhaps she might have forgotten or wasn't successful at getting it done reverberated in my head. But then again, perhaps I would've been denied a green card. I was confused. Fearing that I might be barred from travel, I called Judge Judy to confirm.

"Young lady, it's so wonderful to hear from you. I am a woman of my word and I truly admire you and want you to succeed in life. Yes, you now have a clean slate. Your time in jail never happened," she quipped. "Go on live your life, Gloria. Make those dreams come true. I look forward to seeing you on the big screen."

"Yes!" I rejoiced. "Thanks, Judge!"

Following my call with Judge Judy, I remained hopeful but luck still wasn't on my side. So, I taught catechism classes to kids in the parish and got involved in the youth group. I also offered Spanish, French, and acting lessons at the local library for a small fee.

Thankfully I had saved up a good chunk of the money that I had worked for and still had a couple thousand sitting in my bank account. My decision to not deplete my savings on bail was now clear and, boy, was I thankful I followed my instincts.

Had I done the alternative, I probably would've been deported and gotten myself into deeper trouble—both financially and otherwise—trying to hire an attorney and an immigration attorney to help me stay in America.

In jail I was able to truly show my heart, redeem myself, and do my most important work. For this I was grateful. The ever merciful God is always on my side and His timing is always impeccable.

Fast-forward one month post-release from prison and I received mail from my parents.

> *Our dearest Gloria,*
>
> *We're always so happy to hear from you. Glad you're doing OK. Congratulations, our love, hope you get your green card soon. Of course, we'd give up the world to see you. Dad is also very excited and joked one month might be too short. He's always wanted to go back to Saint Lucia, but you know the money situation kept us from going back as a family all these years.*
>
> *We do not want you to take on this financial burden, so we will chip in. The crops have been doing very well and Dad has been selling a little more these days. Enclosed are your documents. We will renew our passports directly through Saint Lucia because you'd have to send them there anyway to get them back to us.*
>
> *Anyway, we're OK for now. It's always great hearing from you. Take care of yourself, our beloved. See you soon. Yes! Love mom and dad,*
> *XxX*

Explore your innermost desires. Whatever makes you feel alive, do.

Chapter 25

APRIL 2000

Five months later and I was outside tending the sea of flowers that decorated the encirclement of the convent. The birds were chirping, flowers blooming and blossoming, bees buzzing, butterflies suckling the petals of sunflowers and hibiscus and daisies, lizards and small animals scampering the beautifully decorated rocks among the flowers.

With a soul rebirthing, a heart filled with hope, a life filled with gratitude and promise, I added my voice rather loudly to the sweet and soft singing of birds. Beauty was in full bloom.

"Gloria, oh Gloria, you've got mail, my dear," Mother Mary came calling, interrupting my rendition of 'Oh Happy Day!' She joked, "And please cut out the singing, I'm enjoying the glorious sunshine."

"Oh, Mother. Are you insinuating that my singing is a call for rain? Thought for sure you'd appreciate and enjoy the free concert.

Anyway—who is it from?" I asked curiously, walking briskly towards her. I had received mail from my parents two days earlier, so my curiosity was especially piqued.

"See for yourself, my dear," Mother handed me the letter, wearing the most beautiful smile. "Here"

"Immigration!" My jaw dropped. "It feels like there's something in there."

Dropping the watering can at my feet, I used both hands to flip the letter from front to back, back to front, touching every inch to feel the contents.

"Gloria, you know," Mother smiled crookedly, peering at me over her glasses, "if you open it you'll find out what's inside quicker."

"Duh!" I shot her a look. Deliberately turning away from her scrutiny, I excitedly opened the envelope.

"It's here, it's here, it's here!" I turned back around rejoicing, waving the Permanent Resident Card frantically. Then amidst my jubilation, I asked, "It's not green?"

"I knew that was coming," Mother burst out laughing, before squeezing me tightly, "Congratulations, Glo! I know how much you looked forward to this day. You deserve it!"

"What's going on, what's going on?" the Sisters rushed outside.

"I got my green card! I got my green card," I chanted, twirling the document in one hand and wiping tears with the other.

"Congratulations, Gloria!" the Sisters took turns sharing hugs and well wishes.

"And she's disappointed the card isn't green!" Mother added, never missing an opportunity for banter, getting a laugh from the Sisters. "Although I, too, thought it was green. Imagine the shock when I saw a white card."

"Me, too, me too," Sister Theresa and some of the other Sisters admitted, emitting a series of loud guffaws.

"For a moment I thought I was denied," Sister Theresa disclosed.

After a hearty laugh and some more chatter, we headed inside. The Sisters headed to the kitchen to start dinner before evening novena. And I—my heart slamming my chest, bursting with gladness and gratitude and grace—excitedly went to my room to do my cartwheels and write to my parents letting them know the news. As I wrote, the tears and smiles were a balancing act, working in concert, taking turns to show up, sometimes even appearing at the same time. I couldn't stop crying and smiling, knowing that I was well on my way to achieving the American Dream and my ultimate dream.

Before long, the clock struck 6 and its chime had never been sweeter. The Sisters and I gathered for novena. As the prayers ensued, they broke normal tradition to intercede for my family and for me in prayers of thanksgiving.

What would I do without them and God? I reflected. Soon my blouse was spotted, dotted with uncontrollable happy tears. The day I entered this cathedral as a homeless girl flashed through my mind. *The day I spent the night in the back pew over there.*

Turning back around, I remembered the encounter with an observant and compassionate nun who approached me and engaged me in conversation. Deep in reflection, the notion that in life we truly need each other and were placed on this earth to walk each other home couldn't ring truer in my mind. I bowed my head in gratitude.

What a journey it has been getting here. And realizing that achieving certain dreams truly isn't a sprint, I was satisfied with winning small victories at a time. At 7 o'clock, the Sisters and I made our way inside for the lovely feast they had prepared to celebrate my legal status in America.

Oh my, I blushed.

Pumpkin soup. The fig salad was made to perfection; the mashed potatoes—fluffy, cheesy, garlicky and buttery—tasted heavenly; the asparagus crunchy and fresh seasoned with familiar herbs and spices; the salmon grilled to perfection, the skin crunchy and served with hollandaise sauce; the avocado firm and creamy, sitting atop Sister Theresa's specialty vegetable salad; and flan for dessert. It made for a perfect cultural diversity dinner.

"Clink! Clink! Clink!" a few minutes into dinner, I summoned the Sisters' attention. There was a lot I had to get off my chest and the time was ripe to do so.

"Yes, Gloria," Mother acknowledged me. "Oh wait, wait. This calls for champagne."

At Mother's request, Sister Annie rushed into the kitchen to get a couple of bottles of the virgin bubbly they had on ice.

"So, Sisters," I giggled nervously. "You know how appreciative I am of you guys for saving my life. I just want to thank you for all you've done for me. When I deliberately wandered in here and sat on that pew bench, never did I imagine I'd go beyond the altar, but you proved me wrong. Here I am today, occupying a seat at your table."

Forced to swallow, I continued, "Thank you Mother for that fateful day. I will never for-get..."

The tears escaped my welled eyes and spilled down my cheeks. Like a domino effect, everyone at the table got the sniffles. They truly loved me and I truly loved them.

"You know, Gloria," Mother interjected, saving me from having to continue through the tears. "I have a confession."

"Oh?" we snickered, wiping the tears in our eyes. "Do tell, Mother."

"You know, ever since you stepped foot in here you have turned this place upside-down."

"Oh! Sorry, Mother." My heart was confused for a minute.

"Oh no, no... In a good way, in a good way," Mother laughed attempting to explain. "It has never been livelier—infected with a different energy—and I think I speak for all the Sisters in saying that you have a wonderful aura about you. Your presence and your being here have enriched our lives. And for this, we are grateful. Thank you for wandering in here and for sharing your spirit and wit with us. We love you, Gloria. May God continue to bless you! May He continue to honor your wishes and may the pursuit of your ultimate American Dream come to fruition. Here, here!"

Raising our glasses, echoes of "Cheers!" reverberated in the room.

"Thank you, Mother! Thank you, Sisters. I appreciate you more than you'll ever know!" I exclaimed, swallowing my champagne. "Now, tan ta da daaaa, Saint Lucia here we come!"

"Well, some of us will accompany you to Saint Lucia for two weeks and when we return, the other Sisters will be going on a Mission trip to Africa."

"Africa! I've always dreamt of visiting."

"Dreams, they do come true you know, Gloria?" Mother interjected with utmost sincerity, earning an Amen from the other Sisters.

"I believe. I do believe, Mother!" I rejoiced, clapping. "Dinner was delicious, as usual."

"Hope cleaning is just as satisfying, Gloria," Mother responded in a whimsical tone.

"Eh! All by myself?"

"Well," the Sisters laughed, "we cooked, you clean."

"OK, fair enough," I agreed, playfully rolling my eyes.

"No worries, I'll help you, Gloria."

"Thank you, Sister Annie, you're my favorite!"

"Oh!" Mother gaped at me. "Noted, Gloria."

"Jokes, jokes!" I winked.

Laughing, we proceeded to clean up the kitchen.

The Sisters and I retired for the night. As usual, I recorded in my diary and gave thanks to God one more time before sliding underneath my plush comforter to catch some Zzz's. Overwhelmed with gratitude I struggled to fall asleep, but I did—eventually.

"Dream what you dare to dream. Go where you want to go. Be what you want to be."

— Earl Nightingale

Chapter 26

JULY 2000

My parents wrote back letting me know that they had successfully renewed their passports and were ready to go. I wrote back, letting them know of dates and plans, and how the next time we communicated it would be face-to-face.

Ah! I screamed in my head. *This is surreal!*

But before long—within a week or so of their first letter—I received another letter from them, proving me wrong. Unexpected and unsure what it was about, my heart pounding with eagerness, my hand shaking with anticipation, I tore it open.

> *My dearest Gloria Grace!*
> *I have missed you so much. Ever since the news of receiving your green card, I haven't had a full night's sleep. Haha. Tonight is one such night. It's now 2 a.m.*

> *I can't sleep, so I decided to pen you a letter. Dad, of course, is fast asleep. He works so hard that he knocks out before his head hits the pillows. Haha. I'm sure you know what I mean.*

Oh, I remember the sleepy head. He falls asleep anywhere in no time.

> *Oh mi Dios! I cannot believe it's finally going to happen. Woohoo! I'm happy, I'm anxious. I'm nervous, I'm grateful. My goodness, I have all these emotions and thoughts running through my head. I have missed you so much and to think we're finally going to see each other again is beyond exciting!*
> *Anyways Glo, remember to not drive yourself crazy trying to get this and that and buying the whole of America.*

Too late mom haha…

> *I love you Glo and I cannot wait to see you.*
> *Love you eternally,*
> *Madre*
> *XxX*

Aw, mom! Love and miss you guys so much. But phew! Thank God it was an adorable little letter and not… Oh how exciting, surreal and exhilarating!

And as they always did, the tears began to flow.

Although July 2000 seemed to have taken a mighty long time to come around, life at the Convent couldn't have been better. And I couldn't have been more grateful. Except for my battle with sporadic bouts of post-prison trauma, life was good. Thanks to my therapist, prayer warriors, meditation, and workout routines, I was coping the best I knew how.

With one month until our highly anticipated reunion in Saint Lucia, my days were spent disobeying my mom's orders, shopping for my parents and me, throwing in a couple of gifts for mom's best friend, cousins, and the Sisters who would be hosting us at the Convent in Saint Lucia.

And you name it, I packed it—from swimsuits and sundresses to poom-poom shorts for me (*Oh dear!*) and Bermuda shorts for my parents. I also brought disposable cameras, backpacks, medicines, sunscreen, chapstick, and insect repellant. There's no way our much-anticipated vacation would catch us unprepared.

Finally, the eve of our trip was here, although I was still running around buying the whole of New York. *Sorry, mom.* I had to be sure that we were ready for our tropical vacation and reunion in paradise.

With so much to pack in two suitcases—70 pounds each—sleep evaded me once again, but procrastination was getting the better of me. In my estimation everything I bought was essential and leaving any of it behind was simply out of the question. Praying for a miracle, the scale became my saving grace. But that was only after packing and unpacking, moving things around, and repacking several times.

Soon the alarm clock went off, signaling my time to wake. I didn't have to because I hadn't slept a wink. The day was finally here and I was all ready—well, mentally—to embark on this trip of a lifetime. As for physically, not so much. I was tired.

I jumped into the shower and put on the outfit I had laid out— my newly bought white Manmay LaKay tee (because everyone had to know that I was a daughter of the soil, a child from home), blue jeans, Saint Lucia flag canvas shoes. Then I made my way downstairs to eat breakfast. But too excited to eat, I took a few sips of coffee and made my way back to my room to finish last-minute packing.

"Ready, Gloria?" Mother yelled from downstairs in what seemed like ten minutes.

Suitcases? Check. Passport? Check. Camera? Diary? Writing paper? Check. Check. Check. Madras headwrap? Check. What else? What else? Oh! Green card! Green card! Should be in my passport.

Flipping through the pages of my passport, holding it upside down shaking the heck out of it, I found nothing.

Whoa! panic growing inside me, sweat breaking through my pores. *The only logical place it would be is inside my passport and it's not there? Oh My God! Where could I have put it? Where could I have put it?*

Calm down, Gloria. Maybe it's in that letter from immigration.

Going through my stack of mail, I finally found the envelope. Whipping the letter out, flipping the envelope, no green card.

Oh my God! Where the heck could it be? I wondered, wiping the sweat on my forehead. *Did I give it to Mother for safekeeping? But why would I give it to her? I have all my other docs here.* I'm officially panicked. *Should I ask her? What if she doesn't have it? What do I do, then? Oh my God!*

"Oh, Gloria..." Mother called out again.

Hyperventilating, "Uh... I'll be right down, Mother."

OhmyGod! OhmyGod! OhmyGod!

"You don't want to miss your flight, dear. We have to get going," she added.

"Uh...coming, Mother," I lied. I still needed to find my most important document. "Oh, I know! I know!"

Digging into my backpack once again, I pleaded, "Hope it's in there, hope it's there, hope it's in there. Please God, please God, please God, please, please, please..."

Dumping the contents onto the bed, I reached for my diary.

Please God, please God, please please please, I pleaded as I flipped through the pages of the fragile thing. *Nothing.*

Deciding to flip it over, something flew out, landing on the floor and under the bed.

Argh! I griped, getting on the floor to find it. *Was it a leaf?*

"What was that?" I asked, reaching for whatever it was on the floor.

"Phew!" I exhaled, breathing for the first time in ten minutes, although it felt like hours. Leaning against the wall, eyes closed, card against my chest, *'Thank you, Jesus,'* reverberated in my head. Breathing another sigh of relief, now I was ready.

"Is everything OK, Gloria?"

"Coming, Mother, coming," I yelled as I hurriedly jammed everything back into my backpack.

With my backpack on my back, I made my way downstairs, hauling my suitcases. Standing at the bottom of the stairs were ten Sisters. Five waiting to embark on the trip with me, and five others waiting to see us off.

"Are you alright, Gloria?" Mother asked, drawing her brows together. "You look flustered."

"Don't ask, Mother, don't ask. I'm alright now, though." I sighed and smiled simultaneously.

"Have fun in Saint Lucia!" the Sisters took turns hugging us goodbye. "Give our regards to your parents, Gloria."

"Thank you, Sisters! I sure will, I surely will! Woohoo!" I rejoiced, jumping and clicking my heels at the doorway as I exited the Convent. "Whoa!" I lunged forward, barely breaking a fall.

"Oh!" The Sisters gasped. Realizing that I was unhurt, they burst out laughing. Of course, I had to redeem myself, and I did!

"Gloria, Gloria, Gloria." Sister Theresa shook her head smiling. "You are joy personified. I will miss you!"

"Au revoir, Sisters. Enjoy your Mission trip."

"Ready, Glo?"

"Ready, Mother!" I exclaimed. Ready to get on my first plane ride as an adult, ready to reunite with my parents, and ready to embark on a vacation of a lifetime.

"Saint Lucia, here we come! Hope you're ready for these Sisters, GloryAnna, Pedro and, Gloria Grace!"

Made in the USA
Columbia, SC
28 November 2022